Special Agent Booker

SPECIAL AGENT BOOKER

Mimi Barbour
Sarna Publishing

Special Agent Booker

The Undercover FBI Series – Book 5

Contents

Contact me:
383

Special Agent Booker

Undercover FBI Book #5
by New York Times Best-selling author, Mimi Bar-
bour

~*~*~

Suspense lights up in every page of this fast-paced blockbuster of thrills!

When Sloan Booker's father dies tragically, he has no other option but to give up his job as an FBI agent and take over his family's vehicle restoration business in Oahu, Hawaii. Giving up his badge is difficult but having Homeland Security and his old boss request the use of his house in a stakeout, spying on his Muslim neighbors who they suspect are terrorists, is just too damn much for a man already frazzled. It makes no difference that they've offered him a partner to be in charge of the surveillance... until he meets the gorgeous divorcee.

Special Agent Alia Hawkins might look more like a model than a cop but looks can be deceiving. Not only does she rescue street kids, fights their battles and transports them to safe homes, but since she lived many years in Pakistan and speaks their language, she's a sought after agent. So far, she's kept her personal life and job separate. But when Alia's slimy ex-husband threatens to steal her eight-year-old son, she has no choice but to bring him along on her latest undercover assignment – living with a hotshot, sexy as hell agent as his long lost stepsister. Her life suddenly takes some drastic swerves and she wonders if things will ever slow down.

Dedication

This compelling suspense is dedicated to my favorite son, David, who helped me plot the story right from the beginning. I truly feel that it's because of his creative input that this book is probably the best in Undercover FBI series. It was a blast working with him, peering into the mind of a man the same age as Booker and finding the identical large heart and amazing intelligence.

(p.s. I should mention – I only have one son :-))))

Praise for other Undercover FBI books

"I always enjoy Mimi Barbour book's her writing is always so good. Her books are always a hit and this one was another Hit. There is a lot of humor and suspense, keep you on your toes till the end.... WOW this book is so GOOD. Special Agent Maximilian is a must read.... I really wish I could give it more then five stars.... Get it today." *~Reviewed by Chrissybear77*

"I have read every book by Mimi and each one is better than the last. I thought the Vegas series was my favorite but I think this one may just become my new Fav! Love this series and highly recommend any and all books by Mimi!" *~Reviewed by Shirleen*

"Mimi Barbour writes with great strength and realism when it comes to this series of romantic suspense novels. And each one keeps getting better than the last." *~ Reviewed by ajk (avid reader)*

Also author of...

His Devious Angel (Book 2)
Loveable Christmas Angel (Book 3)
***

Elvis Series
— Make an Elvis Song a Book! —
She's Not You (Book 1)
Love Me Tender (Book 2)
***

Undercover FBI Series
— Popular & Compelling! —
Special Agent Francesca (Book 1)
Special Agent Finnegan (Book 2)
Special Agent Maximilian (Book 3)
Special Agent Kandice (Book 4)
Special Agent Booker (Book 5)
***

Holiday Heartwarmers Trilogy
— Truly a Christmas favorite! —
Holiday Heartwarmers Box Collection (Books
2,3 & 4)
Please Keep Me (Book 1)
Snow Pup (Book 2)
Find Me a Home (Book 3)
Frosty the Snowman (Book 4)
***

Other Titles
I'm No Angel
Hotshot Cowboy
Big Girls Don't Cry
Christmas Runaway

The Surrogate's Secret
Mimi's Mix (Box Set)
'Tis the Season (Box Set)
Red Hot Divas (Box Set)
Hearts, Flowers & Romance (Box Set)
A touch of passion (Multi-author Box Set)
Love, Christmas (Multi-author Box Set)
Hotshot Heroes (Multi-author Box Set)
Hotshot Desires (Multi-author Box Set)

***

All Mimi's books can be found on her Amazon
Author Page:
Website: http://mimibarbour.com

Chapter One

Alia scoured the dark parking lot behind the Ilikia Hotel looking for the boy. Palm trees and plumeria decorated the area, but there was no sign of a kid in trouble.

Ruby had sworn he'd be here, and woken from a dead sleep at three a.m. to jump in her jeans and then drive like a maniac to get to him in time, Alia hadn't stopped to ask a lot of questions.

Now she called Ruby using her hands-free in the car. "He's not here. Did he call you back?"

"His name is Justin, and no, I haven't heard from him. He said he'd gotten away from his player; that the guy had roughed him up. He hid out at the Ilikia and another dude came on to him. Scared stupid, he called me, told me he was behind the dumpster."

"Okay, I'll check it out."

Alia pulled the car over, got out and headed in that direction. As she approached, she saw a man bending over something wedged in between two dumpsters. "Listen, kid, I don't want to hurt you. Come out and I'll buy you something to eat. We'll talk. You can stay in my room so you'll have a place to sleep."

"Leave me alone. I'm not going anywhere with you." The boy's voice cracked, his tone going from soprano to bass in one sentence

"Hey, is that the way to act with someone who just wants to help? I'm being nice, but I can—"

"Be a lying prick who wants to get you alone and do nasty things to you. He knows, don't you, Justin?" Alia stood waiting, hoping her insults would piss off the scumbag enough he'd come at her. Then she could kick the shit out of the perverted prick.

Tall, with a kangaroo pouch of sloppy fat in front, the guy shot to his feet as if she'd shoved a stick up his ass. "What the fuck! Who the hell are you?"

"I'm Justin's friend. And I have a real aversion to pedophiles. Actually, I like to arrest the scum, book 'em and hope they never get another moment of freedom to do those icky things they like to do."

The troll looked her up and down and foolishly decided it was no contest. His fist punched air as she dropped in defense and drove her own up into his groin area. Rolling to the side and then to her feet in the nimble way she'd been trained, she tackled the bent-over screamer and pushed him into the steel side of the dumpster. Then she left her fist imprinted on his balls yet again. About this time, Justin slid out of his hidey-hole to level a kick into the guy's ribs for his personal parting shot.

"Enough, kid. Let's go. He'll have some healing to do. Hope it ruins the bastard's Hawaiian holiday."

She ran back to her SUV, and Justin followed. Once in the car, she checked him out. The kid was scrawny with a feminine delicacy many young girls would get surgery to have. His features were ethereal: lovely eyes that looked to be a pale color in the car's dimness, and thick blond hair that hung to his scrawny shoulders curled in ringlets. Justin might have been born a boy, but no doubt he'd pull in top dollar for any pimp who played him right.

"I'm taking you to a safe home, okay? You called Ruby, and that's the way this works. They'll help you. If you want a new start, they'll make it happen."

Slouched in the corner, tears pouring, the youngster sniffed. He looked at her, those big eyes begging not to be judged, and she reached over, her hand open and waiting. Though hardened to some degree by what she'd seen in the past, she still cared about these kids she saved or she'd have stopped taking the calls.

His hand grasped hers and clung. "Thank you for what you did back there. Even if you are a cop."

"I'm actually a federal agent and it was my pleasure. Truly!" She tightened her hand around his and shook it. "I lie... not. It *was* my pleasure." She grinned and waited, taking her eyes from the road for a second.

His fingers squeezed hers tight. "You have no idea what it meant to me seeing you there tonight. No one's ever saved me before."

"Hey, Justin. When you kids call Ruby, either I, or someone like me, will come. It's as simple as that."

Chapter Two

Booker's Restorations.

Sloan Booker finally got it. Why his old man had been so proud of this small business. Seeing your name on a building did give one a kind of chest inflation, even if you secretly resented every minute you were forced to spend there.

His glance took in the immediate surroundings. The big old tree from the back of the place loomed over the roof, swaying in the island's breeze. The paved driveway recently redone that circled the area looked clean and classy. As did the front of the shop they'd remodeled to widen the windows, paint the exterior and install new garage doors.

From the corner of his eye, he saw the stray again. It was like the tabby kitten had his sights on Sloan and had decided he'd be his owner. Blasted animal showed up no matter how many times Sloan put the run on him. He couldn't bring himself to be too fierce with the green-eyed cutie but cats made him sneeze. It was as simple as that. If one happened to be in his vicinity, he'd be using Kleenex, eye drops and suffering.

With a hiss, he shooed the little monster away, feeling slightly pissed at the sorrowful glower from his nemesis. "Sorry, kitty, go find someone else to schmooze. I'm allergic."

Slightly unsettled, he gathered his patience, squared his shoulders and walked into the newly renovated vehicle restoration shop. No one was around and that gave him a few minutes to survey the setup.

While his father had been alive, it had been an old barn of a place, with crap everywhere and corners so dark one never knew what critters might be lurking. The smell of entrenched oil mixed with diesel—a fire hazard for sure—had been enough to make one gag. Most of the equipment had needed upgrading, all the old machinery tossed except the pieces that Les had rescued.

The complete renovation had taken months, plus all of Sloan's savings. But it had been worth it. At least now he didn't dread coming to work most mornings.

Not true.

Maybe it wasn't the same as being an FBI agent, when he'd been totally involved in his work, but it paid the bills. And more important, it kept his two gray-whiskered caretakers working and earning wages, which had been his priority for keeping the place running.

On the days when his talent for detailed drawings to restore cars and trucks was called for, usually when the team first took on a new restoration project, then time passed quickly. During those periods, he came close to being happy, or at least satisfied.

As soon as he turned on the overhead lights that flooded the newly-laid, pale gray-floored room, he noticed that everything had been neatly organized in Roy's area, including his multitude of stacked tool boxes, his old ones having been changed over to the modern dark-gray style with drawers and cubbyholes for all his equipment. This orderliness didn't surprise Sloan.

Neither did the ungodly mess left scattered of dirty rags, paint spills and crap everywhere in Lester's corner. That old man was a slob, no other way to describe him. Shaking his head, a grin hovering, Sloan headed to the updated alcove where there was a small lunch area and, best of all, a coffee machine.

As he got closer, he smelled the Kona beans brewing and knew Les had beaten him there. The old reprobate still got up early most mornings so he could go surfing before work, one of the fringe benefits of living in Hawaii's key island of Oahu.

It had been way too long since Sloan'd joined Les in one of his favorite pastimes. The old surfer had taught him how to ride the waves almost as soon as he could walk and he'd loved every minute. He'd have to make the time.

He grabbed a mug, filled it and headed to his workplace. As he approached, the back of his neck itched, making him damned uncomfortable. He heard voices. Slowly lowering his cup, he picked up a tire iron and slunk to his office door.

When he'd arrived, the garage had been locked tighter than an old widow's house after dark. Which made him question how people could have gotten in there?

What's going on?

He listened at the door to the faint rustling of clothes and a chair's creak. His body tensed, readying itself for action. Suddenly a female voice whispered from close behind him.

"Something wrong?"

Chapter Three

What the fuck...! Sloan jumped, his nerves rioting. "How the hell did you get in here?"

The lady staring back at him didn't blink at his rudeness; instead, his edginess made her grin. "I'm with them." She pointed to the door he'd been listening at.

Disgusted, Sloan waited to hear an explanation. *Where the hell had his skills gone? Eight months ago no one could have snuck up on him like that.*

Roy suddenly appeared and spoke to the light-haired beauty who'd shocked the shit out of him. "Missy, didn't I tell you to wait for me in the coffee room?"

She flipped her head in a saucy way, sniffed and replied. "Can't a lady go to the bathroom in this joint without getting in trouble?"

Roy stepped back. "Oh darn, I wasn't very thoughtful leaving you here alone. Glad you found your way."

She pointed to the washroom sign on the wall and added, "That kinda helped."

Totally off-kilter, genuinely flustered in the way the senior tended to be around females, Roy added, "I'm sorry. I had to take the garbage out. Les left a mess lying around, stinking up the place, and I wanted to catch the truck this morning." Obviously upset, his Santa-like face turned red and he swallowed hard.

Reaching to touch his arm, she spoke gently. "Please, think nothing of it." Blue eyes, as vivid as Roy's own, twinkled at him. Sloan watched his friend melt. He enjoyed the moment until he heard sounds filtering through the door again.

"Excuse me for butting in on your lovefest." Sloan didn't try to hide his grumpiness. "If you two don't mind being interrupted, what the hell is going on here? And who's in there?"

Gesturing his head toward the female, his way of telling Sloan to curb his tongue 'cause there was a lady present, Roy answered, "You mean the other two agents who came calling a few minutes ago? I let them in there to wait for ya."

Heat poured into Sloan's face as he tossed his weapon onto the nearby tool chest. He glared his embarrassment at the old brat, who was having trouble hiding his glee at having caught Sloan off-guard.

"Why didn't you tell me you let them in?"

"I thought I just did."

"Roy, quit messing with me. There've been a lot of thefts in the neighborhood lately. It's made me cautious."

Roy's eyes widened, the vivid blue attention-getters flashing in his otherwise nondescript white-bearded face. Sloan had his interest now. "I forgot about that. Sorry, I should have stuck around to warn you."

Knowing that a situation like this could upset Roy for days, Sloan hurried to soothe him. "No problem, Roy. It's fine."

Paying attention and not trying to hide it, the lady questioned with a no-nonsense attitude, "Have *you* had any break-ins so far?"

"Not since I installed the alarm system with the video surveillance." Sloan shrugged. "I figure even kids know where they shouldn't be messing around." His glance slid past her to Roy. "So, who's visiting?" Sloan arched his head toward the door of his office.

"One of them is your old partner, Don. He's with another man who looked around the place like it was the same dump it used to be."

Sloan knew how much old Roy had loved the changes, unlike the other gray-haired orphan he'd inherited from his dad. Les still grumbled about the updates, muttering about how he could never find anything.

"Don's the only reason I let them in; figured you'd be happy to see him."

"I'm always happy to see him outside of business hours. Not so much if he's making an official call." Sloan raised his eyebrow at the attractive woman dressed in a casual light blue business suit. Sporting a flared short skirt, it showed her tanned legs to advantage. She waited until he'd looked his fill and stared back without a speck of emotion.

Roy broke into the uncomfortable silence. "They badgering you to come back to work for them?"

Sloan didn't break eye contact with her; instead, he stared her down and took a short breath of relief when she was the first to look away.

Roy cleared his throat, obviously still waiting for Sloan's answer. He decided not to bullshit because Roy could read him like a lie detector.

"Not lately. We were pretty close to closing a few cases they'd had on the books for years. But Don's a good guy. He can handle it." Sloan turned away so Roy or the chick wouldn't see his yearning, but the old buzzard couldn't be fooled. He grabbed Sloan's shoulder and squeezed, his way of showing understanding and affection.

"I'll go see what they want and get rid of them. You look after our visitor here... and remember. We've got the Vanguard's vehicle to finish today.

Thankfully, Les is painting the final design trim this morning. We did promise we'd have the car ready after five. I need to get those drawings done for the '66 Stingray, so you can get the boys working on the powertrain build. And you still have the motor to overhaul and the drive shaft."

Back to business, Roy nodded, took the woman's arm like a gentleman and led her away. She hesitated, but only for a minute. Sloan watched them and shook his head, the tubby, slightly crippled senior citizen always solicitous of the opposite sex – Beauty and the Beast.

Sloan's eyes glommed onto the sway of her hips, sexy without meaning to be. Her slender albeit muscular form could stop construction workers in their tracks. But it would be her glorious legs that would bring the whistles. His own lips puckered up but the sound came out so low only he heard it.

Maybe not! As if his eyes burned into her body, she turned and threw him a challenging one-sided grin; no humor, only a silent message: *eat your heart out!*

Sloan wilted; feeling a flash of instant sexual hunger so intense, he had to catch himself. Babysitting these two old guys had put a real crimp in his partying. It was past time to find himself a honey and get some much needed attention to his own drive shaft.

He pulled himself together, arched his back

and tried to wipe off the grease spots from his latest uniform of tight jeans. He tucked in one side of the black golf shirt with the garage's logo, *Booker's*, embroidered in white on the pocket. Then he grabbed his wavy black hair to tie it back with the elastic band he always carried in his pocket. Pissed at himself for letting it get so long, he shrugged.

With no regulations forcing him to keep it trimmed, his barber visits were low on his pole of priorities. Picking up his mug of lukewarm coffee, he faced the closed door and straightened his shoulders.

Chapter Four

As soon as Sloan entered his office, he knew by the look on Don's face this wasn't a social call. Last weekend when they'd bar-hopped together, his buddy had spent most of the night bitchin' about the officious little prick they'd lined him up with, and now Sloan was able to see first-hand what he meant.

"Special Agent Nigel Dullen." The slim dude dressed in a beautifully- designed gray suit with his creaseless navy tie shouting 'silk', looked like a walking advertisement for *GQ 100*. His groomed brown hair, blow-dried and sprayed in place, made Sloan sorry he hadn't dealt with his own messy mop.

He reached over to take the extended hand,

decided the gold watch Dullen sported must have cost him a paycheck, and then wondered how the slick, bug-eyed character whitened his teeth so they positively glowed. "Sloan Booker." He shook hands and purposely turned his back so *Slick* wouldn't see his grimace or the wink he sent his friend. "Hey, Don. What's up?"

"Hey, Sloan. How about I let Nigel fill you in."

Not sure if it was a good sign or not when his pal looked out the window to hide his sudden grin, Sloan felt himself tightening. *Something's going on...* When two men worked together as long as he and Don had, they learned to read each other's body language. This morning, Don's attitude screamed, *Oh man, you're not gonna like this!*

Bracing himself, Sloan went to sit in his chair behind the desk where he would feel more in charge of the situation. On the side section, his drawings for the Corvette job they'd started were laid out. Instinctively, he covered them.

Suddenly there was a tense feeling in the room that warned him the papers had been moved. Though not caring if Don had checked them out, he knew his partner would have waited to be invited or would've asked. Only one other person had had the chance to snoop and this knowledge made his hackles rise.

While he settled himself, Agent Dullen had also made himself comfortable in the visitor's chair, crossing his knee over the other like most women did.

Bristling, Sloan felt the walls closing in and decided to get the party started. "So, Nigel, how about you fill me in?"

Don smothered a chuckle that almost brought a smile to Sloan's face.

"Yes. Good. Here it is. We want you to work with the agency again for a limited time and for a special op."

Cutting him off, Sloan stood. "Not interested."

Shocked and too stupid to hide the fact, Dullen stuttered. "B-but you haven't heard what this is all about."

"So which part of the two-word sentence didn't you understand, Nigel? Not or interested?"

Totally baffled, Nigel looked over at Don, who shook his head, lifted his hands and made a face that clearly read, *I told you so.*

Trying once again, Nigel used a more conciliatory tone. "Agent Booker. You must let me explain."

"No. What I must do is kick your skinny ass out of my place and get back to work on the drawings that I see someone has tampered with."

Now Don let out a bark of a laugh that drew a hateful glare from Dullen and a frustrated growl from Sloan. "Man, you're enjoying this, aren't you?"

"You better believe it. I told the bosses you'd be a pig-headed idiot who'd refuse to listen to our perfectly-conceived plan. I'm so glad you didn't disappoint me."

Sloan narrowed his gaze. Figuring Don was playing him didn't alter the fact that his damned curiosity had been stroked.

Sitting back down, he said. "Okay, then. You've got five minutes."

"Oh, good." Dullen's sigh was overdone.

Sloan first pointed at Dullen. "Not you." Then swivelled to aim his finger at Don. "Him."

Now alert, leaning forward on the small couch he'd chosen when entering the well-lit office, Don began, "Actually, man, it's not you we need so much as your house. It's about the Amans, the family of five who moved into your neighborhood recently, right across the street from you." Don pulled out his cell phone and within seconds began reading from his notes. "The father is Samir and the mother's name is Janna. The children range from nine to three—a boy called Faisal, and two girls. The five-year-old is Dina, and the youngest girl who's three is called Anya. She's the only one who was born here on the island."

"Hold it. I know their names as well as you do. They didn't just move in, and you know it. They've been living here for five years. And they're nice people. When they first came, they reached out, held a barbecue to introduce themselves and made a lot of friends in the neighborhood."

Nigel's snort of disgust interrupted. Sneering,

he added, "Many terrorists appear to be nice people. They're trained to be good pretenders."

Chapter Five

Sloan had the biggest urge to drop the idiot right there and then. Only respect for the badge and the prick's relationship with Don stopped him.

"Seriously, man? Terrorists? Give me a break."

Don interrupted. "Sloan, listen. No one's being accused here. There've been some strange goings-on in that house. They're expecting visitors who we've ascertained have ties to other suspected terrorists back on the mainland. And Mrs. Aman—"

"Her name is Janna, as you well know."

"Janna, then, has a brother, who's recently become of interest to Homeland Security."

Involved, unable to stop himself, Sloan fired back. "How do you know all this?"

"We've had a few of our Muslim operatives join with a certain community in California and they've reported information about her brother and his family. Look, we're not saying these people are involved. What we are saying is they need to be watched, and you've got the perfect house from which we can do so."

Shaking his head, Sloan cut in. "Hold it, buddy. I work twelve hours a day at this garage. And... I have to be here, you know that. So how do you propose for me to be in two places at once?" He came around the desk and leaned against the edge. Crossing his arms, he tried to hold in his aggravation. Tormented by his longing to dig into the story more, his voice harsher than he would have liked, he added. "No can do, pal. Sorry."

"Hey, do I look like an idiot? I know your situation better than anyone, so when this was discussed back at the agency, we came up with a foolproof plan."

Tantalized, Sloan waited to see what this fabulous proposal was.

"Since you can't be the one to investigate these people, we have an agent who's perfect for the job. Al has been involved with Muslims, grew up with an aunt who married a Pakistani man and lived with them for a number of years in that country, and... understands their faith and the language. You have a roomy house, three bedrooms, and can have a new roommate without anyone getting suspicious."

Instant rejection filled Sloan's expression. "That won't work for me. I like being alone after my long days here at the garage. I don't need some slob of an agent hanging around, disturbing my belongings and leaving his gear messing up my place."

Sloan had always been a neatnik, one of the quirks of his personality that had driven his father, Tommy, around the bend. It had forced Sloan to move out at an early age and buy a place of his own as soon as his wages with the FBI had allowed.

It had also started a lot of fights at the garage when his father had been in charge, and where Sloan had worked quite often, helping them out in a pinch. His amazing talent for drawing the specifications for remodeling the vehicles they took on had been passed down from father to son.

The last few years, probably because of his earlier boozing habit, Tom's hand hadn't been quite steady enough for the more detailed sections. Mostly, he'd relied on Sloan. But every time Sloan had walked into the place, his hackles had risen and he'd gotten that same claustrophobic feeling. The mess in the joint had driven him nuts.

Snatching Sloan's attention with a cough, Don shook his head. "We weren't thinking of a full-on, typical undercover stake-out. We'd thought of a more casual kind of surveillance, unless things get hot and then we'd make a change. But for now, we just need to get someone in closer with the family, who can kind of infiltrate into their everyday lives, get involved on a more than casual level, meet their acquaintances, learn who they typically spend time with, what activities they're involved in, you know—that kind of thing."

Totally stymied, Sloan didn't hide his suspicion. "And how the fuck do you figure to make all that happen?"

Don's chuckle and his hands rubbing together brought Sloan to attention. "My man, trust me. Our secret weapon will make even you go along with this operation."

Hackles raised, not too stupid, Sloan visualized the woman who was even now wandering his garage and entertaining his mechanic. "Does the chick outside have anything to do with this hackneyed, crazy-assed plan of yours?"

"She is the plan. And it's beautiful. Let me introduce her and you'll see what I mean."

"Not gonna happen. If you're thinking I'd hate rooming with a man, you're right. But living in the same house as a broad with legs like hers is a total no-goddam-way-in-hell." Sloan meant every word. "Have a heart, bro."

"Wait, you haven't heard it all." Don wiped his hands on the sides of his pants, his tell for when he felt deeply about something. "She'll be your fiancée, girlfriend, ex-wife, hell... for all I care, your common-law floozy. Whatever you want to name her. But she's our best hope in uncovering secrets to stop possible terrorist activities from taking place on the island. Like I told you, she's got a background of living with Muslims and understands their ways. If you don't agree with going along with this plan, you won't believe the lengths the department is willing to go to. They're serious, Sloan. Homeland Security will harass those poor people, and you and I both know the damage they can do. If you care about the Amans at all, let us set this up."

Sloan pictured Sam and his family at the latest street barbecue, the shy way they interacted with the neighbors, little Dina running to him to be picked up and comforted after a fall she'd taken from her bike, her small arms confidentially circling his neck. They were a nice family. How could he let the government pursue these people, pester them until their lives were ruined or they were forced to move?

Still hedging, he asked, "What qualifications does this agent have? When did she move to Hawaii? How come I never met her?"

Nigel finally spoke up. "Her name is Special Agent Alia Hawkins and she transferred in from San Diego last month. She has impeccable credentials. Both her aunt and uncle belonged to the Muslim faith and after her parents died, she lived with their family until she'd graduated high school with honors through correspondence. Then she returned to the States and went to university in Chicago. After getting her Bachelor of Science in Criminology, she took her training at Quantico."

Don moved between Sloan and Nigel to draw Sloan's attention. "For the sake of Sam and his family, man, you need to do this."

Sloan replied, his voice filled with disgust. "Well, fuck!"

Chapter Six

"Now that's exactly what I said." Alia Hawkins entered the room in time to overhear Booker's snippy comment. "Sorry, boys, we got a call. There's a hostage situation happening in Waikiki and all agents in the vicinity have been ordered to assist."

Dullen flew to his feet, shock visible. "Yes, right. We'd better be off. Think about our offer, Mr. Booker."

Don stood in front of Sloan and didn't break eye contact even after Dullen's interruption. "She's a good agent, bro."

Sloan swivelled to assess the person they were discussing. The woman had longish, thick, light-brown hair she wore pushed up at the back, off her neck. Probably so the Hawaiian heat didn't affect her as much. He'd seen other girls mangle their hair in the same way.

This chick could be a model for a top agency, her makeup – and there was a lot of it – had been applied flawlessly. The black outline around the striking blue eyes added depth and made them appear huge, as did the false eyelashes. If he'd been asked, he'd admit that his first impression was of a princess who'd be high maintenance.

Her classy yet simple outfit looked like she'd just slipped into it, no wrinkles or sweat marks, kinda businesslike yet feminine. His eyes were drawn yet again to her legs; an image of them could keep a guy awake at night thinking how soft they'd feel wrapped around him. *Shit! Don't go there, man.* There was a small glittery bit of bling on her sandals, the only sign of frippery she'd allowed, and that little detail caught his interest.

Quickly, sensing her need to get moving, he searched her eyes once again and this time he read the dare she didn't try to hide.

"Okay. I'll go along with the set-up. But there's to be no love interest. Agent Hawkins can be my troubled stepsister, needing refuge. Set it up and call me to come in for briefing. Better move now; looks like you people have work to do, and so do I."

***

Alia heard Booker's statement about her being his sister and breathed a sigh of relief. She could handle living with a man as his relative, but there was no way in hell she wanted to fight off another agent's advances while being stuck living with him in his house on a covert assignment.

She'd had her experiences with harassment while doing her training at Quantico, guys thinking because she was a female they could push her around, take advantage, even force their attentions on her and she'd be willing to put up with their pawing bullshit.

In fact, at the beginning of her training, one drunken, overzealous student had tried trapping her in her room to have some fun—whether she'd wanted to or not. Thanks to being fit and fast, he'd ended up with a bruised face and feeling sorry for himself by her form of refusal.

His words the next day – "You could've just said no" – made her laugh sarcastically. "Buddy, you weren't in the mood to listen. Trust me, I tried. I guess all you wanted was to, ahh, feel… therefore I made you feel. So report me." She'd glared her challenge and watched the hustler back off, disgust plain on his face.

After he'd turned to go, she'd stepped up close and spoke to his back, her warning tone low, fury seeping through every word. "Creeps like you have no place in the FBI. I won't report you this time but I'll pass out the word to the other female agents that you need to be watched. That you're a pig who tries to take advantage of girls, overpower them and then pretend we asked for the treatment. Keep acting like – because you have a prick you're special

– and you won't last a month."

He'd stomped away and she'd followed through on her promise, warning the others. She'd been wrong; he'd lasted two months.

Don spoke up from the back seat and interrupted her thoughts. "Alia, Booker's good people. He's had a raw deal, what with his father dying unexpectedly and the garage being in such a mess that he had to step in. It's been a bitch for him not being able to do what he loves."

She turned to look at Agent Howard, a man she'd respected from the first day she'd arrived in the Honolulu agency's office. Sure he'd made a pass, like most of the single guys had, but he'd taken her refusal with grace and had offered friendship rather than trying to get her to change her mind. She liked that.

"So why didn't he sell the garage if he hates it there so much? He was admired at the agency. I still hear people telling Booker stories." Her question was fair and she waited for Don's answer.

"You met one of his reasons, Roy Parker. But you didn't meet the other, Lester Williams. A beach bum and surfer with a gift for incredible designs that would leave you astounded. Only reason he still's able to do the work God gave him the talent for is because Booker keeps him on the straight and narrow, like his old man used to. As it is, the reprobate falls off the wagon every once in a while and it takes the combined efforts of Booker and Roy to get him back in shape. But without Sloan being there every day to babysit, no telling what trouble those two old orphans would get into. Sure as hell, they'd lose the garage."

So... that bad boy, Sloan Booker, had more going for him than she'd thought. Not that a muscular body, thick black waves and deeply dangerous brown eyes with the slant of the island's heritage in their shape wouldn't be enough for most females.

Her initial judgement had taken a bit of a shit-kicking after listening to Don's explanation of his hunky friend's responsibilities. She'd considered Booker a swelled-headed egotist who looked down on women and thought highly of himself.

Maybe she was slightly off.

Maybe...

Chapter Seven

Following directions from Central, they finally arrived at a scene where destruction ruled. A group of misfits calling themselves *We're Bad*, a band who'd risen to fame almost overnight, had taken over the penthouse suite of one of the major hotels along Kalakaua Avenue. And they were out of control.

Partying was one thing, but taking the room maid hostage and trashing the joint was another. The management had called in saying the boys had weapons and shots had been fired.

When they arrived, other agents had cleared the lobby, shutting down all the exits. They'd sent an officer to every floor to stop the guests from leaving the safety of their rooms. Taking every precaution, they'd covered the stairwells too. Only one elevator was left working and Don, Nigel and Alia used that to join the SWAT guys on the top floor.

Being the lead, Don questioned the captain, "What's up, O'Brien?"

"We just got eyes in the main room and it looks like there're four in the band. Two are totally wasted, while the other two are crazy-high, I'd say probably cocaine lased with something else that's driving them loco. The girls have locked themselves in the bathroom. We think one room maid and a couple of groupies the guys picked up after the show who're terrified and refuse to open the door."

"So what are they shooting at?"

"Everything. They killed two TVs, shot the glass out of both front windows and are now aiming at the bathroom door, trying to coax the girls out."

Alia snorted. "Like that's gonna work!"

"Kinda what we've been trying to tell them. Didn't seem like they wanted to hear it though. They sent the next few shots toward us; we just dove out of the way in time. If we don't put a stop to the nonsense soon, those idiots are going to end up hurting someone."

"Maybe a woman's voice will calm them down. Here, let me try."

"Fine." The captain handed over a loudspeaker

and stepped back.

"What're their names?"

"The two still functioning are Slade Trolling and Dave Raster. Better known as Troll and Ras."

"Okay, here goes." Alia stepped toward the door, keeping to the right so she wasn't directly in front where bullet holes could be seen, and cleared her voice.

"Hey there, Mr. Slade, Mr. Ras, may I have a word? It's Special Agent Hawkins here."

Suddenly, a crash sounded in the room on the other side of the wall and everyone dove behind the bullet-proof barriers—everyone except Alia.

"Wow! I don't usually get such a reaction when I ask men if I can speak with them. What's happening?"

"Whaddya want, baby? Wanna come and join the party? Those other fucking whores won't come out from their hidey-hole. Crazy bitches." Another volley of shots was heard, and faint women's screams followed.

Alia banged on the door to get the shooter's attention. "Hey, calm down in there. You're terrifying those poor women. No wonder they won't come out. You're behaving rather inappropriately, don't you think?"

"Jus-s trying to have a little fun."

"Well, they're not having fun. Look, you need to stop this nonsense before someone gets hurt. If you and Dave drop your weapons and unlock the door, we'll get this settled."

"Can't, we're having a party. Need more booze, broke this stuff. Need more girls, wanna get high, forget..."

The voice dwindled down as if the speaker had lost his functions. They heard the sound of some-one falling, and within a few seconds, the SWAT member with eyes inside announced that Dave had crashed, leaving only Slade still performing.

"Slade, are you okay?" Alia kept her voice con-cerned, hoping to reel him in so he'd calm down.

"Whadda you care?"

"I care, my friend. You're obviously upset. Wanna talk about it, I'm listening."

They heard a body slide down the other side of the wall, his voice clear through the holes in the door. "We got a sell-out crowd tonight, people loved us. We're big stars. Did you know that?"

"Actually, I didn't. It must be pretty cool having everyone cheering for you."

"It's fr-frightening, is what it is. All those faces, people yelling, everyone wanting a piece of your soul."

"Never thought of it like that before. I guess I was under the impression that was why you per-formed on stage."

"Why, because we make a lot of money?"

"No, because you make a lot of people happy. They love you."

"How can they? They don't know me. I'm just

plain old Oliver Trolling from London." A sobbing note crept into his voice, warning her that whatever he was on was wearing off.

"Well, I'm very pleased to meet you, Oliver Trolling from London. Any chance we can shake hands like normal people, maybe share a cup of coffee?"

A loud sigh could be heard before a sound of something being tossed. What made Alia's heart swoop lower than her belly was the gunshot that followed and the grunt from a man who took a bullet. Oliver's scream "Dave!" was the final straw.

Moving out of the way, she waved on the SWAT team with the battering ram. Once the door flew open, first on the scene, she dashed inside.

With officers surging into the room behind her, and commotion happening everywhere, all Alia focused on was getting to Oliver. Unable to stand upright, the stumbling fool hovered over the body of his buddy. Blood gushed from a gaping wound on Dave's shoulder and swear words oozed from his mouth. He screamed. "Ollie-man, why the hell did you shoot me?"

"I didn't mean too, Ras. I was throwing the gun away. I didn't know it would go off." Oliver's tears were making it difficult for him to speak. "Shit man, I'm sorry."

As Alia moved in, Oliver reacted to having a person near him. He went for her, gripping her shoulders harshly, hurtfully. Without a second's hesitation, she reacted and flipped him over so she could restrain his movements. The guy was out of his mind and taking chances wasn't in the cards. He needed to be shut down.

"Okay, Oliver. Just relax now. We'll get your buddy to the hospital and let the doctors repair the damage. Unfortunately, you'll be downtown answering questions."

"I jus-s wanted to spend some time being happy."

"Once the hotel hands over the bill to your agent, you'll be spending a hell of a lot more than time."

Chapter Eight

Weary, slouched at the bar in a local drinking establishment at the end of twelve frustrating non-stop hours of work, Sloan's attention became riveted on his friend.

"You should have seen her, Sloan. Cool as a cucumber. Bullets flying and she didn't even flinch. Christ, Nigel had worked his way behind the barriers as soon as we arrived and she'd moved right up in front of me, like you used to. Craziest damn thing I ever saw."

"She's got balls, so what. Are there any brains working at the top end? Or is she a hotshot show-off? We've seen them before. They get themselves and other people killed."

"No, she's not like that. Used common-sense

when she talked that idiot down—had it settled. If he hadn't thrown the gun so it went off accidently, we'd have been in there without any casualties. As it was, her tactics were pretty to watch and she moves like a warrior."

Sloan eyeballed his old partner. He couldn't stop the knowing grin that plastered itself over his face. "I gather you've made your play already and it didn't go over. That's not like you."

Dan picked up the cold bottle of Koko Brown beer to rub it over his forehead. Then he did the sideways glance he always used when embarrassed. "Yeah, well I wasn't the only one. She's made it pretty clear she's not interested. Korver took it personally, says she's a lesbian."

"Korver would. His tiny brain couldn't visualize anyone smart enough to turn him down."

Sloan scratched at the beard that always appeared halfway through the day. By nightfall, it shadowed his face. Sensing his partner's unease, he searched Don's brown-eyed gaze and saw the hard-jawed cop he'd fought beside through many battles return his stare. "You wanted me to take this assignment. It matters to you, I can tell. I just don't know why."

After another gulp at the bottle, Don put his elbow on the bar and leaned his head on his palm. "Last weekend at the street barbecue you invited me to, Sam Aman sat with me for a while. He's a proud man, and the dude had tears in his eyes watching his family interact with everyone else, being accepted as if they belonged."

"He's a softie."

"I know." Don grinned at Sloan. "Your cul-de-sac is a little United Nations. Your next-door neighbors, the Newmans, are black like me, and the rest are a mixture of white families, Chinese and interracial Hawaiian. It's kinda nice to see everyone being friends, the kids all playing together and the pot-luck food tables filled with such a variety."

"Yeah, yeah, get to the point. You planned for me to do this because...?"

"Because I don't want to see that family get hurt. Sure there's enough circumstantial evidence to flag Sam and Janna and you'll hear it all, but it's not enough to make any arrests or convict them. Far from it."

"So, I'm to prove they're innocent rather than find confirmation of their guilt."

"I just hope you find the truth."

"Hey, fuckie, you're gonna ride me on this one, aren't you?"

The stubborn lines around Don's mouth appeared. "What do you think?"

"I think I'm screwed."

Chapter Nine

A certain ring tone, one that sent vibes of tension detonating inside Alia Hawkins, jangled from the special phone she kept in her pocket. This small phone never got left behind and never ran out of battery. It was a lifeline for some poor youngster who needed help, and Alia would ultimately be their savior.

How the hell she got into this role, she'd never know. Life had a way of manipulating one and she'd been suckered by a pro – her son's nanny, Ruby. The woman had often been described as an angel. True, Ruby did have a big heart. But it was her disciple, Alia, who had a soft head or she'd have put a stop to this nonsense a long time ago. But she hadn't and each call brought action.

Quickly closing the drawer of her desk at the Honolulu FBI bureau's office, she turned her chair to the wall and answered. "Hey, Ruby, what's up?"

"This one sounds really young and scared, Alia. She's being followed but managed to give them a slip and is at the ABC store on Kalakaua Avenue, the one near Koa. Her name is Sara."

"Where do I take her?"

The slight hesitation left Alia under no illusions. Anger sizzled but resignation won out. "Not again, Ruby."

"I'm sorry, Alia. Every place in the city is brimful tonight, Harvey can take her tomorrow. I'll keep her in my room until then."

"This isn't—"

"I know. Can't be helped. She said she's clean. Are you on your way?"

"Heading for the car right now. See you soon."

Alia walked out of the office, breathing a sigh of relief that no one stopped her. Since she often operated alone, the times she'd be forced to leave with no explanation had worked in her favor. No one thought to question her about her destination.

Heading to her black issued SUV, again she wondered how she'd gotten roped into these mercy missions. When they'd left San Diego, she'd sworn they'd stop and Ruby had agreed. But it hadn't taken long for the big-hearted one-time-victim to set up a network here in Honolulu, and the next thing she knew, Alia, vigilante and street rescuer, had been revived yet again.

Not that she'd fought against it too much. Truthfully, it made her feel good to know she'd helped a lot of the young misfits find a way out of the messes they'd unfortunately gotten themselves into.

So many were teens with either problems at home, or had gotten with the wrong man or had a drug addiction that enslaved them. Hell, there were too many reasons to name. And they all led to a future that none of these kids had ever imagined for themselves.

Her nanny, Ruby, knew this all too well, life also had a way of engulfing those who couldn't swim fast enough. And now every fallen angel had to be helped.

Alia arrive at the convenience store, leaving her car double-parked and hoping to get away with it. She entered the store and quickly found her victim, a young girl with a bright pink bathing suit cover-up wrapped around her like a native dress. Her long hair looked like a rat's nest, her legs and feet were bare. And her eyes were full of terror. She couldn't have been more than fifteen.

When she saw Alia, she flinched and began to cry.

"You're Sara, right? Ruby sent me."

"Yes. I'm Sara. It's too late. He's found me and keeps walking past the store, waiting for me to come out."

"Tall dude, struts like he owns the world, long hair and a mean face?"

"Yes. He's my friend. But I can't be with anyone else. I just can't." Her voice began to get louder until Alia motioned for her to keep it down. "He's going to kill me for calling you."

"He'll have to get past me first, honey. And that ain't going to happen. Let's go."

Alia took the girl's hand and pulled her to follow. Sara held back and began crying again. Just as they came close to the cash registers, the store manager ran up to them, waving his phone and hissing a warning. "I don't want no trouble in here. I call the police if you make trouble. Get out now." He pointed at the door, his face mottled with anger and his finger shaking with fear.

"No trouble. We're leaving. Come on, Sara. Just do as I say and we'll get away. You'll never have to see that prick again, I promise. Let's go."

Sara locked eyes with Alia and must have seen the calm, the absolute certainty. She swiped her arm over the mess on her face, gathered her courage along with the cotton wrap and squeezed Alia's hand harder.

As soon as they moved onto the street, the stalker dude stepped up. "Ah, here you are, baby. I was waiting for you." He reached to take what he considered his possession and ended face to face with Alia instead. "Get into my car, Sara. The black Honda SUV double-parked." She blocked the way so Sara had a clear path to the vehicle.

"Wait, girlfriend. Don't leave me. I need you. We'll talk things out, I promise." The phoney good-looking actor, trying to con the young teen, could star in a porn movie, but for Alia, his syrupy whine, full of sexual coaxing, made her want to heave.

"Hey bud, back off. Sara, get in the car." The girl only hesitated for a few seconds and then quickly dove to safety.

Once his charm wasn't needed, the mean streak appeared, no doubt the same one responsible for the swelling on the Sara's face. "Get out of my way. That bitch is my property."

Alia grabbed the front of his shirt and pushed him up against the wall of the store, her body blocking the view of her gun stuck into his side. The little gray shooter convinced him to let her do whatever the hell she wanted.

"You mean son of a bitch, back off. She's no one's property but her own. If I see you near her again, I'll come after you with the full force of the law. You won't get away with just a warning."

His breath, stinking of cigarettes and beer, had her gag reflexes kicking in and she quickly stepped away. "Just accept Sara got away and write her off."

"Ain't gonna happen, cop whore. We'll get her back. I'm just her handler, but she's the boss's property and he don't like anyone messing with his girls. You're gonna be sorry."

"Who's the boss? Tell me and I'll go visit him myself, have a little talk."

"Yeah, like I'm that stupid. Fuck you, cop."

Alia saw the uniform first, making his way over to see what the fracas was all about. Knowing she couldn't answer any questions, she started towards her car as if she hadn't a care in the word, got in and drove off.

Sara watched out her window. "He's so pissed."

"Look, Sara, he doesn't matter. Not anymore. You're safe now and you never have to do what he says again." Alia watched the rear view mirror and sure enough, as suspected, she caught sight of the red Camaro zig-zagging through the traffic, trying to keep up. Loving this part of the game, she drove through the streets she'd mapped out in her getaway plan. In every area of the city she had a perfect route charted, and Waikiki wasn't any different.

As she led them in a merry chase, she listened to Sara crying. "Are those happy tears? You got away, they should be. You know Ruby's promises are solid and the people she supports don't deal with cops or government agencies, it's just street people looking out for others. Most of them have been where you are now and they want to help you."

"I know. The others told me, gave me her number, said to call if it got rough. But I never thought I'd have to. Roger was so nice at first. I thought he loved me."

"Yeah, a lot of girls think the same thing. He's a shit, like all the other pimps. And eventually, he'd have forced you into doing things you never imagined he'd ever ask of you."

"That's why I ran away today. He wanted me to let those men... Oh crap, they were old and ugly, one was fat and slobbered all over my chest. I kneed him and ran."

"Good, I hope you crippled the son of a bitch."

Sara gave a sad giggle and carried on. "They started offering me pot but it makes me sick, so they backed off. Then they had booze, but I saw them add some pills so I refused to drink it. I hate alcohol, but they kept trying to coax me and I knew why they insisted. Get me drunk so they could do whatever they wanted. Oh, God... They were so gross."

"And we both know what they had in mind, don't we? You would eventually heal physically but those mental scars, they'd be scored into your memory for life. Look, I gotta ask. Are you on any drugs, Sara? I need to know because you'll be staying with me and Ruby tonight and I've got a kid to protect."

"No. Sometimes, I drink beer but that's it. I swear." She started to cry, deep sobs that sprung from her disgust, her revulsion ripped through her throat, harsh and ugly, pain-filled and real.

Alia hoped this would happen. The cleansing

needed to begin. She drove around, giving the kid time. Purposely, she headed to the busy Ala Moana Boulevard for long enough to see if they followed and sure enough, there they were, still tailing her. She took a few fast corners and headed for the parking lot where they'd make good their escape.

Once she'd backed into the slot she paid monthly rent for, she hustled Sara from the car and hurried over to the next row where a duplicate model and color SUV sat waiting. Taking a bunch of magnetic stick-ons from the floor of the front seat, she applied them to the back bumpers, the side doors and one on the hood; goofy stickers promoting the sun and fun of Hawaii.

"Hurry, get in the back and cover yourself with this blanket. Don't look up." While Sara did as she was told, Alia opened another bag in the front seat and took out a long blond wig with masses of ringlets. Adding pink-framed glasses and applying red lipstick, she quickly got behind the wheel, opened the window and cranked up the hot rock. While driving, she added net gloves, pink and flashy, to her costume, and as she drove past the red Camaro, she banged her hand on the steering wheel, a tourist out for a night's entertainment.

Within a block, she knew her little circus had paid off. She'd evaded the asshole and it was safe to head home. She turned down the volume, threw the wig to the passenger seat and retrieved a tissue to wipe off the lipstick. "We've lost them, Sara, but it's safer if you stay down."

"Are we going to Ruby now?" Sad and weepy, Sara's muffled voice had Alia gripping the wheel harder.

"Yeah, sweetie, we're going to see Ruby. When we get there, I'll take you in through the back door to Ruby's place downstairs, where you can decide if you want to press charges against those bastards or you just want to start fresh, maybe grab a shower."

"No charges." Fear snaked through Sara's voice. Just the thought made the volume rise to near hysteria. Alia knew she'd reached the end of her courage.

"Your choice, kiddo. You're free to make them now."

Chapter Ten

Alia left Sara in the downstairs room and headed up to find her eight-year-old son, Kean, still up watching TV, waiting for her. The nanny, twenty-five-year-old Ruby Cruz, lay sprawled beside him on the sofa, a half-empty dish of popcorn leaning precariously between them.

Alia bent over the brown leather furniture to fondle her boy's hair. "Bedtime, son, it's after eight. Pajamas and brush your teeth. I'll be up to visit in a few minutes."

"Aw, Mom, you just got home."

"And yet you haven't taken your eyes off the screen."

"I'm watching this documentary on building ships."

"Record it and you'll have it for tomorrow. Scoot now."

His grunt of displeasure didn't deter her as he knew it wouldn't. He picked up the remote, pressed the necessary button and gave Ruby a gentle hug before disappearing up the stairs.

Alia removed her weapon and locked it in the safe hidden in the side table. Then she moved closer to Ruby, who looked worn, the black shadows under her eyes telling a tale of sleepless nights and a worried soul.

"Don't rush away, Ruby. Sara is fine. She's downstairs having a shower so you can take your time going to her. Have you heard from your family in the Philippines today? How is your father?" Alia sat beside her employee.

"Not good news, Alia. He's not getting any better. My sister, she's worried, but her family's so large she can only spend a little time with him. He wants to go home, only she can't take care of him there, and in her house, there's no extra space."

Tears began forming in Ruby's already reddened eyes and they tore at Alia. She and softhearted didn't go together except when it came to her family and old people. Then she was pure mush.

"Ruby, we've been together since Kean was born and there's no one I trust more with him, you know that. You're an amazing woman. Not only have you taken care of us, but look at the numerous other people you've helped over the years. All those countless hours you put in, walking the streets, handing out your cards, urging the young ones to call you for help whenever they need you."

Ruby's expression lightened. "I know in the last year or so you wanted me to back off from the program in San Diego. And I promised not to get involved here in Honolulu. Then I broke my word. You've never given me hell for that, Alia. And I never told you I was sorry."

"Never? Only maybe a hundred times. Look, you know why I hoped you wouldn't get involved here. Kean is growing up and I'm not sure I want him around some of the messes we get tangled up with. So far, he's accepted the occasional 'friend' staying over, young girls who are here for a short time, but soon he'll begin to ask questions. So let's not bring anymore stray kittens to the house, okay?" Alia grinned away her sarcasm, and Ruby's theatrical look of sorrow melted away. The little actress kept trying but her skills needed a lot of polishing.

Besides, Alia knew that there was no way in hell that Ruby would turn her back on a call. Even if it meant paying for a hotel room herself, something she'd done many times. So had Alia, if the truth were known.

In San Diego, Ruby had set up a network of ex-street people who'd banded together to save lost souls. She'd started this arrangement secretly until one night a frantic call had come. No one else was available to pick the kid up, so she'd turned to Alia for help. After that first time, Alia had become a regular transporter. But she'd hoped that once they'd left the mainland, it would end there.

Sadly, within a week of them moving to Honolulu, Ruby had begun to organize the youngsters on the street here, and Alia was again carrying a special phone.

"I'm sorry, Alia. I can't help remembering how you saved me when I was in a similar situation, how much it meant to me. Without you, I would have taken those pills I stole from the hospital. I meant to kill myself. You knew it, and so did I."

"And Kean and I would have had to manage on our own, without your wonderful cooking and having you picking up the messes we leave everywhere. I don't think we could have survived without you, my friend."

No matter how hard Ruby worked for the discarded kids from the streets, she was totally loyal to Alia and Kean. Years earlier, Alia had saved her from human traffickers who'd kidnapped her and others from the same village.

Only fifteen, Ruby had been ripped from her family, brought to San Diego and forced to do all kinds of horrific things to stay alive. She'd lost count of the number of men she'd been forced to service but had pushed the nightmares of that brutal life to the back of her mind, only for them to be reignited whenever she saw another poor helpless girl.

Enslaved for six month before Alia and her people had broken into the warehouse, poor Ruby had suffered horribly. Beaten for trying to protect one of the younger girls, she'd been taken to the hospital where Alia found herself almost daily, visiting, supporting the homeless teen.

Ruby's guilt had stopped her from taking advantage of the city's provision to send her back to her homeland. Instead, with Alia's help, she'd chosen to stay and work in this country.

Alia, pregnant at the time, had gladly found the girl a job and even a place to live. Until after Kean was born. Then she'd moved Ruby in with them and they'd become a family of three.

For eight years, Alia had marvelled at her good fortune. But now, she needed to think of Ruby. The young woman was hurting, and Alia had the cure.

"I'm going to buy you a ticket for Manila tomorrow. You have to go home, Ruby. Be with your family and make peace with them. What happened to you wasn't your fault. Hasn't Father Bowen continually told you that? And so have I."

Ruby nodded reluctantly. "You don't understand. Maybe my body's been cleansed, Alia. But I'll never wash the filth from my soul. That's why the young people we save matter so much."

Alia took Ruby's face into her hands and forced the other to look into her eyes. "Think of all those kids you've helped over the years, Ruby. Even now, you have a fifteen-year-old downstairs crying her heart out, a girl who will have a chance because of you. Do you ever wonder if the nightmare you suffered had a purpose?"

Ruby blinked, but the tears still streamed. "Alia, you save them. I only pass on their names and locations."

"Maybe I deliver them but it's you they trust. You who visits the streets to talk to them and hand out your card. You, not me, who cares so much about what becomes of them. You're their savior. I just deliver. Look... you have everything under control now. I can take the calls direct rather than you passing them on."

"No. You have too much to do. Cassie can take the calls and give you the messages like I do. She's offered to handle the phone when I wasn't available."

"Okay, good. Think about my words. Think hard. In the big scheme of things, I'm about to give you the same advice you pass onto the girls you save. Those assholes who stole you don't really matter anymore. Neither do the ones that used you. The only people who really matter are your family. If you feel regret for what happened to you now, I can't imagine the remorse you'll feel if you don't choose to help your people, who really need you."

Ruby's soft brown eyes grew large. For the first time, Alia didn't see the usual shutters closing off her words. Instead, Ruby listened. Her expression became thoughtful and then lightened. "I must go."

"Yes."

"How can I leave you and Kean?"

"We'll be fine. He goes to school all day and I can find a babysitter for afterward. It's only until you come back. We can manage. We have to."

Excitement filled Ruby's face. "I can go home."

"Yes." Alia hugged Ruby hard, shaking her so she'd understand the emotion. Then she whispered, "It's time, Ruby."

***

Explaining the situation to Kean later didn't go quite as smoothly as Alia had hoped. "Why can't Ruby Skype them, talk to them online? Does she have to go all the way to Manila?"

"Her father's ill, Kean. He needs her. She has to go."

"We need her, too. We're family, aren't we?"

"Yes, but families do what's best for each other, and right now it's best for her to go back to the Philippines and make peace with her past. You've asked me before why Ruby gets so sad sometimes. Well, it started there. She needs to go back and face it."

"I guess."

"We'll be fine, you and me. I'll find the best babysitter on the planet and I'll cut back on my hours at work."

"O-kay. I'll miss her so much though, Mom."

"Me too."

She kissed him goodnight, something she forced herself to do every night even though showing the affection was so difficult. Her lips lingered on his forehead longer than usual. Then she left his room to go to hers.

The minute the door closed behind her, she sunk to the floor and covered her face with trembling hands.

So where's your courage now, idiot? You're sending Ruby away. Now you'll be alone to deal with everything. Being the mommy. How are you going to survive without her? And what about this new assignment?

An image of Sloan Booker unexpectedly slipped into her head and she felt the fear swell and her muscles clench. Agitated, she forced herself to take a few calming breaths.

Having Hawaiian blood had only added to his rugged handsomeness. Amber brown eyes that didn't stop probing were going to be hell to live with. And his tall physique and muscular frame wouldn't bend to any woman's demands; she knew it. Just like she knew she'd be making them.

Friggin', shittin', hell… Why did life have to throw so much crap at a person all at once?

Chapter
Eleven

Swiping at the unexpected tears, Alia gave herself a mental kick. *Okay, stop it. Booker's not Paul.* He wasn't anything like her ex-husband. That asshole had screwed up her life enough and she refused to give him any time in her head or let him have any more power in her life.

Her last conversation with Paul, the one that had made her flee San Diego, had almost convinced her to pull her weapon. Silly bastard couldn't believe she'd refuse his offer.

It had only taken two years of living in hell with a workaholic drunk, for her to throw in the cards. Young and naïve, she'd never known a person could be both but it turned out she was wrong.

She was also wrong about him being an

upstanding citizen; his work mostly hovered on the borderline between criminal and shady. She'd never regretted her decision to leave him, especially after Ruby had entered the picture to help her raise Kean.

Veering back to their conversation, the one that had prompted her to relocate as far away from San Diego as possible, Alia felt the anger rise yet again. The same fury that had flooded when she'd sat in front of him... her mouth hanging open and disbelief raging at his stupidity.

"You want me to—what? Be a surrogate for you and your new wife? Are you insane? Working all those hours, drinking all that booze and hiding your business dealings from the law has finally disintegrated the last of your smarts. You're over the edge, pal."

Paul had leaned forward, earnest, the hot-shot dealer selling the biggest deal in his life. "We just want you to donate your eggs for the IVF process. You have Kean, *my son*, and I've never intruded or interfered in your life with him, have I? I knew he was happy with you and Ruby, and during those years, I'd have been a piss-poor dad anyway."

"Hey, bud, if we're being real here let's at least be truthful. You never interfered because work came first; it's your mistress, your fun... hell, your whole reason to get out of bed every morning. You didn't give a shit about me or your son. Give me a break; as long as we didn't interfere with things important to you, life was good. "

"Okay, true. But that was eight years ago. I've changed, remarried to a lovely girl and she wants a baby. I mean, she *really* needs a baby... my baby. Adoption won't work for her. I've tried everything, trips, gifts, big brand new house, pets, hell I'll do anything, but she's miserable for a baby. And the final tests prove she's infertile."

"You're breaking my heart."

"Look, I've made a lot of money. I know you haven't taken any from me; my lawyer has come back time and again to say you've refused and that you only signed the trust papers for Kean."

"As if I didn't know you were using us as a way to shield your profits."

Paul had waved away her reply. "As his biological father, I have rights too."

Furious, she'd pointed her finger in his face and spat out her anger. "You gladly signed those rights away in court to give me full custody."

Paul had smiled sadly. "Something I've always regretted. Nowadays, with all my influence in the political arena, Alia, my pet, I could have that over-turned just with a snap of my fingers."

Hardly able to breathe, she'd hissed, "You'd go that far?"

"He's a good kid, strong and smart. Any man would be proud to be his dad."

At that point fear had paralyzed her. "What are you talking about?" She'd moved to San Diego after Kean had been born for just this reason—to keep Paul out of her and her son's life. "When did you see him?"

"Oh, don't get your shit in a knot. I haven't broken our agreement. But I could so easily. Drop a few lies, talk to some valuable allies I've amassed along with my fortune, and things could be totally different. You and I both know it, so don't mess with me, Miss Bigshot FBI Agent."

"Let me get this straight. You're blackmailing me for my eggs, so you can give my child to a woman half your age to raise. It ain't gonna happen, bud. And if you so much as touch a hair on my son's head, I'll come for you and I'll be carrying my bigshot *FBI*-issued weapon." She'd stood to leave but he'd held her wrist, leaving a bruise to remind her of that conversation for many days.

"Just think about it. You've had Kean all to yourself. The baby I gave you. Now I want a baby for me. It's not too much to ask."

"You're crazy, Paul. Nuts! Loonier than a bat with rabies. What you want from me is more than I'd ever be willing to pay. Leave me and Kean alone. Get yourself another donor and lie to your wife."

"That's just it. I guess I didn't make myself clear. You're *my* choice for the mother, not hers. I want another kid like Kean. And I always get what I want. Think about it. I'll give you a month."

Two weeks later, Alia had settled in her new home on the island of Oahu. A helpful realtor had found a house with high walls around a good-sized yard. She'd added a top-of-the-line security system. Then she'd tried to forget about the shadow hanging over her.

Tried...

Chapter Twelve

Before heading to the agency the next morning, as promised, Sloan stopped at the garage first to find Les working in his area. Airbrushes, spray guns and paint surrounded the beaming man immersed in his specialty.

A few days before, he'd taken a custom detailing on a Harley for a demanding customer. With the steady hand of a master, he was working the ultimate touches on his intricate dragon versus angel design.

The purple and dark pink hues of the swirling angels offset the vibrant reds, golds and oranges of the dragons. The battle between the two sets of warriors waged on, encircled by filmy smoke, burning flames and sparkling mist that swirled around the heavenly beings.

Sloan shook his head, still not able to understand how this old genius could come up with such details and then replicate it exactly on both fenders.

"Hey, Sloan, whaddaya think? Figure Bo will like it?"

Since Bo, the Harley's owner, weighed in at over three hundred pounds, sported a Hell's Angels vest and carried himself with a hard-assed attitude that screamed... *Don't fuck with me*, Sloan sure as hell hoped so.

"How can he not? You've outdone yourself, Les. I think this is the best one yet."

"Crissakes, boy. You say that about all my work. Can't you spit out an original compliment?"

"Quit angling, you old fart. I like it already."

A twinkle appeared in the sapphire sparkles of Les's still attractive eyes. He stretched his lean, muscular body that almost reached Sloan's own six feet, three inches before speaking again. "I'm thinking Bo's gonna get his shit in a knot when I tell him the price has doubled. The son of a bitch paid me, but the ugly asshole's laughing behind my back."

Visualizing the invoice from the new system that'd been recently instigated, Sloan shook his head. "You charged the man fifteen hundred. It's fair."

"Ratfink bastard added stuff to the design after

I wrote out that stupid bill; wanted two angels instead of the original one. And he decided I should cover the whole area rather than the smaller picture we'd agreed on. To top that off, he wanted the image replicated on both sides. Fuck's sake, Sloan, I can't afford to work for nuthin'."

Roy climbed out of the pit from under the Stingray. He dropped his tools and joined Sloan and Les. "*Pfft.* You jus' gotta make trouble, old man, don'tcha? Sloan's been working so hard to get this place in shape, and ya buck him at every turn."

Les winked at Sloan, put his hands on his hips and grumbled, "Watch yer mouth, Roy. You never let *me* say fuck. Not without getting shit."

Red exploded in Roy's cheeks as he spit his indignation. "I said buck. B-U-C-K. Get your ears cleaned, and while you're at it, get them to wash out your mouth too."

Les laughed, delighted that he'd riled Roy. The two were at it all day. "Who said you could come out of your cage?"

"I heard you trying to make trouble. That Bo's a mean one."

"Yep, bat-shit crazy. And cheap as a pimp trying to cut down the booze for his alcoholic whore. I know that already, nosey-parker. I'm havin' a discussion with my boy here so butt out." In a way that no sixty-five-year-old should be able to do, Les lifted himself on the counter as easily as a man half his age.

Red-faced, agitation bristling his whiskers, Roy yelled. "He's not your boy, you old fool. He's your boss and you treat him with respect. If he says you charge what you invoiced, that's the end of it."

"But he never said that, did he? How could he when you interrupted before he could get a word out... nosey asshole."

Sloan recognized the beginnings of a full-out battle between the two old co-workers. He'd heard them going at it all his life and had learned to either take off or cut it short at the start.

"Hey, enough! Did you tell Bo you'd have to charge more when he told you to change the plans?"

Les pushed his long ponytail over his shoulder and leaned forward, both hands now on his knees. "Fuck him. He's got a brain, don't he? It makes sense it'll cost more."

"What costs more?" Bo ambled into sight from around the corner. Soon as he saw the finished bike, he moved swiftly and bent to his knees. "Dammit all to hell, dude. You got it perfect."

Les drawled his response, "I knew you'd like it. I added the stuff you wanted but it's gonna cost you more. You told me to double the image and that means double the price."

Bo straightened.

Sloan stiffened.

Roy groaned.

"I don't think so, Les. You gave me an invoice,

overcharged me as far as I'm concerned, but I'm a fair guy and I paid you." Bo's beady eyes glowed, almost obliterated by the bushy eyebrows and overgrown whiskers that covered his face. "Don't fuck with me, man."

Les didn't hesitate. "Sure you paid for the image on the right, you cheap prick. You want I should erase the other side, I can do it. You gotta understand, my time's worth money, man. Seems only right you should pay for it—if you want your bike back."

Sloan, wishing Les had cleared the cost with Bo before doing the work, clenched his fists. He could see Bo wasn't taking to being dissed from the likes of a garage employee.

"Okay, let's all calm down. We can talk about this." Since he'd never interfered with Les's prices and his way of charging before, Sloan had no idea if the estimate was fair or not. Every designer set his own rates, which was as it should be. Some were geniuses like Les, and others... not so much.

Provoked, Bo started to walk towards Les, his hands clenched, his manner that of a man who was pissed.

Sloan blocked his path. "I said we'd discuss this, like professionals—"

Before he could finish his sentence, Bo pushed him aside to get to Les. Not willing to let that happen, Sloan hauled back and slugged the guy in the stomach. Before he could follow through with a blow to the head, Bo swung his arm and brushed Sloan off like a bug. He had Les in his sights.

Roy, not liking this treatment, stepped into the fray and got himself shoved aside in a similar manner.

Throughout the skirmish, Les never moved. Not until Bo reached for him. Then his feet came up and the strong surfer's muscles in his legs kicked out, sending the big man went flying ass-over-tea-kettle, crashing into the steel cabinets lined up along the wall.

Totally wild now, he rushed back to Les, whose fists were up and ready, but met Sloan who wasn't about to let Bo loose.

First he kicked out Bo's leg using the tackling method taught to him during basic training. Then he forced the man to his knees. He had Bo's hands behind his back in seconds. Restraining his arm in a move-and-you'll-be-sorry hold, he hissed. "Bo, I swear I'll break the goddamn thing if you don't stop. Then how'll you ride your precious Harley?"

Bo's struggling ceased. He cussed a fine string and then heaved a sigh. "Okay! Fine. I'll pay."

Les, seeing as how he'd gotten his way, decided to be magnanimous. He pushed his long silver tail of thick hair back over his shoulder and crouched down. "If I halve the price because it wasn't discussed beforehand, will you accept it? Don't wanna make enemies. Jus' wanna get paid for an honest day's work."

Bo stared into Les's eyes, taking his measure. "Seriously, man? You gonna take seven-fifty?"

"I will."

"I don't have that much on me, got a couple hundred. Can I take the bike and bring back the rest?"

"You can. Let him up, Sloan. We gotta shake on it so I know the man won't break his word."

Sloan let go of Bo's arms and helped him to his feet. Without a break in his movement, Bo slugged Sloan in the face and then stuck his hand out toward Les. "I didn't hit him hard, but the man's gotta know he can't be punching me and getting away with it."

Sloan stayed Les's fist and rubbed his cheek where he had no doubt a bruise would be showing up soon. "Just get this over with so I can leave. Bo, give Les the money."

Bo made a point of handing Les the money, and then waited for Les to finally shake hands. Once the deal was settled, he wheeled his bike to the entrance and the three left behind listened as the motor clicked and then clicked again without starting.

Taking the two spark plugs and a wrench from the drawer where they'd been hidden, Les threw them at Bo and watched as the man fit the parts into place and retried the bike, which started with a roar and disappeared.

Les turned to Sloan and grinned. "Let that be a

lesson to you, son. Don't ever let anyone ever take advantage of you. Know your worth."

Roy pointed at Les before he disappeared back to his own area. "One thing I know, you ain't worth a punch in the face."

"I love you, too, Santa Claus."

Roy flashed him his middle finger and an unholy grin split his face. "Hope Bo gets a lot of use from your wrench he just rode off with."

Chapter
Thirteen

Alia saw Sloan's arrival in the main area at work and watched the others crowd around to welcome the good-looker. She knew the crew at the agency liked him. Many times, they'd indulged in their hero-worshipping tales until she'd felt nauseated and left.

In the coffee room, they told funny stories about his exploits, women troubles and, with awe in their voices, talked about the times he'd put his life on the line to save others. Their favorite was when he'd taken a bullet while dragging a fallen co-worker to safety during a shootout at a drug bust.

From their respectful summary, she'd discovered that his comrades admired him. But in her mind, he was nothing but a womanizing prick with no fear for his safety, and he epitomized a man who always got his way. Well, she was one woman he wouldn't be getting his way with.

Don't talk so fast, chickie!

Riiight! She'd been assigned to live with him for an unspecified amount of time. Him and his friggin' dimples and sexy buns and his melting, brown-eyed stare. That 'him'. The drool-trigger who could be a game-changer.

Shaken, she remembered her promise to Kean about how she'd spend more time with, because the one person in his life he'd always depended on for every meal and bedtime story was leaving.

Her stomach knotted and the world began to close in. She made a silent plea to the big guy upstairs. As if in answer, a spark suddenly lit up some dazed brain cells that, due to all the stress, hadn't been wholly functional. An incredible idea surfaced.

It could work.

And be the perfect solution.

She'd take Kean along as her son. He'd stay with her and out of Paul's reach. And, be a part of her cover as Sloan's stepsister. *After all, there's nothing saying you have to be a single sister, right?*

Her clenched muscles began to unwind as did the tightness in her chest. Kean would also be a safety net in case Sloan attempted any of his womanizing tricks on her. Not that she couldn't handle the prick if he tried any hanky-panky, but in her state of sexual deprivation, would she even want to stop him?

Her brain went into overdrive and began creating a story to tell Kean about her and Sloan being separated as youngsters. About how she'd found her stepbrother and now she wanted to get to know him better. *Good. That's good.* And, with them having to leave their house because of the termites, maybe he'd invite them to stay with him for a while.

It was plausible.

Okay, it was thin, but with Ruby leaving, it might fly. Especially if she hired the contractors to do the work needed in her house and presented the whole package well. Her eight-year-old was smart as a whip, but he usually accepted whatever she said as gospel.

Besides, he wouldn't have any reason to be suspicious. Thankfully, she hadn't talked about her childhood a lot, other than to say she had been adopted and her parents had died. If she brought in a fictional stepbrother, he'd have no reason to doubt the truth.

So far, all the dialogue surrounding the case had been about the Aman family, discussing options and strategies. No doubt, bringing her son into the picture at this late date might be like throwing a lit match on a propane barbecue but what could she do?

As far as Kean's safety went, it wasn't expected

there would be any danger during this undercover investigation. It was strictly surveillance: record Samir Aman's visitors, get close to his wife, Janna, and see if she could discover information about their earlier life, mainly zeroing in on Janna's family.

Homeland Security wanted her and Sloan together before for the Amans' anticipated visitors from Pakistan arrived. They were expected in the coming week. The agencies had their sights on those people especially, and wanted to know the reasons for the trip, where they spent their time while in the city and with whom.

Previously, Ruby would have been there to look after Kean and they would have managed. Alia's lifestyle of long hours and undercover cases had taken her away from him many times and they'd always dealt with those situations fairly well. How ironic that she'd been pissed at Paul for having let his work rule his life, and she'd become his female equivalent with the same sin.

In fact, lately, she'd worried that Kean's attachment to Ruby overrode his love for his mother. But then she'd always stifled her affections, kept them to herself, unable to openly show him her devotion.

As an only child raised by stoic Brits who didn't believe in coddling or displays of affection other than a pat on the head, it was hard to overcome that kind of early training.

After her parents died within a year of one another, both from different cancers, her aunt, who'd married a man of the Islam faith had taken her from her home in Chicago to live with their large family halfway across the world.

Everyone had treated her kindly and they were always willing to listen, but again, they weren't an affectionate family either. Her uncle had been the Imam in the mosque close to where they'd lived, a very gentle, knowledgeable man. He'd prayed for a daughter and believed Mohammad had sent Alia as the answer to his prayers. He was probably the only person in her life who'd made her feel truly cherished.

She'd returned to the US to attend university and attain her Bachelor of Science in Criminology, and then signed up for her FBI training at Quantico. Her first assignment had taken place back home in Chicago, where she'd met Paul.

For a short time, she'd been madly infatuated with him. He'd been a voracious lover, demanding but equally giving. Every minute they'd shared, he'd lavished her with affection that she'd sucked up like a person who'd been on a starvation diet for years.

Which she had.

In turn, she'd adored the man, and in those first few glorious months of marriage, she'd floated through each day with blinkers on her eyes and a song in her heart, that had soon turned into a wail of disappointment.

Like everything that was too good to be true, her romanticized reality *was* too good to be true. She'd found her hero was actually a dud, a phony. Having been with the agency for a few years, she'd seen the signs that his business buddies weren't of the highest calibre, and that corruption tended to be their way of making a living, but she'd turned a blind eye.

After she'd gotten pregnant with Kean, Paul was never present. A night or two a week he'd show up late and basically ignore her. By then, she'd accepted that not only did he care more about the scads of money he made, but his mistresses had superseded her place in his life. Problem was, she hadn't given a damn.

She'd locked her bedroom door, and when he'd graced their home with his presence, he slept in a room down the hall.

Once the baby arrived, sick of the pretense, she'd divorced him, gotten sole custody of Kean, a son he'd never wanted, and moved herself, Kean and Ruby to San Diego. This way, she wouldn't be aware of his shady dealings. And her small family could begin to live a normal, happy life.

Over the next years, her job had ranked number two in her life, second to only her son. Because of her reputation as a dependable agent with certain skills and knowledge about Muslim customs and the Islam faith, on occasion she'd gotten loaned out to different cities.

Her career had blossomed and she'd found a certain happiness in being the person in charge of her destiny. Men had come and gone but none made any difference to her way of life.

During these years, she'd been as gentle as she knew how with her son. She'd even gotten used to his demanding goodnight kisses and the hugs he spread around, but instigating this affectionate behavior was still hard for her.

Unlike the Filipino woman who showered him with all kinds of embraces and smooches. Ruby had a huge heart and her very openness was what had attracted Alia to her in the first place. Such opposing personalities, and yet they'd managed to build a strong and healthy family unit.

But now things were different. With Paul's threat hanging over her and no one around who she trusted to step into Ruby's place, this latest option could work. Kean would be safe, they'd be together every day, and maybe he could begin to rely on her as his mother, rather than Ruby.

A wall of insecurity spread over her like syrup. Just thinking about this new mothering role made nerves rattle around in her stomach causing pain and doubts. Fearful of a revolt, with eyes down, she started making her way to the ladies' room, swallowing the whole time.

"Are you ignoring me on purpose?" Sloan stood in her path, and she looked up, gulped and exhaled slowly.

"Sorry? I was thinking about something and didn't know you'd arrived."

"Liar! I noticed your face when you saw me, and I want to know why you looked so angry and just now so frightened. Am I that scary?"

"Don't be an ass. The only thing that scares me is a loaded gun pointed my way and the IRS." She gestured to the men waiting in front of the meeting room. "They're ready for us. They'll be briefing you on what's been discussed so far and see if you have anything to add. Something's come up for me that we'll need to deal with too."

Chapter
Fourteen

Alia led the way to where Don, Nigel and his former boss, Jack Harrison, the assistant director in the criminal investigative division, waited.

"Hey, Booker, it's nice to see you back here." Jack held out his hand, a cordial expression of pleasure covering his face.

Sloan accepted the gesture and politely turned aside so that he didn't block Alia's way. *Score one for the hotshot!* No doubt chivalry came easy to a man who, according to his mates, had scads of women falling over themselves to get into his bed.

Soon they entered the conference room and settled around the oval table, tablets in front of each person. They began scanning the data until Jack called them to order. "I'm happy to announce that Agent Booker has agreed to work on this case with us and will be temporarily reinstated. We also have Alia, Agent Hawkins, who's agreed to pose as his stepsister, recovering from a broken romance. She'll be moving in with him until—"

"Me and my son."

Sloan's head swiveled and he aimed a laser-like stare her way. "You and your *what?*"

"Sorry, gentlemen. Something has come up with my personal situation. I've lost my live-in babysitter, and since I don't trust anyone else with Kean I'll have to bring him with me to live at Agent Booker's."

Sloan's voice hardened. "Not gonna happen! I'll have enough trouble accepting *your* presence at my place. A bratty kid's out of the question." He crossed his arms, his obstinate attitude totally impenetrable. "No bloody way in hell."

"Fine. Then you'll have to find another woman to play the part of your live-in."

Jack interrupted. His voice sounded low and calm. "Let's just talk about this. Al, what's going on? Why are you insisting that Kean comes with you? What's happened with Ruby?"

She'd only discussed her personal situation with one person at the agency. When she'd come for her initial interview, Jack Harrison had made the effort to welcome her to Hawaii. He and his lovely wife, Marla, had taken her out for a scrumptious diner at the Cheesecake Factory, and their warm kindness had lulled her into talking about her personal arrangements.

Not about Paul though, only that she was divorced, but that she had a live-in nanny who she thought the world of, and that she was happy to be self-supporting and established.

Alia linked her fingers in front of her on the table, posture erect; she looked around at each person. Finally she cleared her voice and started, not sure of just how much she needed to share.

"Ruby's my son's babysitter and our live-in housekeeper. Her father's recently become ill and needs her to return to Manila." Her glance skimmed around the table and she saw everyone's attention centered on her. Tightening her grip to where the bones in her fingers protested, she went on, "As you all know, I've only been here a little over a month and I've had no time to become acquainted with facilities where they care for eight-year-olds, or with any other sitters who I'd trust. Therefore, it's my responsibility to keep my kid with me, and that's what I intend to do... either at Sloan's or not. Your decision!"

Sloan slid his fingers through his still uncut hair, shoving it to the back of his head. With his elbows on the table, his head cradled between his hands, he didn't move. And neither did anyone else. Silence reigned until he finally began venting.

No one interrupted as he mumbled to himself, yet they all heard his words. "Shit! You gotta be kidding me – a stepsister and a kid? I can't believe I've agreed to this. I must be crazy. Those two old bastards have finally driven me around the bend."

Suddenly, he glared at Don, the one person who was grinning like an idiot and shot his forefinger at him, a gesture that produced a chuckle, and that seemed to piss Sloan off more. He growled a warning at his old partner, "You laugh, you son of a bitch. Guess who's going to be taking care of this lot while I'm working my normal twelve-hour shifts."

***

Everyone around the table knew Sloan's penchant for overreacting, everyone except the woman glaring his way. They knew it for what it was: a way for him to deal. They also understood that he always made things work and usually in the best manner for everyone.

But he needed his rant time. And if she didn't like it? Too damn bad. How much more could he take on and not blow. Caring for Les and Roy had pushed his patience to the limits these last few months. How in Christ's name did they expect him to look after an eight-year-old used to a *nanny* and a female with a burr up her ass so deep, he wondered how the hell she sat down?

He glanced her way and saw her perched at the edge of her seat, hands clenched, her eyes cold and impenetrable.

Next he looked at Don and saw the slight nod

his pal didn't try to hide. He knew it for what it was, his way of saying... *I'll have your back, bro.* Then he checked out Jack Harrison and knew that the smart man waited for his decision, with no doubts that he'd kick in and do his duty.

Their gazes met and Jack's face wore his usual cool expression, composure in every line of his body. Then suddenly, Jack glanced at Alia first and then turned back to Sloan and winked. That spoke more loudly than if he'd demanded Sloan's instant compliance.

Slapping both hands on the table, Sloan stood and went to the water dispenser to refill his glass. "Fine! Let's get on with this session, so I can get back to the garage and maybe finish the day's work before midnight."

Chapter Fifteen

On his drive back to the garage a few hours later, Sloan thought about the strange meeting he'd just left. Near the end, they'd been joined by others from Homeland Security, who'd presented the intelligence they'd collected so far. Information they'd journalized about Samir and his family and their previous lives in Pakistan. They'd had scads of lists and reports he'd have to read as soon as he found the time.

Also, they'd organized the equipment Alia would need for surveillance and just looking at the list made his ass tighten. Where the hell would they store all this shit?

Come to think of it, his house had two bed-rooms and a sunroom at the front. The square footage worked well for one person but add two more, along with all this crap, and it would be a disaster.

Taking a deep breath, he'd swallowed the cuss words and scanned the table instead. He'd observed that the agents in the room were comfortable with each other, with one exception.

There'd been a noticeable constraint with Agent Hawkins. The only ones who seemed at ease with her were Don and Jack Harrison. He'd heard both of them refer to her as Al; probably a nickname and she'd gone along with it.

Guess if she liked someone, she'd let it pass. From the icy attitude she threw his way, he figured he'd be calling her Agent Hawkins, rather than something friendlier, like Alia or 'little sister', till the end of the case.

According to the plans they'd prearranged, she'd be arriving Sunday at lunchtime, when the Amans would be at his house for a barbecue. Everyone in the neighborhood took turns cooking outdoors and had gotten into the habit of going to a different house on the cul-de sac-each week. As it turned out, his turn to host the event was this coming weekend. It couldn't have worked out better.

Don, Roy and Les would be there to help with the arrangements, do most of the work, and he'd be the guy manning the barbecue. That he *could* handle and do it well.

He thought back to the arrangements they'd

discussed earlier. Don had suggested, "Al and Kean should appear as if by magic and Sloan can act totally shocked... but welcoming. That way, the whole neighborhood will get the story all at once."

Sloan had broken in there. "What story?"

"That Sloan Booker has family staying for an unspecified amount of time. She'll have her cover and you won't have to tell everyone about her. They'll see her arrival with their own eyes and the word will be out."

The rest of the people around the table had nodded, agreeing, even Alia. Sloan's groan hadn't been heard by anyone but himself. He had two days left of freedom, a neat house and no gorgeous chick running around in her undies... one he had to keep his hands off.

Chapter
Sixteen

Once back at the garage, Sloan decided to approach Roy first to explain about his short stint as Special Agent Booker. He'd always known the old man had fretted about him wearing a badge and his involvement with the lower life forms that cops had to deal with – Roy's words for the scum who broke the law.

Sloan had thought his joining the FBI and getting off the streets as a beat cop would lessen Roy's anxieties, but that hadn't happened. He'd known the old worrywart had carried a St. Christopher's medal for him, exactly like the one he'd forced on Sloan. Hell, if it would have given the old man peace of mind, he'd have worn fucking pearls!

He remembered that after his announcement,

while he'd trained to take a position with the Honolulu Police Department, Tommy, had been proud, strutted around and bragged to anyone he could corner.

Les had enrolled him for training in martial arts and made sure he knew how to take care of himself.

But it had devastated Roy. Danger was danger and, as far as Roy had been concerned, anyone wearing a badge was a target for every crazy with a gun.

Instead, Roy had celebrated when Sloan had quit law enforcement and began working fulltime at the garage. But sensitive to Sloan's feelings, he'd not done it overtly. He just couldn't seem to wipe the gleaming grin off his face in contrast to Sloan's scowls.

Approaching the pit area where Roy and his small crew worked their magic on any overhaul they had, Sloan heard his two reprobates talking, their voices low. That caught his attention immediately because the norm was for Les to tease and Roy to holler in defense.

"I still think we should tell Sloan about that phone call you overheard, man. He deserves to know our suspicions about why his old man died."

Roy argued back, his voice shaking with conviction. "Tell him what? That I overheard Tommy threatening somebody, ordering them to leave town and take their illegal activities with them, or he'd blab to his FBI agent son about what was going on? I don't think so. That's no proof that Tommy was killed."

"Get real, genius! We both know the man hadn't taken a bloody drink since the time after Wai took off. He'd lost his mind for those two years following her leaving him, but he'd straightened out."

"I know." Roy's grudging words were spoken low, leaving no doubt that he didn't want to agree.

"Remember the day he swore off the booze? He'd been driving shit-faced with Sloan in the baby seat and he drifted into the oncoming traffic. He came close to killing both of them. I've never seen you so mad, dude. I thought you were going to kill him."

"I almost did. He had our son with him, the idiot."

"You scared the shit out of him, threatening to get a paternity test to see which one of us was Sloan's real dad. It smartened him up. After that, the dumbass seldom touched a drop, right?"

"Right."

"Then why – on that very day – did the son of a bitch get liquored up, drive off the cliff at Laie Point and kill himself?"

"I don't know," Roy groaned the words. "But it was months ago. Why do you have to keep bringing it up?"

Sloan stepped out from where he'd stayed hidden. "Yeah, Les, why do you keep bringing it up to Roy, and yet not once have you mentioned it to me?"

Both of the old men twirled his way, shock covering their faces. Roy looked devastated, while Les appeared relieved.

"Shit, man. You sure know how to make an entrance."

Sloan leaned against the side wall, his arms crossed and every muscle in his body clenched tighter than a stripper's legs on her pole. "Spill. I want it all. Les, you go first."

Les shrugged. "It's like the old fool says, kid. I'm making a mountain."

"No, sir. You don't get to back off now. I heard you, Les. You were seriously suspicious about Dad's accident. Why didn't you say anything when I got back from L.A.?"

Same as Sloan, Les caught Roy's expression and must have seen the tears there. "There's nuthin' to say. The bastard took a few drinks, obviously had no tolerance and drove stupid. End of story."

Furious, Sloan turned to the fidgety man who'd suddenly taken a seat on the nearby stool. "I want the truth, Roy. You're controlling Les and preventing him from telling me everything, but it's wrong and you know it. Tom Booker was my father..." He saw the quick glances shared between the other two and a sledge hammer of doubt weakened his knees.

Chapter Seventeen

Alia couldn't believe Sloan had given in after his initial outburst. His over-the-top reaction hadn't affected the others but she'd taken it personally. Now she was stuck with the plan.

She'd be moving into his house in a couple of days, and Kean would be coming with her. And there was nothing she could do to stop it. Fretting over her options, she drove home and noticed what looked to be the same car parked down her street that had been there a number of times.

Yep! It had the exact sticker on the trunk revealing the name of a rental agency. From her front window yesterday, she'd seen a glint from sunlight on glass and her suspicions had risen. When she'd gone out to confront the person, they'd driven away. This time, she'd sneak up on them and get some answers.

Fury driving her actions, she pulled up on the street, parking behind random cars rather than turning into her driveway. Making sure her weapon was visible on her waist, and her badge next to it, she strolled past the vehicle and saw the woman busy with binoculars aimed toward her house.

Backtracking, she snuck up on the driver's side and blocked the woman's view. In seconds, she jerked the binoculars away and appeared shocked to see Alia bent over, leaning into her window. She arched away, her expression laughable. Except for Alia; this wasn't a laughing matter.

"What the hell are you doing?" Blonde, with too much eye makeup, chewing gum and bright pink lipstick smeared on her teeth, the woman's attitude ramped up to obnoxious in the time it took for Alia to inspect the front passenger seat and look for a weapon.

"Funny thing – that's what I want to know too. What are you doing on my street, across from my house, spying with those?" Alia pointed at the field glasses the idiot hadn't tried to hide. The weirdo quickly threw them on the floor as if by putting them out of sight, she could pretend they hadn't been there in the first place.

"I was checking out the properties on the street, 'cause, ahh... I'm thinkin' of buying a house."

"Ain't none for sale around here."

"Yeah, well, I was just looking. No law against that."

"How about harassment? I've seen you spying here before, and that constitutes a criminal act in my book."

"Your book? What the hell would I care about you for? Get out of my face." Pushing open the door so it forced Alia to back up, Blondie stepped out of the car.

Alia didn't care if the female topped her by twenty-five pounds and stood a foot higher in her spike heels. She wanted answers. "You have a license to snoop on me? I can't imagine Paul hiring someone who isn't legal."

"What the fuck are you talking about?" Suddenly the wiseass noticed Alia's gun and her face paled.

Raising her hands, she changed her attitude. "Look, I don't want no trouble. Some guy hired me to watch the gardener; he figures maybe his wife and the dude are getting it on and he wants proof."

Gardener? "The only place on the street able to afford one of those pretty boys is my next door neighbor. You workin' for Ralph Graves?"

Eyes narrowed, the woman pretended a deviousness that gave away the truth. "I might be. Not in my best interests to say, not if I want to keep any clients. I'm just doing my job. "

"You got a card?"

"Why?" Blondie's gaze became focussed, her act diminishing.

"To prove you are who you say you are."

Reaching into the open window for her purse, the PI slipped her hand in a back pouch and passed over a white card with one name—Libby—and the name of her firm, *Private Lies*. A byline, *Your secrets are ours!* was emblazoned on the front in gold embossed type, and one website address sat alone on the back.

Taking the card, Alia added, "You stay off my property, you hear? Otherwise I'll get you for trespassing."

A crafty look appeared and the other nodded. "Yeah, I know. Just trying to make a living. Won't bother you no more." Moving faster than Alia would have imagined, the other woman got in her car and, in no time at all, her taillights had turned the corner.

Alia hated having to let Blondie go without questioning her further but she hadn't really broken any laws, at least none that would stick. Harassment would be thin, not easy to prove.

One thing she did know: Ralph Graves and his wife were in their seventies, and the gardener was their grandson.

***

"Hey, Paul. Libby here. She made me. I had to back off. But the kid and the nanny live with her, and you were right about the street."

"Only because I was fortunate when old friends of ours said they'd seen Alia running one morning. When they pulled up to talk with her, she disappeared around the corner and by the time they'd turned the car, she was gone. They didn't know we'd split, and wondered if we had a summer house in Honolulu."

"Pure bullshit luck that they remembered the exact area."

"It happens. So she approached you?"

"Yeah."

"Told you to be careful. Alia's smart and trained. Hope you took care of tracking her."

Libby giggled. "Hey, you take me for a newbie? Of course I did. Slapped that cute little ole GPS device under her fender last night with my own hands. She's not getting away from me, honey."

"Good. It's why I pay your agency the big bucks."

"Hey, we're the best. Our PIs always deliver. You can depend on it."

"Fine. But can I depend on you?"

"Does the sun come up every morning?" Libby giggled again as she hung up.

Jackass!

Chapter Eighteen

Sloan eased off when he saw Les's glare. It wouldn't do any good putting both his and Roy's backs up against the wall; they'd pull together and shut him out. He knew Les would always go along with Roy, protect him. As a boy, Sloan had seen it numerous times.

It was one thing for Les to taunt the other man, push him till he was furious, but they all knew his teasing behavior camouflaged an abiding loyalty; a fierce respect and affection.

No way could Sloan fight that. But he knew how to get to Les, and at this point, he'd use any weapon in his arsenal.

"Look, let's go in the coffee room and take a break. I'll lock the door so we won't be disturbed, and you'll both come and we'll talk. I think it's time for some explanations, right, Les? You know me. You know I couldn't go on now that I've found out this much."

Les looked at Roy, waiting. Roy walked toward Sloan. He stood in front of him, staring at him, pleading, a look of love in his eyes that brought tears to Sloan. He knew the old man was begging him to stop.

To pretend he hadn't heard what they'd said was what was being asked, but he couldn't do that. He never flinched, nor did his look waver. Finally, he sensed that his beseeching stare did the trick.

Roy's shoulders slumped and his head dropped till his eyes only saw the floor. "You won't let this go, boy, will you?"

"Not a chance."

Again, Roy shot Sloan an imploring look. "Not even if I ask you to?"

"Sorry. I'd do most anything for you, Batman, you know I would. But not this. If you care about me at all, don't ask me to." Sloan used his nickname for Roy, one he'd started as a little boy when Les and Roy would play with him – Les was Superman, and of course, he'd play Superboy.

Roy looked at Les. "Go lock the door. I guess it's time."

A short while later, all three men had coffees and were sitting around the same table they used every day.

Sloan knew they were stalling, so he opened the discussion by saying, "Who wants to start?"

Les cleared his throat. "First, how about you tell us what you heard."

"You know already. Roy listened in while Dad talked on the phone. That's as good a place as any for you to begin, Roy. Tell me everything you remember about that conversation."

"It's a long time ago."

"And yet it hasn't left your mind. Quit stalling."

"You know how proud Tommy felt about you being a cop? Well, when you switched over to the FBI training, his bragging went to a whole new level. He told everyone about his boy being one of the good guys."

"Quit playing me, Roy. Tell me what you overheard."

"I was getting to it. Either let me tell it in my own way or we'll forget about it. I need to lay the groundwork."

Sloan heard Les snort, but his glare shut the other man up before he could start riding Roy. "Fine. Just get to it."

"That morning, sitting right here having morning coffee before we started work, Tommy told Les and me that you two had talked the night before. He said you'd shared a bit about a drug trafficking case you couldn't crack. Your frustration had gotten to him and he didn't know how you could work one file for months, slowly gathering evidence when you had no doubts about the perpetrator. It boggled his mind."

Les broke in. "It's because that dude never took his time at anything. He'd go full bore at whatever life put in his way, and never mind the consequences."

"You're right. Anyway... he'd planned to start working the Ashtons' Cadillac that morning when suddenly, he cussed and jumped up. We've always wondered if it was something you'd said the night before that had light-bulbed and sent him muttering to check the car. By the time I'd cleaned away the coffee stuff and followed to see what was wrong, he'd ripped off the passenger door panel and found something."

Roy held his hand toward Sloan to stop his question before he could form the words. "Don't ask me what. I don't know. But whatever it was, he became incensed. Then he checked in the glove compartment, and ran into the office to make a call. When I heard him yelling into the phone, I stopped to listen."

"What exactly did he say?"

"He basically said, '*Tadeo, you bastard, you've worked for Kroller for years. He's always driven a blue Caddy just like the Ashtons' vehicle that was brought into the garage recently. I found your stash in the car, same place you always keep your shit. Now you better come and get that effing car out of my garage and take*

Kroller's business elsewhere, or I'll tell my FBI son about his uncle and the gang he runs with.' Then he smashed down the receiver so hard I thought he'd broken it for sure."

"What happened next?"

"A customer caught me and started yakking. Before I could get away, Tommy had taken off. It was the last time I ever saw him alive."

Les added, "He stopped by my corner and said he needed to look after some personal shit. He wouldn't be back that day." Les hunched his shoulders, a weary look replacing his normally sardonic expression. "He looked pissed, which happened sometimes. Anyway, I had a job to finish that morning. Besides, you know your ole man. He'd get in that souped-up GTO of his, act like a stunt-car nutcase and get a speeding ticket out on the interstate. Then return all smiley and feeling better. So... I backed off."

Roy added sadly. "And he crashed."

"And you never told me any of this because...?"

Les looked at Roy first and, after getting his go-ahead nod, he continued. "Because Roy figured the accident had nothing to do with the threat your dad had made on the telephone—"

Roy cut him off. "And because I forced Les to keep quiet about it. We had no proof that someone killed him. Why put you in danger?"

Sloan got that Roy was trying to protect him; hadn't he done that all his life? So he turned to Les.

"What aren't you telling me?"

"I hadn't seen Tommy that upset since Wai left. It might have driven him to buy that son of a bitchin' bottle they found in the car. He could have drunk the half that was missing. The coroner said that he'd had enough in his system for him to be impaired. Roy's right, kid. We had no proof of anything. I only got suspicious when he came to pick up the car."

"Who came?"

"Your mother's brother... Tadeo."

Chapter
Nineteen

Stunned, his body so tight it felt like one slight nudge could shatter him, Sloan didn't even try to hide his fury. "My mother's brother? How come no one ever told me I have an uncle?"

"Because him and your old man didn't see eye to eye. Look there's a lot about your mother you don't know." Les refused to look at him.

"A lot? Fuck, man. I don't know anything. None of you musketeers were forthcoming about her. I learned early on to stop asking questions and just accept that you three were my family."

"We did the best we could, Sloan."

Sloan reached out to Roy and squeezed his arm. "Don't take that the wrong way, man. No kid had a better upbringing than I did. How many other brats had three dads hovering around, and you playing the mom role when you sensed I needed it, or the buddy role when it seemed appropriate? All my friends thought I was the luckiest bastard in the world."

"And you? What did you think?" Les had a shrewd look in his eye and Sloan knew he expected the truth.

"I was a kid. What the hell did I know?"

Roy broke in. "We saw the poster you always had hanging in your room of the Hawaiian princess, leis around her neck, long hair streaming in the wind and her muumuu flowing. Every time I saw that picture, it stunned me just how much it looked like Wai. When you were little, you told me the girl was your mom, and we never argued with you. If it made you happy – it was fine with us."

"The day I spotted the poster, Dad stopped next to it, stunned and shaky; he said the girl looked just like Wai. I made him buy it for me so I had an image of her. That night when he hung it up, he finally talked about her, the one and only time. He stared at the image, said she'd been a loving girl who'd had so much to give, but she couldn't be tied down to only one man. I was too young to understand what he meant then. But as I got older, it always stayed with me. I guess because there wasn't any censure in his voice, only love, I never held it against her that she'd left. The three of you more than made up for her absence."

Roy wrapped his arm around Sloan's shoulders and squeezed, a loving gesture he made often. "She was lovely, son, inside and out."

Sloan caught Les's eye and saw how Roy's words had touched him. Staring, unable to look away, he dared Les to finally admit the truth about their family. About the strange life of three men and one boy living together in a rambling place attached to the garage where they worked.

Secrets had always simmered underneath their everyday normal routine, but Sloan had been brought up to respect everyone's rights to their own memories and to stay out of where he wasn't invited.

So questions hadn't been asked and no one had volunteered any information. When a sensitive kid perceived that the people in his life wouldn't take kindly to demands, he stopped making them.

Les began slowly, inching his way forward. "Your mother was as beautiful as your poster. Everyone loved her."

Sloan knew his voice came out rough but he had to know. "Roy did. How about you, Les? Did you love her too?"

A long silence followed with Les leaning down, clutching his hands between his knees; hands that shook visibly.

Roy broke in. "Tell him, Les. It's past time."

"Look, kid, we all loved her." He waved at Roy and then at himself. "I met her at night school where I used my drawing talent to learn how to actually paint. She took classes too because she worked with fabrics, designs on materials, had a dream of starting her own line of clothing. In those days, Wai wasn't ready to settle down, she was wild and free. She dazzled me, and I brought her here to meet my two friends, Tom and Roy."

Roy took over. "The three of us had worked our passage across from 'Frisco and had been shoved in the same stateroom. After Les and Tommy stopped the squabbling, we settled in and became kind of attached. Decided that once we arrived, we'd open a garage in Honolulu and go into business together."

"That's how you three started *Booker's*. I often wondered."

Les answered. "Hell, we fit together as if it was meant to be. With Roy's mechanic skills, he could handle the repairs. Tom could do the body work and eventually became skilled at the drawings, and I could do the finishing and detailing. Worked like a hot damn. Tom had the only bankroll, so he invested in the property and we started building up the business, gaining a reputation, and we became known for not cheating or bullshitting our clientele."

Sloan had grown up knowing about *Bookers'* reputation. "Tell me about my mother. What happened?"

Les stood and began striding from one end of

the room to the other. "We all happened, is what happened. Your mom was a free spirit, she couldn't be tied down. She loved people and took to Roy because of his gentle spirit – her words, not mine."

Roy added. "She loved to ride the waves and talked Les into surfing with her. Even though she'd surfed all her life, he taught her a lot."

"Guess she liked doing more than riding the waves—"

Roy came back at Sloan like a tornado touching down. "You don't get to talk about her that way, son. She wouldn't hurt a fly; she caught them and released them outside. She never meant to break our hearts. She just loved everyone. But in the end, when she found she was pregnant, she chose your dad as the father and wrote his name on your birth certificate. Once you were six months old, she disappeared and we never heard from her again."

Les added, "She'd seen the way we all fawned over you. Hell, the three of us were like fucking love-sick idiots all over one tiny baby."

Roy nodded. "It's true. She knew we'd never let you go. In the end, after she disappeared, Tommy always blamed Tadeo for her desertion. He'd found out that Tadeo had given her the money to move to San Francisco, to start her own business. Tommy went to Tadeo for her address, laid a beating on him, but the man wasn't sharing. Tom went after Wai but he never found her. Came back to his new baby and we all carried on."

"So... which one of you bastards is my father?"

Chapter Twenty

Roy looked to Les, leaving him to answer. "Does it matter?"

"Christ! Of course it matters."

"Well, it never did to us. Wai made up her mind she wanted Tommy to be your father, and so Roy and me decided we'd honor her decision. Far as we're concerned, you're Sloan Booker, Tommy Booker's son."

Sloan looked from one to the other and saw Roy nodding in full agreement. He couldn't help himself. "I'm taller than the old man – more like your height and build, Les. And, I have a lot of your mannerisms, Roy. Only thing I thought I had from Tommy was his drawing talents, and I could have gotten those from Wai."

Roy looked pleased, almost superior, as he raised his eyebrow toward Les, who glared and then said, "You're the spitting image of your mom and her side of the family. You have her island eyes; your brows are full and slanted like hers were. You have her bloody personality too. Dedicated and fixated, you don't give up, and she was like that, knew what she wanted and went after it... no matter what."

"You're talking about her as if she's dead."

Roy piped in. "When she left, we knew she'd never come back. She had a dream to follow, made a name for herself. About ten years ago, we found out she was killed in a car accident. We never did see her again."

Though Sloan had just discovered facts about a mother he never knew, the news of her death made his heart lurched crazily. He gripped his hands together, his shoulders slouched. "How did you find out?"

Les shrugged. "You can find out anything you want to on the fucking Internet nowadays. She kept a low profile, but her designs eventually became very popular. You wanna know more, look her up. She used the name Wai Sloan."

"She chose my name."

"Yes. Said it stood for 'warrior'."

"Did she eventually have another family?"

"Not that we know of. But more than likely, she did. Your mother was a loving woman. I can't see how she'd have remained single. Did you want us to look it up for you?"

"No. What I want to do is talk to my uncle Tadeo and find out what the hell happened on the day Tommy got killed."

"Oh, for crissakes! You mean on the day your *dad* got killed." Les made a point, one he meant for Sloan to accept.

"Whatever." Sloan narrowed his eyes and waited for the explosion. He didn't have to wait long.

Both Roy and Les stood, both glared just like they had on the day the cops had picked Sloan up for smoking pot when he was thirteen. That day, all three of his dads had surrounded him, hands on hips, and stared him down. He'd never smoked the shit again.

Roy tried placating, calming the tension. "Sloan, we agreed. And you got no say. Tommy Booker loved you and dedicated his whole life to raising you right. He was your father."

Sloan stood and faced them. "Looks to me like *all three* of you dedicated your lives to raising me and I'm grateful. Don't ever think I'm not. But this time you're not gonna stop me. First, I'm gonna find out if Tommy was killed, and if it's the last thing I ever do, I'm gonna catch the bastard who murdered him." He stomped away and faintly heard Roy's groan.

"Why'd he have to say it like that?"

Chapter
Twenty-one

Sloan headed to the agency office, his reinstatement coming at the perfect time because he'd have access to their data banks and other facilities that made getting information so much easier. He intended to find out everything he could about Tadeo Kealoha, his uncle.

First he stopped at Jack Harrison's office, schmoozed his secretary to find out if the AD was free and then knocked on the door. "Hey, boss, you got a minute?"

Jack pushed the papers to the side of his desk, settled back into his chair and crossed his right leg over his left knee. "Sure. I had it on my agenda to call you in today, so this will save me having to do that. What's up? You look rattled."

Sloan slumped in the chair across from his former boss and tried to figure out how to start without sounding like a man on the edge.

Jack beat him to it. "Did Don get the equipment to your place? I know you've decided to use the sunroom for the stakeout, and he was going to set up the monitors, the long-lens camera and bring the binoculars before Al and her kid showed up. That way, if Kean sees the stuff, you can pretend to have a star-gazing hobby or some such thing."

"No problem. Don's coming early tomorrow before the barbecue, as far as I know. You're right. We wanted to get organized before Hawkins and her son arrive later."

"So what is it then? You look riled. I hope you're not backing out of Operation Relatives."

"No, nothing like that. I just got a shock and I'm still trying to process it. Look, there's a chance my old man, Tommy Booker, was murdered and didn't die in the car accident as we all thought. I want to do some digging and I need your permission to use the facilities here, get the guys researching on an old case Don and I were working on at that time."

"What's that got to do with your father?"

"I'm not sure."

"Which case was it?"

"Kroller. I think there's a tie-in between him and Tommy's death."

Intensely interested, Jack leaned forward. "No

shit? You're telling me you believe they were linked? We've been hitting dead-ends with Kroller for years now; every time we get close, the bastard shuts us down. I'd give my left nut to get something on that slimeball. If you think you have some pertinent info, give it to us and let us run with it."

"Nope. It can't happen that way. I need to be in on this one. Look, I just found out I have an uncle on my mother's side who works for Kroller, has done for years. Tommy called him the day he died and they had words. I need to look into what happened."

"How the hell can you do that? What about Relatives, and the fact that you'll be having some of your own visiting you the day after tomorrow?"

Sloan groaned and swept his hair back. "Shit!"

Jack stood and began pacing. "Look, Booker, we need that operation to go smooth as fucking lake water on a still day. No screw-ups, nothing. Intelligence has intercepted some communications that there's a lot of underhand activity happening on the island. The details they've collected so far allude to some form of an attack here in the holiday capital; we're thinking bombs."

"Crap! You're kidding me?"

"Not at all. We both know that ISIS wants the US to quiver in fright; and to that extent, the fear mongers have done their job well. We all understand the cold, hard facts; they have people everywhere who are willing to die for Allah. And what better place for them to hit than the city where everyone comes to have their vacations free from danger."

"And no doubt, like every other state in the union, Hawaii has given sanctuary to their share of new supporters to the cause."

"Exactly. Knowing what we do, we can't afford to mess up with these neighbors of yours and their visitors."

"You've managed to attain proof against the Amans' relatives?"

"That's just it. They aren't relatives, no more than Hawkins is your fucking sister. We've been able to ascertain that much. As far as we're concerned, they're strangers who have somehow forced their way into the Amans' lives by pretending a relationship to Janna's brother."

"Crissakes. You're serious."

"Like prostate cancer. We have other leads we're following, but the people planning to visit Samir Aman have shady shit in their background, enough for us to keep a close eye on all their activities. That's why we need you and Agent Hawkins totally focussed on that family. There has to be someone watching their house all the time."

"Seriously?" Sloan moaned. "How the hell—?

Interrupting, Jack waved him quiet. "Look, I know you have commitments at the garage and we've taken care of that for you. One of the other agents has a brother who took his mechanic's ticket and needs a job. I was going to tell you about him today. We'll pay his wages if you put him to work and free yourself so you can help Al in the stakeout. With her kid around, she won't be able to man the binoculars and other equipment all the time. Either you or Agent Howard will sub for her when she needs assistance. I'll leave you to work out the details."

"What about Kroller?"

"With your reinstatement, you'll have access through the computers into most of the files, and in time, I'll make sure you have total clearance on that case. But for now, we expect you to do the job you've been assigned to."

Chapter
Twenty-two

Sloan left Jack's office and slumped against the wall. Jack's secretary had left and he grabbed this moment of privacy to gnaw on the inside of his mouth while he let his screaming nerves settle to a dull roar.

Every instinct in his body said he should search for Tadeo Kealoha and beat the truth outta him. Find out for sure if his dad had been messed with, if he needed to arrest his killer.

Unfortunately, training had a way of messing with a guy's intentions. Plus his respect for Jack held him from acting crazy and following his instincts to get to the bottom of the mystery.

He'd always taken his career seriously, respected the badge and played by the rules, like he'd been taught by the three men he loved. But, he wouldn't let this go. Even after eight months, the grief of missing his father ate at him.

Unlike the cliché, the pain hadn't lessened with time. It was as raw today as the day he'd returned from his undercover case and found out he'd missed the funeral. That horrible, gut-wrenching despair of not being there when he should have been fueled this need for revenge.

Breathing deeply, he unclenched his hands. Through the glass walls, he scanned the main office and noticed Alia Hawkins at her desk, head down, light-brown hair gathered on top of her head.

As if she sensed being watched, she looked up and found him instantly. They made eye contact and a question appeared in her expression. She started to rise. Then others in a roomful of workers walked between them and he lost her. The following irritation loomed way out of proportion. Damned if his crazy-assed heart had kicked into overdrive and that left him reeling. *Jesus! Why would his body react just from seeing the woman at a distance?*

He rubbed his hands over his face.

"You looking for me?"

Straightening, he tried to grin but it fell short. "Now why would you automatically think I came here to see you?"

"Maybe because you were staring at me and I

had the feeling you wanted to talk. My bad." She turned to walk away, her back stiff and her attitude kinda sour.

Sloan had seen her expression, wariness mixed with concern and knew his stupid remark had bothered her, and that bothered him. *Shit! Women! Who knew what would turn them off?*

He made sure he softened his tone and added the appropriate amount of remorse. "Well, thanks for checking." Roy had told him years ago that women liked to be appreciated for any little thing they did, and he'd earned many favors, including sexual, applying this rule.

She stopped. When she looked at him, questions loomed in her stunning blue eyes and she hesitated.

He'd noticed before that she wore a lot of makeup; false eyelashes and intense colors applied generously. Her face appeared satin smooth, her skin covered with creams and powders that made him think of a magazine model rather than an ordinary working girl. To him, she didn't seem fake as one might think, just untouchable... a poor, sad soul hiding behind a mask. *Now where in the hell had that thought come from? You're losing it, bud.*

"Did you want to talk? I can grab a coffee." She leaned on the wall next to him, her hands tucked in the pockets of her short black skirt. Worn with a white shirt-blouse, open at the top and tantalizingly revealing, she looked efficient and sexy as hell. It was probably her black shoes with three-inch heels at the end of those gorgeous legs that changed her outfit from mouth-watering to fantasy-creating.

He cleared his voice and straightened. "Thanks. That's nice of you."

"Just so you know, I'm not nice. In fact, I think *nice* is truly overrated. But we'll be working together for a while and I make one hell of a good partner."

He searched her gaze, holding it until she finally looked down. *She's also a liar. Hmm!!*

"Then we make a good pair." He smiled his winning grin that had gotten him a lot of tail over the years. "Rain check on the coffee. I have to get back to the garage. I'm winding up as much of the work there as I can so I'll be free to assist you in the stakeout. Jack just promised he'd send over a mechanic to take on most of my smaller jobs."

As if she didn't want to let him go, she added. "We talked earlier and Jack mentioned he was going to contact you. They're really concerned about the Amans' visitors. I think the bombings on the mainland aren't helping to calm worried politicians. Those bigshot power-mongers are applying a lot of pressure to the various agencies to get on top of the threats."

"Well, we'll do our best. But you've never met these people, so I'll wait to see your thoughts about them after tomorrow."

She studied him more intently. "I can tell by the tone of your voice, you don't believe them capable of terrorism."

"I don't."

"Right! It's funny how the neighbors of extremists always tell the reporters, they were so normal... so *nice*." Her grin invited his.

He picked up on her taunt and liked her way of mocking him. He chuckled. "True. I get what you're saying. These people are all that, but they're also honest and caring. You'll see what I mean."

"I guess I will. Later..."

He watched her saunter away, as if she hadn't a care in the world, and every male hormone in his body stood to attention, including the mister down below that should have known better at his age. *For fuck's sake.*

Chapter Twenty-three

Kean wouldn't stop asking questions. The next morning, all the way back from taking Ruby to the airport, he hounded her. "This guy owns a garage, right? And he's my uncle?"

Alia had tried to tell Kean it was make-believe, but the boy had glommed onto one word, *uncle*, and he wouldn't let it go. Believing he had a male relative had made all the difference, so that even Ruby's leaving had taken second place.

Sure, he'd held on to his nanny at the departure gate, but there hadn't been the expected tears. Not like Alia, who had disgraced herself. She and Ruby had hugged tight, swaying back and forth, unexpected emotion making it impossible for her to say the calm good-bye she'd planned.

Once the door closed behind the last passenger, Ruby… Kean had taken Alia's hand and dragged her to the car, excitement making his eyes glow. "We get our bags now and go to the barbecue, right? My uncle will be expecting me."

"Kean, remember what I told you? He kinda knows we're coming but not when. He'll be surprised to see us today."

"I know. He just wants us to live with him for a while so he can get to know us. And you decided with Ruby leaving, now was a good time. Right?"

"Right." The kid had almost verbatim what she'd told him the night before. She'd wanted to stop his tears, take away the sadness he'd suffered ever since he'd found out his nanny would be leaving him, and her news had worked like a charm.

"You don't know him, right? You didn't live together. He had another mommy and daddy who brought him up. That's what you said."

"That's right. I never really got to know him. So now that workers are renovating our house, I decided we'll surprise him today. You and me. We'll get the gear we packed yesterday, call a taxi and away we go."

"What about your car?"

"My car?"

"Why aren't we taking your car instead of using a taxi?"

Thinking fast, Alia answered, "Because it's the agency's car and they're going to pick it up. I'll get another one later. But for now, we won't have any wheels."

"You're not working for the FBI anymore?"

Okay, now what should she say? This lying stuff was hard, something she never did, so she hadn't realized how one lie could lead to another and before a person knew it, the bullshit was so deep, they'd better stay upright.

"Remember, I warned you. We can't tell anyone I used to work for the FBI. It's our secret. We'll surprise your uncle and I can also spend more time with you."

"And get to know Uncle Booker too. That's a weird name.... Booker."

"I told you, his name is Sloan Booker. You can call him Mr. Booker."

He giggled. "Mom... you don't call an uncle mister. Maybe my uncle can buy you some."

Lost in the labyrinth of his boy-mind, she asked. "Buy me some what?"

"You know – wheels."

Yeah, like that's going to happen!

"So you can pick me up at school like Ruby does."

"Right. Pick you up." How could she have forgotten? Her son needed to get back and forth from his school every day, and it was up to her to get him there and back home again. Circulate among all those other mothers and pretend like she knew what the hell she was doing. As if the mother role came naturally.

Oh God!

***

Later, shutting up the house, locking doors and windows, gave Alia a jolt she never expected. Between her and Ruby's efforts, the house had become a home. Lime green pillows decorated the gray sofa and chairs, and there were lots of sparkling glass vases usually full of garden flowers.

Most of the artwork was from local artists who loved the islands and focussed their paintings on where they lived. She'd slowly invested herself into these surroundings, so much so, that it felt like a real home.

As she went from room to room, making sure she hadn't missed anything, she stopped at the arch in the hallway to the kitchen and fingered the dated cut mark she'd made when they first arrived. It was to be Kean's new monitor which would show him that he really was growing.

The phone in her pocket rang and her heart dropped. *Not now. No way!*

"Hey, Cassie, you're messing with me, right?"

"Don't get your panties twisted, kiddo. We're cool. I just wanted to let you know we're thinking aboutcha. Ruby said this new assignment you're on will be tough, and that you were nervous as a chicken being chased by a hungry farmer with a cleaver."

Shocked that Ruby said anything about her at

all, she bristled. "What did Ruby tell you?"

"Calm down, missy, she only said you'd be stay-ing with relatives and you needed a break, warned us not to pester you unless we were desperate. I've got a couple of others carrying phones so you'll be my last resort. I promise. We've got you covered. Go and have some fun."

Tension released too sudden made Alia drop to the kitchen stool and hold her head in one hand, her loose hair fanning over the counter in a cascade of waves. "Shit, Cassie. Don't mess with me like this. I figured you had a call for me."

"Nope, just sending some sisterly love your way, and telling you if you need anything from those of us in the group, we're here for ya. Bye now, chickie. Love ya."

"Yeah, yeah. Bye. And thanks." Alia threaded her fingers though the soft mass of golden-brown strands, lowered her forehead to the counter and took a few deep breaths. Then she gazed around her lovely kitchen, which had been mostly Ruby's domain, and stood to gather the cookbook and the other articles Ruby had insisted she'd need if she was to look after Kean properly.

The list of directions that sat on top of the pile gave her pause and she quickly scanned them to see her son's favorite snacks for school, his best friend's phone number and loads of other informa-tion she didn't know. What kind of a mother didn't know her own kid needed his soccer shorts clean for Mondays and Thursdays, and that he preferred the white ones with the red stripes rather than the red ones with white stripes?

And... that he hated fresh bananas but loved banana muffins, recipe on page 102. OMG! There were more instructions here than in the FBI Manual on self-defense.

How the hell was she going to cope with this besides keeping Sloan from having a breakdown with a strange kid around and still do her job?

"Mom. The taxi's here."

"I'm coming. Just locking up in here." Before she left, she snagged a tissue, wiped her eyes and blew her nose. *Time to toughen up... chickie! This won't be that bad. Good lord, girl. You've stood up to men twice your size and never thought to back down. Now you're just being a wuss.*

She grabbed another tissue.

Chapter Twenty-four

Just as the taxi pulled out of the driveway, Alia spotted a familiar blonde head in a strange car parked up the street. The woman looked like Libby, the same PI she'd stopped a few days ago.

Not having believed any of the lies that'd slid out of the woman's mouth, she'd done a search on the firm and on its owner, Libby Holt. Turned out, Libby had a good reputation, was older than the mid-forties Alia had thought she was, and had a decent clientele. Paul would have chosen the best; she'd never underestimate him in that way.

But right now, the last thing Alia wanted was for Miss Libby Holt to know her destination.

Alia leaned over to talk to the large Hawaiian fellow behind the steering wheel. He was all dreads, big-ass sunglasses and sporting a loud, orange-flowered shirt that brightened up the interior of the older model taxi. Making sure that Kean had his earphones on and connected with his iPad, she took a hundred from her purse and slipped it in front of the driver.

"There's a blue car following us, my husband's PI. She's blonde with big hair and driving the Focus. Look, the jerk wants to take away my kid. This money's for you if you can lose her."

Brown eyes checked her out in the rear-view and he grinned. "You got it, *wahine*." Suddenly he took the corner on the left and, going against the traffic for a short distance, he sped up the street. Then he veered into a gas station that led to another intersection. He did a u-turn halfway down that street and ended up driving through a yard where a driveway was accessible from the back and a garage sat in the middle.

As they approached, he pushed a button and the garage door magically opened and shut, enclosing them into the small area.

Alia laughed. "Whose house is this?"

"Mine." The driver grinned back, and she noticed Kean was now looking shocked and slightly worried. "No problem, *keiki*, I just have to pick up something from my house. Your mama's okay with it. I'll be right back."

Kean's eyes were huge. "Mo-om!"

"It's like he says, babe. He's got to pick up

something, and I told him we weren't in a hurry. Personally, I figure he has to hit the bathroom and knew he was so close to home, he decided to come here." She winked, and Kean picked up her lack of tension and relaxed.

Minutes later, their driver reappeared carrying a fancy blue coffee mug and waved it at them. "All clear." He grinned at Alia in the mirror and turned to speak directly to Kean. "It's the coffee, kid. Don't ever get hooked on this stuff."

The garage door rose and they backed out slowly, then they pulled out onto the street and drove the speed limit to Sloan's house.

The driver helped them from the car, took out their suitcases and passed her his card when she paid him. "Just in case you're ever in a spot and need to lose anyone else on the road."

She checked the name on the card. "Hey, thanks, Koko. You never know." She slipped it into the side pocket of her handbag, nodded her appreciation and shook his hand, taking no offense when he held on a few seconds longer than necessary. She just gave one more shake, grinned into his concerned expression and quickly took the larger two cases, leaving Kean to get his smaller two.

There was a lot of noise coming from around the back of the house, Hawaiian music playing loudly, voices laughing... the distinctive sounds of a party going on. Kean hesitated for a few seconds before following her along the winding path toward the garden. It gave her time to scope out the neighborhood.

She could see that Sloan's house sat quite close to the road, promising anyone inside a view of the other buildings across the street. More importantly, the sunroom, front left, had a perfect line of vision to the house they'd be watching.

No wonder, Don suggested Sloan's house for their investigation. One thing that bothered her: there was a huge hibiscus plant smothered in white blooms in front of the window which could block one's view. It should be trimmed as soon as possible.

"Mom, are we going around the back?" Kean's expression held fear mixed with curiosity, and a whole lot of shyness.

"Yeah, *Mom?* What do you say?"

Alia's glance shot to the man slouched against the side of the house; his long silver hair tied back giving him the look of an older hippy. But it was his grin sparkling with youthful vitality that made her take a second glance at his tall, lean body. This man sported a classic Romeo personality, though he had to be in his mid-sixties.

"Can I help you and your boy?"

"We're looking for Sloan Booker."

Kean piped up. "He's my uncle."

Dark blue and now intense, the man's eyes lost their smile and flew from Kean back to her. "You got the right place, Sloan lives here. But as for the uncle part—"

Alia cut him off. "He didn't tell you about me? I'm his half-sister from San Diego. We just found each other. I'm sure he can explain." Not wanting to blow her cover before she started the assignment, Alia didn't stop talking. "This is my son, Kean. We decided to come for a visit. Surprise him. Is he here?" Sweating internally, Alia wished her acting skills were better.

"Oh, right, he did mention that you'd been in touch. I'm one of his partners at *Bookers*, Lester Williams. Who's this little dude?"

Kean's eyes sparkled with excitement. "I'm Kean. She's my mom. I'm not so little. I'm eight."

"And I'm sorry. Guess you looked kinda little to me 'cause I'm way too tall. Sorry about the misunderstanding." Les winked at Kean and grinned Alia's way. "Why don't we go out back and give Sloan's friends the shock of their lives."

Chapter
Twenty-five

Sloan had the hamburgers and pork cooking just fine on the barbecue. The kebabs, filled with peppers, mushrooms and onions, gave the grill a colorful appearance that started his mouth watering. The smells of the meat wafting everywhere drew a lot of expectant looks his way.

The table had been arranged earlier by Roy and Don, who were setting out some of the food now, though a few of the women present rearranged things as soon as the guys put the dishes down. It made Sloan smile when he saw Roy furtively fix the just re-arranged plate back to the way he'd had it in the first place, then smirk at Don who sent him a thumbs up.

Sloan's glance swung from one group to

another. His neighbors were having fun and inter-
acting the way of people who already knew and
liked each other, creating a real party atmosphere.

To his left, the Newmans, a black couple adored
by everyone on the street, were laughing with
friends from further down—a Hawaiian male and
his wife, a well-endowed blonde Swede, who often
acted as bartenders. They were lovers of Mai Tai
cocktails, guzzlers who tottered off a little tipsy at
the end of every party. Both couples had small children who loved swimming, and were happily playing and making a lot of noise in Sloan's pool.

There was another group milling around closer
to the house on his newly renovated patio. The
wicker furniture had been bought online and
delivered just the day before, with yellow-flowered
cushions and glass table tops to impress Sloan's
house guests.

The Chinese wife of another Hawaiian friend,
who'd loved the dishes brought to last week's barbecue, was talking recipes with Janna Aman, while
her husband chatted with Sam, both laughing
uproariously at Anya, the Amans' beloved toddler.

Happy at being the center of attention, the little
doll-like child performed for them. Swaying to the
music while trying to move her hips and tap her
feet at the same time proved too much for the pre-
cocious child. Tripping over and stubbing her bare
toes, she ended up in a heap of wails.

Sloan quickly set down his meat flipper and

rushed over to pick her up before the others could. He knew just how to bring back her smiles. She was his favorite of all the kids, and the rainfall of tears pouring down pudgy cheeks that only seconds ago were full of laughter couldn't be allowed.

He lifted her high, lowered her belly so it rested on his head, then jiggled her in the way she loved. This made her laugh as he knew it would. Her chubby arms wrapped around his head hugging him, while her face lit up with adoration and her tears changed to giggles.

Suddenly the noise level lessened. A model-like female stood looking as if she'd just walked off the cover page of Cosmopolitan. At a complete disadvantage with a small child draped over his head giving him slobber-kisses, Sloan watched her approach.

Sweet Jesus. The woman was striking and way too much for these laid-back neighbors of his. They needed her to fit in, not stand out. *Shit!*

Les was with her, his grin stretching his face out of its normal sardonic expression. And so was a small boy who looked like he was heading straight into a pit of flames. His mama-blue-eyes were wide and terrified of rejection.

Just then, a ball of slobber dripped off Sloan's hair and landed on the end of his nose.

Shit! Seriously?

Chapter Twenty-six

Seeing Sloan's disadvantage, Alia knew she should say something, continue the act they'd discussed previously about her surprising him. From the look on his shocked face, he was playing his part perfectly.

Having the adorable child clutching his head in such a loveable fashion, well, that just turned her to mush while her new partner scored a ten. One of... strike that. He was undoubtedly *the* most handsome man she'd ever met. The memory of this moment wouldn't soon go away.

With her knees acting all weak and her head spinning, Alia wobbled forward, her high heels on the grass not making it any easier. Without knowing she would, she reached to caress the little one's face, and had her hand grabbed by the cherub who was now arcing her small body toward her.

A woman intercepted and pulled the child away. But the stubborn tiny miss howled at not getting to her target. She'd spotted the large multi-colored stones in the necklace Alia had used to detail her slim-cut white dress and, as most little ones would, she wanted them.

Still sensing all eyes on her, the noise of the guests having all but receded when they'd spotted her and Kean arriving, Alia awkwardly reached out and hoped the mother would let her hold the adorable wriggler.

Janna hesitated. First she looked at Sloan, who said nothing. Shy now that she was the center of attention, shushing the little one who still cried, Janna let her daughter slide into Alia's waiting arms and peace was suddenly restored.

Sloan, playing his role, finally spoke. "Can I help you?"

Taking her cue, Alia hugged the baby a little tighter and began Act One. "Hi, Sloan, I'm Alia Hawkins... your stepsister." *Okay that hadn't gone well. Where was all the lead-up she'd rehearsed? The explanation of why she'd come and how she'd found him.*

Sloan's eyes hardened slightly but his grin remained. "There's gotta be a mistake. I don't have a stepsister."

Alia sensed Kean's distress as he leaned into her from behind. "I *am* your stepsister." This time she put emphasis on the one word she needed everyone to believe, her voice hardening and her eyes spitting fire.

"Don't get me wrong, if I did have a stepsister, I'd be over the moon. Who's your mother?"

"Wai Kealoha Booker, formally known as Wai Sloan. She was a fabric designer and lived in San Diego."

"She was my mother too. You don't look like her."

"I know. She was beautiful. I recently moved to Honolulu, only to find my house full of termites and so it's being renovated. I hoped you'd let me and my son stay with you. Didn't the lawyers contact you?"

Sounds of shock filtered through the group of onlookers, but no one spoke until Sloan asked the next question they'd put into his script.

"Yes. Some time ago. I told them I'd be willing to meet you but they needed to do all the background checks before they sent you to me. I haven't heard from them since. What's your name?"

"Alia Landon is my married name, though I'm now divorced. Look, they promised to contact you and let you know that I was moving to Hawaii."

"They didn't. How did you find me?"

"The lawyers gave me a letter from my mother when she passed, which explained that she had a son from an earlier relationship with Tom Booker, your father. Since you're now my only family, I wanted to find you... meet you. I have a son. You're his uncle." *Okay, she was now back on script.*

Sloan slowly crouched down and reached out his hand toward Kean. "Hey, kid, you want an uncle? I have a pool, lots of good friends and I cook a mean hamburger. Whaddaya say? Ya wanna stick around with me so we can be a family for a while?"

Kean hesitated. He looked up at his mother, waiting for her approval. This whole farce had been stressful for Kean and she felt terrible that he'd had to suffer through this damn act so necessary to introduce her into Sloan's life and his house.

She nodded at him and hugged the little girl tighter, who was now trying to get the necklace to go over her head too. Being choked to death at this point seemed preferable than having to live out this charade for one more minute.

Kean searched Sloan's features. Being his mother's son, he didn't jump head first into any situation. Even though earlier he'd seemed stoked by having Sloan enter his life, when the chips were down, wariness kicked in. "Do you like kids... boys?"

A sigh went around the group, who'd all moved closer to watch the newest episode of a day in Booker's world. Sloan looked stunned, as if the words had punched him in the gut.

He reached out to hold both of Kean's arms and his voice turned solemn, the joking tone vanished.

"I used to be a boy myself. It's a tough world for us guys. I had three dads to help me make things less tough. If you like, I can share two of them with you, and if you add me in as your uncle, that's three of us in your corner. Work for you?"

Kean lit up, his face now wreathed in smiles. "Okay!" He nodded, his head resembling a bird bobbing for feed, and then he dropped a bombshell. "I'm kinda hungry, but I think your hamburgers are burning."

Those words broke the spell and everyone moved to the rescue. Sloan, who'd taken Kean by the hand, rushed to see if their dinner could be saved, and left Alia holding the proverbial bag, meaning the kid doing her damnedest to strangle her with her own necklace.

Janna, insistent with Anya, took her from Alia's arms and shushed her renewed cries, until Alia removed the jewelry and placed it around the toddler's neck. Instantly Anya's cries turned to happy hiccups, and her large brown eyes sparkled.

"No, please, miss. You mustn't. The necklace is expensive, and she's little more than a baby who doesn't understand. She'll break it."

After almost taking a header from having her heel stick in the grass, Alia kicked off her shoes and moved closer, wanting to calm the lovely woman... who was now her suspect.

Their eyes met, and Alia saw the essence of Janna, her spirit and kindness, her open friendliness in welcoming a new person into the group.

They'd just overcome the largest hurdle in their plan, initiating Alia's entry into Sloan's world. But now she had a different problem that wouldn't be as easily conquered. A link had formed between her and Janna Aman, an instant liking from the minute their eyes had taken each other's measure.

Dammit! How the hell was she to do her job now?

Spying on her new friend...

Chapter
Twenty-seven

Sloan had no idea whether it was the burnt hamburgers everyone jokingly consumed, or Anya's instant acceptance of Alia; the child was now sleeping in her father's arms still clutching the fancy necklace. Or because Alia had kicked off her shoes and joined them as if she belonged. But the day had become a success.

Sloan had motioned Faisal over, the Amans' nine-year-old son, and introduced him to Kean. Hoping that the boys would be pals, he'd encouraged Kean to get his swimsuit on and play with the other kids in the pool.

Faisal, a little seal in the water, a gregarious kid who loved to tease his sister and the other little girls, would be the perfect friend for the shy boy who'd hovered near him since he and his mom had arrived.

However, the next time Sloan looked, instead of being with the rest of the kids, Kean was sitting happily near Roy, who was in his glory. Roy's manner of calm knowledge, his way of teaching lessons without anyone even aware they were being taught had turned Sloan's childhood into a wonderful experience.

Comfortable now about the kid, whose big eyes had almost unmanned him, Sloan checked out the laughter coming from the group around the patio. Chatting with the rest of the females, Alia was sipping a Mai Tai while her feet were tucked under her in one of his new garden chairs. Her dress had slid up and her tanned legs, curled in that way women had when they wanted to be comfy yet ladylike, drew his eye.

Until... he caught her watching him. Then his cheeks grew hot, and not from the heat of the barbecue.

Well, damn...

Quickly, he skimmed the rest of the yard, where, just that morning, Roy had performed his usual miracle as the main gardener. His eyes strayed from one colorful, tropical plant to another in the newly trimmed gardens; a perfect backdrop to where his neighbors were enjoying their day. Everyone looked relaxed, exactly the way they'd planned.

He sauntered over to the patio and crouched next to Alia. His move brought a lull to the conversation which suited him perfectly. "You and Kean are welcome to stay with me for tonight. Tomorrow I'll call the lawyers. If you are my sister—"

"I am."

"Which I have no reason to doubt, since I never knew my mother, you can stay as long as you want."

"Thank you, Sloan. I really appreciate you taking us in. I have a lot of personal stuff to share with you about your mother."

"Fine. We have time. I'll get your suitcases." He got up and went to fetch the forgotten luggage that Les and Kean had left by the entrance to the back yard. Les jumped up to help, as did Don, and they hauled them into the smallish back bedroom he'd designated for his two visitors.

Les waited until they were out of earshot and talked low. "You didn't tell us your new partner was a bloody princess. I never thought I'd see an FBI'er who looked like her. She could be a movie star, for fuck's sake."

Don piped up. "She's a sweetheart, Les. Give her a chance."

Les eyeballed Don, his attitude changing slightly. "I already came to the same conclusion on my own, Special Agent Asshole." He turned away from Don's grin and looked at Sloan. "As per your instructions, or should I call them like they are:

your orders. I watched for the cab, but when I first saw her I gotta tell you, I figured it was a frickin' joke."

Sloan held up both hands. "Hey, I didn't know she'd come dressed for a night in Vegas, for crissakes. For a guy who likes the ladies, you're being rather asinine."

"Am not."

"Are so."

"Hey, who you calling an arsehole?"

"Cut it out, you two." Don broke into their typical nonsense. "At least she's broken the ice. They all like her, especially Janna and Sam."

Les became serious. "There's one thing that kinda worried me, could be a game changer. Figured you should know."

Both Don and Sloan stiffened, acknowledging the change of tone in Les's voice.

"After the taxi took off, I saw a car pull in across the street. A blond chick with huge hair seemed very interested in the house and your new sister."

"What the fuck? She has someone tailing her? Is that what you're saying?"

"All I'm saying is... yeah! I guess that's what I'm saying."

Chapter Twenty-eight

Sloan smelled Alia's perfume wafting through the room, the subdued sexy smell snagging his attention in the same way it had the other times he'd stood close to her, wanting to touch.

While she settled her kid in the strange bedroom, he sat on the brown leather couch in the living room, waiting with two mugs of coffee in front of him. Paying little attention to the big-screen monster most men only dreamed of owning, he turned the sound low.

Since his two token daddies had hauled it in last Christmas as their joint gift, he'd had no choice but to set it up. Working the hours he did, he seldom watched the bastard, never made time until baseball season started. Then drawn into his favorite sport, he'd have continuous company. Between two old brats fighting over the remote, and Don hogging the popcorn, things could get out of hand.... in a fun way.

Last year, Sam had started joining them. Sloan's mind wandered back to earlier, when his neighbor had come to thank him after the barbecue.

He liked Sam, who was a gentle soul with a strong core. A man who loved his kids and was constantly thankful they'd chosen to become US citizens. Both the Amans spoke reverently about their new opportunities, which had been stifled in Pakistan after Sam's press editorial exposing his government's treachery.

Dawn, one of Karachi's leading newspapers where Sam had worked as its well-respected reporter, had released his editorials, but stepped back when his words had inflamed those in power.

He'd been active in providing important evidence showing that – after the arrest of terrorists – some in the security establishment acted behind the scenes to set the suspects free. After his exposé, Inter-services Intelligence was no longer to consider ISIS terrorists groups off-limits for civilian action. This underhand support, which Pakistan had been giving to these extremists, and now revealed by Sam, had put his life in danger.

It wasn't unheard of for hand grenades to be tossed through windows, or for people to be shot because of their actions in exposing links to radicals. He'd taken the advice of his co-workers who knew of others who'd previously emigrated and pulled every string imaginable to get visas for himself and his family and make the move before it was too late.

Now, living in freedom, he worked happily for the Honolulu *Star-Adviser*, Hawaii's chief source for breaking news. He often reflected about how a man could write the truth here and not be persecuted.

Although, earlier, he'd seemed worried. Fidgety. Not himself. Sloan wondered if it had anything to do with the imminent arrival of his so-called relatives.

Using Alia as an example, he'd broached the subject of unexpected visitors, hoping Sam would open up and tell him about these people. Though Sam had looked anxious and even at one point on the verge of sharing, the moment had been interrupted and had passed.

Alia returned and began scurrying around the room, picking up the messy shit he'd been trying to ignore. "What are you doing?"

"Tidying up."

"Well, don't. I can do it later." Others messing with his shit made him uncomfortable. She'd already shoved dishes into cupboards that were clearly for other things. And... she'd used his towel to wipe a counter when everyone knew there was a dishcloth to do that. And then, she'd used the same towel to clean the floor when she'd dropped a dish full of food.

Feeling his obsessive impulses kicking in – Les called him an OCD prick, which he wasn't, just liked things done properly and everything in its right place – he patted the seat next to him. "Your coffee's getting cold. Come and sit."

"I don't drink coffee."

Christ! "Then get a beer or whatever the hell you want. We need to talk and make some plans." He tried to stifle his sigh when she came back with one of his fancy glasses. *Of course the princess would drink wine!*

"Did Don show you the arrangements we set up for the stakeout?" *Why would any woman wear a formal dress to a barbecue?*

"Yes. We snuck away at one point and he waved me into the sunroom. It's perfect. The camera is adequate and so are the binoculars. My only suggestion is for us to cut back the plant in front of the window that obscures the view to the left."

"Roy meant to get to that this morning, but he wanted to clean up the back yard for the barbecue first. He'll be here tomorrow and finish the rest." *She's redone her make-up. Her lips were brilliant red again.*

He liked natural...

"Good. We can't afford to disrupt the operation due to something preventable."

"Speaking of preventable, if Central knows who these people are, why don't they just detain them at the airport and refuse them entry into the country?" *Why didn't she let her hair down? The mound of curls on top of her head did nothing to soften her face. She reminded him of a marble statue...*

"Because, we don't know exactly which of her relatives are being impersonated. We've been able to ascertain that there'll likely be two people and their destination is staying with the Amans, but we don't have any official grounds to refuse them entry."

"Can't the Custom's people question all travellers from Pakistan to single them out?"

"Sure, but these individuals have ties to some very important people in Pakistan and our government can't appear to be unfriendly for no justifiable reason."

"So... associating with known terrorists or signs of dangerous activities is what we're on the look-out for." *Why are you sitting so far away?*

"And, if necessary, stopped. That's our core mandate." She bit her lip, looking over his shoulder rather than meeting his stare. Her hands continuously rubbed the top of her legs as if smoothing her skirt would add length.

Mesmerized by her edginess, he kept the conversation going. "Got it! Protect the island at all costs and try to get along while doing so." *Did you know when you sit like that; I can see up your skirt... Of course you do. It's why you keep tugging at it.*

"We'd get along a hell of a lot better if you'd quit ogling my legs."

Still lost in his reverie, Sloan only heard the words as an afterthought and he immediately hit the defensive.

"Then quit sitting like that." He slid forward on the seat and slammed his mug down on the table, his hands clasped between the knees of his khaki shorts. He levelled her with a stare that he'd perfected when wanting to get a point across. "And while we're at it, quit with the model-look. We're laid back around here, regular folks who don't appear as if we've just finished the last take of a scene in a movie. Dress in shorts and holiday clothes, look like you belong."

As soon as she flinched, he realized his grouching had hurt her. And he'd have given anything to take back the rant. He was just being a cranky bastard.

Sure, sharing his house with a partner and her kid sucked, but when she had breasts that invoked fantasies, lips that made him squirm and legs that turned him into a jibbering idiot, well, that didn't sit well either.

Now it was her turn to let him have it and she didn't hold back. "Look, I never asked for this assignment. They forced me to take it because of my understanding of the Pakistani language and my knowledge of their customs. I lived with my uncle and aunt in that country through my teens, so I was the ideal choice and my agreement was taken for granted."

Feeling like an idiot, he wanted to wriggle out of the pickle he'd started but didn't know how. *Dammit, Sloan!! You and your big mouth...*

Unaware of his discomfort, Alia didn't stop. Instead, she sat forward and kept talking. "My mandate is to insinuate myself with the family, try to understand their dynamics and learn what I can about each member. Getting along with you is secondary. But to keep the peace, I'm willing to tolerate and abide by your rules... to a point. If they get too crazy, we'll be having this cozy little chat again."

Her sarcasm hit him hard. The clenching in his guts, sharp and intense, clued his response. Rejection, not something he normally dealt with, especially with the opposite sex, confused him. He reached out to touch and apologize, except her instinctive pulling away had his seesawing temper rising once again.

Not at her, but at himself for being such an ass. He looked at her, his remorse openly visible.

Without flinching this time, she held his stare; her daring him to disagree was visible and understandable. The woman wouldn't put up with his nonsense.

"I'm being a prick."

"Yes, you are."

He deserved her affirmation and she knew it.

Her voice softened. "Once we'd finalized the assignment, Don warned me you were compulsive about your house and your belongings. I wish I'd have known that beforehand. I'm not the neatest person and I'll admit Ruby did most of the housework. In fact, she cleaned up after me and Kean a lot. We'll try and keep things nice, but you'll have to tell us how you like everything so we don't screw up too badly, okay?"

Now he felt like a whiny little bitch. He slid closer. "It doesn't matter. What's important is that you both feel at home. Look, we can do this." He reached out and was relieved when, after hesitating, she slipped her hand into his.

The minute that happened, rockets went off.... the big guns. No warm fuzzies, no sweet breathlessness. More like, strong urges, instant arousal, steamy need, a craving as essential to his well-being as his next breath.

Chapter
Twenty-nine

Once they'd touched, the warm brown of his eyes became flames of golden intensity. Half-opened, the molten magnets drew her toward him like a regretful, *I-should-have-known-better* moth to a flame. Her feeble attempts to tug her fingers from his clasp failed.

"Let me." Voice husky, he drew her closer while his other hand released the clip she wore to keep her hair up and off her neck. She felt its bulk cascade over her shoulders and then his hands threading through the strands. How could she have stopped him? Her bones had liquefied. He scooped her up, his strong hands sliding under her bottom.

Weakened with the instant passion incited by his entreaty, her good intentions fled, taking her will with them. *Good Lord, the man's charisma devastated.*

Her body's instant approval: breasts swelling, demanding pulsations between her legs, muscles clenching – draining the moisture from her most sensitive place. All these sensations melted her resistance.

"Yes. If you want..." Rapid heartbeats forced her breathe out in gasps she couldn't control. *Was she this easy?* There was no doubt in her hazy mind... the man could do with her as he chose. She had no willpower.

Thank God. My inhibitions are saturated in Mai Tais, wine and hunger! It had been so long since anyone had tempted her surrender, the compulsion was too hard to deny.

She moaned and words burst out. "It's been so long."

"Trust me, darlin'. Me too."

He had his face buried in her hair. Sniffing her neck, he licked the soft, sweet-smelling skin under her ear. His following breath cooled the dampness, and shivers of excitement stormed her body. "You smell like heaven."

Breathing erratically, she swallowed the next moan. "It's Pure Poison.

He kissed the spot again that should have tickled but didn't. "Poison's not the term I'd use. You smell *good*."

"It's the name of the perfume. Never mind..."

He moved to lay claim to her lips. The man's kiss held nothing back; rather, he forced her surrender. Excited beyond recall, she arched closer, driving her chest against his, needing the contact, wanting to give, share... heal.

His hands cupped her face and he began kissing downwards, working his way to where her breasts mounded in slopes of white, satiny skin. His small, playful nips, licks and teasing caresses created tingles as she watched while he paid homage to her willing body.

Of their own accord, her hands sifted through his hair, the black thickness curling around her fingers like strands of silk.

"You have goose bumps." His warm palm stroked the skin he'd just kissed so lovingly, his wandering fingers delved further under her dress, searching...

"It's a sign of pleasure. Ignore them." A sigh escaped when she felt his finger touch her ultra-sensitive nipple. The sound erupted as somewhere between a whimper and a groan full of raspy frustration.

"I want to touch you too." Her hands pulled at his shirt.

Sloan quickly worked at the buttons until her fingers got in the way. With a growl of irritation, he grabbed the Hawaiian shirt from under the back collar and pulled it over his head.

Then his strong arms lifted her to straddle his

lap. Warm hands pushed her dress up past her hips, his desire to touch as compulsive as hers. Their mouths connected, driven by a need so strong it melted her rational brain cells to soggy putty. She couldn't get enough of him, not when he tasted like raw honey and she had a sudden craving for sweetness.

Hi tongue did wicked things in her mouth, making her aware of what his intentions were for her body. Breaking lip contact, he reached for the zipper along the back of her dress and fiddled with the blasted thing until it drove her half wild.

"Let me." Shivering, heart racing so hard she hoped she wouldn't pass out; she jiggled her butt while still perched over his thighs. His subsequent groan made her try harder. If she could just get the blasted dress off, the protrusion in his pants, promised a grand reward. Jerking upwards, his impatience was obvious as he waited for her to fix the problem.

Not willing to stop, his warm hands began to slowly stroke her legs, her thighs, their warmth seeking the ultimate prize at the junction, wet and throbbing.

Why was he taking so long? Touch me...

Concentration destroyed, she squirmed, rubbing herself against his body to relieve pressure growing, building, pouring out, demanding to be fondled. She heard his husky whisper. "I hate your dress."

"I'll burn it tomorrow, I swear. See if you can reach—"

A ringtone sounded from the special phone in her handbag, which was draped over the chair nearby. The jolt was like greased paddles shocking the return of her heart to a normal its rhythm.

She pushed back from the man whose hair she'd just been grasping so she could hold him in place while her lips roamed his throat. Their eyes caught and his wicked mischievousness instantly turned to awareness.

"What is it?"

She glared at him as if placing all the blame for the insistent, demanding ring on his shoulders and then slipped off of her perch. She stumbled to grab the offending phone.

The huskiness in her voice didn't surprise her. Hell, she was that shocked, she could barely form coherent words at all. "Cassie, you promised!"

"I know, girlfriend. But I really had no choice. It's Sara. She's hysterical, scared shitless, and all she whispered before hanging up was to tell you to come and save her. Only you. Fuck me! I have no idea where she is, so I couldn't send anyone else."

Shaking as much with worry as well as unfamiliar passion, Alia's voice cracked. "Well, I don't know what the hell she meant either... unless it's the same place I picked her up from last time."

Envisioning the slimeball who'd been after the young girl then, her anxiety ramped into anger, hot and mean. "Okay, I'm on my way. If she calls back, tell her to meet me outside if she can. If not, I'll come into the store. That perverted shit-face, Roger, must have found her again."

She hung up and for seconds she didn't move. *So close...*

Chapter Thirty

Shaking from supressed desire, her dress gaping, her hair in total disarray, and her jumbled mind trying to kick into gear, Alia spun around to leave the room. Only to have Sloan's voice stop her in the doorway.

"What's up, Al? What can I do?" He'd fetched his shirt and was working at doing up the buttons, his fingers having a hell of a time.

Fighting to overcome her unleashed emotions, to slip back into her usual uncaring role, her voice came out harder than she meant it to.

"There's nothing you can do. I need you to stay with Kean. Oh, yeah, and I need to borrow your car."

"Well, that ain't gonna happen. That car was

my dad's. No one but he ever drove it, and after his crash I put it back together myself. Now it's mine. And I'm the only driver." He clicked a link on his cell and within seconds spoke into the devise. "Don, can you come over and babysit Kean right now? Something's come up for Alia. We need to go out for a little while. Great, the door's open."

Still fighting with her clothes, she demanded. "What the hell are you doing?"

"I just called Don. He'll be here in a few minutes. His place is only two blocks over."

Not sure if she was okay leaving her son with a man who was barely known to him, she hesitated and he picked up on her reluctance. "Seriously? You know Don; the FBI agent... loves kids. The same man you've worked with, who played badminton with Kean and Roy earlier and had them both laughing. Don would never hurt a child."

Alia thought back to the friendly interaction Don had instigated with Kean and knew instinctively that Sloan spoke the truth. "Fine. I'll be right back."

She tiptoed into the room she was sharing with Kean for the next little while and stopped by the bed to replace his covers. Her son looked small and defenseless—a priceless gift.

Mine!

The usual swell of pure adoration hit her and she leaned over to place a soft kiss on his cheek, something she'd have trouble doing if he was awake.

Then she grabbed her luggage to take into the bathroom. Opening her makeup case, she used removal pads and wiped her face clean, only adding a slight touch of lip gloss. Next she whipped her hair back and swirled it into a clip, then stripped to pull on stretch yoga pants and an overly large black Hawaiian T-shirt, the uniform she usually wore to these calls. Her gun was the last item she claimed.

Fitting it into the special pocket she'd sewn to her waistband, where she also slipped her slim wallet holding her badge and driver's license, and another slot for her phone, she headed downstairs to where Don now stood with Sloan.

"I'm sorry Sloan interrupted your evening. He wouldn't let me borrow his car, and I need to go out for a while."

Don's eyes grew large. "His car? You wanted to borrow his car? He's never let anyone else drive that baby. But it's no problem for me to hang out while you're gone. I'll check on what's happening next door and if I get bored, I'll just watch TV."

Considering the remote was already clutched in his hands, Alia had no doubt he meant it.

Once in the muscle car from the 70's, a dark wine GTO Judge with the requisite strips, she buckled in and inspected the interior that gleamed with loving care, the man's attention to detail apparent. "I need to go to the ABC store off of

Kalakaua and Koa."

"Right." With the ease of someone comfortable behind the wheel, he pulled a U-turn and headed in the direction that would get them there quickest.

"I wish you would have just let me take the car. Or even your truck. I'm a good driver. I hate this, sitting here and fretting, with nothing to do."

"No doubt. Why didn't you bring your own vehicle again?"

"Don worried someone would recognize it as an official FBI SUV. He thought it best for me to rent a car while we're with you. I'll do that tomorrow."

"Didn't your Ruby have a car you could use while she's away?"

Alia hoped her voice didn't change when she admitted that her nanny had promised another friend—Cassie—the use of her wheels. And when Alia had found out, she hadn't had the heart to argue... nor the right. After all, the pink and black Smart Car belonged to Ruby, bought and paid for with her wages, and she could lend it to whomever she wanted.

"Yeah, well, she made other arrangements before we knew I might need it. No biggie. Like I said, I'll get my own tomorrow. Look, could you step on it. The kid we're going to pick up is most likely in danger, and the quicker I get there, the better I'm gonna feel."

Already exceeding the speed limit, he sped up and passed two more cars in front. "I noticed Kean took some time to settle in tonight? Was everything okay?"

She looked at him, saw the grin he flashed her way and knew he was trying to settle her nerves with blah-blah and kindness.

"Truthfully, he had to tell me verbatim what Roy had said at the barbeque, and then how him and Les goofed around. How much they made him laugh. And... best of all, they invited him to visit the garage. Promised they'd show him around the joint. His words, not mine."

"That's Les. He's a colorful character, but his heart's bigger than his attitude and Kean's already gotten his number."

"Okay. Pull in over there. Wait in the car and keep the motor running."

"You got it."

She exited from the passenger door and ran behind the parked vehicles until she was directly in front of the store. Looking in the window gave her no clue. Nothing seemed out of place. Tourists dressed in their new Hawaiian garb were milling up and down the aisles, shopping and laughing. No one appeared to be concerned or worried.

She entered, looking everywhere, her eyes scanning the place, especially where Sara had waited the last time by the wall of sandals. Quickly she checked the ladies' room and even the men's room and found both empty. Next she caught up with a store employee, showed him her badge and questioned him. "Has there been any trouble in here tonight?"

"No more than the usual shoplifting, breakage, denied credit cards and fighting spouses. You know, the regular nutcases, but nothing out of the ordinary."

She nodded and headed out.

Friggin', shittin' hell!

Chapter Thirty-one

As she slid back into the car with its motor purring, Alia's adrenaline settled into a dull roar. No doubt Sloan saw the confusion and exasperation on her face. He didn't say anything for a few moments, giving her time.

Finally, she admitted, "Sara wasn't there."

"I kind of suspected. Where to now? And while we're on the way, tell me a bit about this kid you're trying to help."

The phone's ringing interrupted her. "Cassie, Sara's not there—"

"I know. She called back a few seconds ago in a panic. Said her stalker followed her. But he's just circling the house. Then she hung up again. You need to come now. The kid's losing it, Alia."

"She said *house?*" Alia figuratively smacked her forehead. "I should have known. Okay, we're on our way."

She looked at the man next to her and gave him directions. Then she held onto the door handle as he whipped the car around and drove like a bat out of hell.

Realizing she still held the lit phone in her hand, she added, "Cassie, where do I take her?"

"Bring her to me. I don't want the kid traumatized any more than she already is."

"You're an angel, you old softie. Between you and Ruby, I don't know which one's worse."

"Look in the mirror, Sunshine."

Alia chuckled to change the subject. "Gotta go. We'll have her there as soon as possible."

"Who's we? Hope it's a handsome dude who can't keep his hands off you. Time you had a man."

"Speak for yourself, *Chickie*. Soon..."

She shut off Cassie's laughter—the woman was a huge romantic—and became aware that Sloan's shortcut had them closing in on her neighborhood.

Glad he wasn't a showy driver using a lot of excessive actions, she watched as he held the wheel firmly and controlled the car as if they were connected. She liked that. She'd been told she was a gifted driver, so it was easy to recognize the familiar skill in others.

"Are you ever going to tell me what's going on? Don't get me wrong. I don't mind driving you around Waikiki, but it might be a good idea if I know what to expect when we get to this place."

"It's my house. I took Sara there the last time I picked her up. She must have memorized the security code for the back entrance and went looking for me. I told Ruby we can't be having the kids coming to our place, but when we're in a fix, sometimes there's no choice."

"The kids? Who are they? From the backstory I've overheard, I gather she's young and in trouble."

"They all are. Young and in trouble, I mean. We help them. Save them. Give them a chance. It's Ruby's deal, not mine." Scanning the road, she noticed the same red Camaro that she'd outrun before. "We're here. Slow down and pull into the driveway on the left. They're neighbors and away this month. Drive right up to their garage and turn the car around. We might have to leave in a hurry, so it's best to be facing the right direction."

He did as she said, reversing the car with minimum effort, and soon had them facing the road.

"Great. Wait here. I'll go and get her and we'll be back."

He opened the door, but her hand grabbing his arm stopped him.

"Stay here. It's easier for me to sneak in and out alone."

"No. You're not going anywhere without me, so suck it up."

His tone didn't waver and neither did the hot

determination in his eyes.

Seriously? The dude was going to give her trouble when she had no time to argue. "Okay. Whatever. Let's go."

She snuck through the archway hidden by the mass of trellised, rich purple Bougainvillea between their yards. Skimming along the greenery, keeping clear of any lights that might set off the motion detector, Alia directed them to a concealed entrance off the kitchen.

She keyed in the code and slipped into the house in time to hear the sounds of a hand slapping flesh and the ensuing scream. Bloodcurdling, it set off every alarm in her body, ramping up her adrenaline, only to have it controlled by her training. "She's in trouble. It's coming from the basement. He must have broken in."

"He who?"

"Her worst monster. Follow me."

She pulled out her weapon, headed in that direction and slipped down the stairs, Sloan covering her back. Once at the bottom, he reached for Kean's baseball bat standing up in the corner. With hand movements, she pointed him to the opposite hallway. He nodded and slunk off in the other direction.

Screams changed to whimpers and then pleas. "No. Stop it. You don't own me, Roger."

Another slap rang out. "You're mine, Sara. And you'll do exactly as I tell you to do. I treated you good, tramp. And this is how you repay me – running away, hiding, making me search for you? Well, little girl, here's the proof that I own you. I'm gonna let my friend Joey here teach you a lesson."

Alia watched from around the rec room door as Roger's phone rang and he lifted it to his ear with his left hand, while still gripping Sara's hair with the other. His foot was pressed on her chest, holding her in place. "Yeah, boss. We've got her. Joey's taming the little bitch and she'll be ready for your party. Okay, you know where we are. Come meet us and we'll pass her over." He slipped the phone into his shirt pocket, shared an evil grin with his partner and gave him a go-ahead nod.

Alia entered unseen. Both hands were on a gun that never wavered. She saw there were two men, Roger, and another who she didn't recognize but had to be the aforementioned Joey.

The sicko worked feverishly to undo his pants and a look of excitement colored his ugly, scabby face. He'd straddled the now struggling Sara, ripping at her clothes like a starving animal that'd been promised a feast. When she tried to scramble away, he raised his fist.

"You touch her just once more, Joey, you piece of shit, and I'll shoot off your pecker first and then your ugly face. And you, Roger, you look surprised? You figure Sara has no one who cares?"

Sara pushed away from Joey and, covering her naked chest with the pieces of her blouse, she crawled quickly toward Alia.

"It's you again, you annoying bitch. You made me run all over the fucking place to get my merchandise back. This time it's not going to be so easy for you to get her away from me."

Roger had stood sideways to Alia, but when he turned, she saw the gun he'd concealed by his leg that was now aimed in her direction.

Chapter
Thirty-two

If Sloan hadn't driven the bat into the back of Roger's knee just then, his shot might not have missed her, striking Sara instead. She'd never know. Nor did she have time to wonder.

By now, Joey had pulled his gun too, but with his pants at half-mast, his movements were hindered. Alia quickly kicked the weapon from his hand and then pistol-whipped him and knocked him down.

Sara, sobbing in pain from the unexpected flesh wound on her arm, nonetheless scrambled to get his gun. Then she slithered close to the asshole and took aim.

From the corner of her eye, Alai saw Sara's intent and turned so she could stop the girl. "Hey, kiddo, don't do it. Joey's no threat to you now."

"Maybe not now, but he will be again. Could be he'll pull this kind of stuff with some other poor chump who can't get her shit straight."

"It's up to the law to decide that, Sara. Not you."

Joey followed the conversation, his hand trying to stem the blood on his cheek while his widened eyes, the whites gleaming, lit on Alia. He nodded vehemently in obvious agreement with her.

Screaming, saliva emitting in white bubbles of froth from her bruised lips, Sara continued. "Where was the fucking law when my own father was raping me? I was seven. And then my brother decided he needed to get some. So where were the cops then, huh?"

A thick cloud of social conscience hit Alia, who crouched down, conflicted but pissed. "Fine, shoot the bastard. They'll arrest you but maybe a jury will be sympathetic. You might only get justifiable murder because of the special circumstances. Hell, girl. You'd be out of the pen in your thirties. Is that what you want – to ruin the best years of your life?"

Sara laughed, the evil in her spirit ringing clearly. "It's worth it," she said. Then she aimed the gun and pulled the trigger.

Good Lord! No way had Alia seen that coming.

Chapter Thirty-three

Alia wrenched the gun from Sara's hand before she could take the second shot. "That's enough. You've had your fun. We've gotta go." Alia hauled the girl to her feet and pushed her in the direction of the stairs. "His friends will be here soon. We need to get out while we still can."

Joey lay curled and sobbing, no threat to them now. Blood poured from his head where Alia had pistol-whipped him, but it wouldn't kill him. Nor would the wound in his hand. The one he'd held up trying to ward off the shot from Sara.

Noises of a TV screen crashing attracted Alia's attention, and she watched the other two men grappling, punching... destroying her rec room. Evenly matched, the difference was that one fought for the right side and his training and brains drove his strategy.

But the other fought to win.

Sloan, pinned under the man whose hands were clawing at his throat, aimed a powerful punch into Roger's side that broke his hold. Then he flipped him over and drove his fist into the prick's face, the crunch of something breaking a satisfying sound.

Backing off, he turned when Alia called to him. "Let's go."

"You're kidding, right? These two bozos broke into your house and assaulted an underage minor. We need to arrest the assholes."

"Not gonna happen. It's not how this works." She grabbed Sara, who'd whipped around behind her and was wildly kicking Joey. "We need to get out before the others come to collect her." She pushed a struggling, reluctant Sara in front of her, seizing her before she could aim yet another kick and headed up the stairs, an annoyed Sloan following.

"You're law enforcement. You know better."

"Be quiet. They don't know I have a badge. And they can't know. I'll explain. Come on. Let's just get Sara to safety."

"Then we'll talk?"

"Okay, fine." She got to the kitchen door and looked out before she led Sara to the hidden entryway, Sloan bringing up the rear.

Before they could get to the car, Roger, hugely pissed but running on fear and hate, had gotten his gun, come up behind them and began firing. The first bullet went wild, but the second hit Sara and she went down.

"Goddammit!" Sloan reached for her and had her in his arms while Alia covered his exit. Then she ran to the car and opened the back door for him. "Get in."

Sloan backed in with Sara wrapped in his arms, and Alia dived into the front seat. "Thank God you left the keys in the ignition." She started the motor, heard the powerful roar and stepped on it, missing the concrete gate post with only inches to spare. A whimper from the back seat sounded in a male voice.

They skidded into the street and saw the headlights of another car coming towards them, beginning the turn into her driveway, only to stop and pick up Roger.

"Friggin', shittin' hell."

"You can say that again." A Sloan's sarcastic tone let her know that once they escaped, he'd be asking her questions. A lot of questions...

"Friggin', shittin' hell."

Chapter Thirty-four

Alia hadn't had the experience of driving a muscle car before, especially not one that ran like a souped-up race car, purred with power and was as responsive as all hell.

She put the pedal to the metal and they swerved up the street, only for her to see a familiar face behind the wheel of a rental a little further down.

Libby!

In the rear-view, Alia saw the savvy broad pull out of her parking spot and cut off the following SUV. She chuckled and saw Sloan's answering grin. "Someone you know?"

"Kind of. I think she's my ex's PI who's been spying on me."

"She must be the one who tailed you to my place."

Alia eyeballed him through the mirror, her heart missing a few beats at his words. "Not sure I know what you mean."

"I'll tell you later. You maybe want to keep your eyes on the road."

She grinned before returning her attention to the traffic. "It's a sweet ride."

"And I'd like to keep her that way... please."

"Her?"

"She's precious. My baby."

"Seriously, dude. You need to get a life."

"That's what Les tells me all the time. But I like my life just fine, thank you. No inconveniences or responsibilities."

"You mean like Les and Roy?"

"Besides them." His chuckle sounded forced.

Deciding to leave that subject for another time, Alia switched focus. "How's Sara?"

"She's still out cold. The poor sweetheart took both bullets near each other, one in her arm and the other in her upper shoulder."

"Not such a sweetheart. She shot Joey point blank."

"I knew there was another gunshot. You can't deny her provocation."

"You're sticking up for her?"

"No. Just understanding things from her point of view. We weren't the ones staring up into those beady little eyes full of malicious intent. Look, she's lost a lot of blood. Better get us to the hospital as soon as possible?"

"No can do. I'll take her to Cassie. She's a nurse, and they have a clinic that looks after these kinds of things."

"You're kidding me, right?"

"Not even for a minute. It's the deal. Unless we have their permission or they're mortally wounded."

"A deal... With who?"

"Oh shit, they're back. Hold on."

Wrenched sideways, Sara, still unconscious, let out an involuntary squeal, which made Sloan react. "Alia, ditch these guys. We need to get her some medical attention now."

"On it."

She took the next corner on two wheels, and Sloan's groan coming from the back seat almost had her sympathy.

She did her usual tricks to get away from the others, but this time no amount of playing Hide-and-Seek worked. So, she fell back on the one trick that never failed.

Moments later, after she'd jumped a yellow light and earned a few seconds, she pulled the stunt. The others had dropped back, forced to stop at the red light behind another car.

Putting Sloan's baby through its paces, she screeched around a few more corners and headed into the parking lot, whipped up the four levels at an unhealthy clip while Sloan whimpered, and then shot into the empty stall next to her hidden SUV.

"Quick. Bring Sara. We're transferring."

Thankful for his accepting orders and not taking time to question her right to give them, she pulled the tarp off her stored vehicle and transferred it to his.

Once she had Sloan holding Sara in the back seat, behind the blackened windows so no one could see in, she flipped on another of her wigs. This time, bouncy red curls framed her face and a lacy white blouse with ruffles around the collar completely changed her appearance. Moving fast, she got behind the wheel and drove out of the garage.

She glared through her oversized black-framed, golden lens glasses at the sight of the crazies, who cut her off and yelled obscenities. Then with her music blaring, she backed up to let them pass and drove sedately on her way.

Chapter
Thirty-five

Later, after transferring Sara into the care of Cassie, they headed home, Sloan happily ensconced behind the wheel of his GTO. He'd watched Alia shut down, close into herself, signaling she didn't want to talk.

Well, for crissakes. He needed answers. The place they'd taken Sara to had been adequate, though a bit rundown. The clinic portion, like a small operating room, was well-stocked, had a couple of hospital beds and enough paraphernalia to appear professional. There was even a doctor, besides Cassie, waiting to look after the girl.

But he still wasn't convinced of the propriety of taking the girl there rather than a regular institution. He'd just followed Alia's orders and done what he was told. But now he needed her to share. What the hell was going on?

Before he could break the stilted silence, Alia's cell rang with a different ringtone than earlier. Her side of the conversation kicked in and he unabashedly listened. "They left before the cops got there? Good. Who called them? You?"

She listened.

"True. I guess gunshots do freak out neighbors."

She listened again, this time with a slight smile on her face.

"Thanks for the heads-up, and for stepping in earlier and slowing the pricks down. Now can you just stop spying on me and go back where you came from?"

The smile slid away.

"I didn't think so. Fine, just don't mess with my kid." She hung up and her disgruntled sigh let him know she wasn't pleased.

"I've been a darn good sport so far, Alia, but I need to know what you're up to and if it's going to hamper the mission we're on."

Her hands continually rubbed her thighs, from her crotch to her knees, over and over as if she could massage away conflicting emotions. Finally, she spoke, low but steady.

"My nanny Ruby was taken from the Philippines, brought to the US and forced into prostitution by a ring of human traffickers. This happened over eight years ago."

So, she was going back to the beginning. That worked for him. "How did you meet her?"

"I was one of the first responders on a tip from a neighbor. He'd suspected there was something not quite right about the old warehouse they'd housed the girls in."

"You saved her life."

"Me and others in the FBI squad who were on that mission."

"Why didn't Ruby return home after her rescue?"

"She was too ashamed. This trip will be her first time back. Her father's illness forced her to overcome her dishonor and face her family. It's been very difficult for her. She's a soft-hearted woman with only one flaw – as she calls it."

Interested, and not wanting to hide it, he egged her on. "And... it's..."

"Hatred for people like Roger and Joey. You have no idea how many confessions that poor girl has made at mass on Sunday mornings." Alia chuckled, the sound soft and loving. It made him squirm. He liked it.

As if once started she couldn't stop, Alia added. "Because of those horrific experiences, she formed a network of other people who've been hurt in the same way: street people, prostitutes, even drug dealers and pot heads. But they have no confidence in the cops. Or respect or liking for law enforcement. Instead, they've formed their own rules, and try to the help the youngsters who are just starting out down the path."

Fascinated, he questioned the one part of her story that puzzled him. "How do the young ones find out about this group?"

"Ruby, Cassie and a few of the others are on the streets, talking to the kids, trying to help them make the right choices. When the kids won't listen, they pass out cards with a number only. And that phone is always monitored."

"By Cassie?"

"Sometimes Cassie or Ruby, sometimes one of the others."

"So what's your role?"

"I'm just a transporter. When someone's in trouble and needs assistance to get to their safe place, they call me, or someone like me, to go and bring them in."

Sloan soaked in her words for a few minutes, aware of her changing positions frequently, nervously awaiting his condemnation. As an officer of the law, he should feel annoyed that, given her role as an FBI agent, her involvement in this kind of anti-establishment system was against their very principles.

The thing is, in his opinion, anything that helped those needy kids, especially the runaways who ended up on the street because of family dysfunction, had his total sympathy.

"You've only been here a short time. How did Ruby organize so quickly?"

"It was a blog post on Social Media that Cassie wrote a while back about street kids. Once Ruby read it, she hooked up with her and explained what they'd set up in San Diego. Cassie loved what Ruby and her friends were doing and had already begun setting the system in place here before we arrived."

"Why no cops?" He already knew the answer but had to ask.

"They wouldn't have anything to do with the group if they thought the law was involved. That's why I don't flash my badge, make arrests or force the kids to regular hospitals, where they'd have no choice but to call in the police for gunshot wounds. Look, what we do is save them any way we can. I'm just a person who comes to their aid when they're in the most danger. My training allows me to help them and so I do what I can. No biggie."

"You're a real softie, aren't you? Trying to be the iceberg princess when deep inside, you're all gooey."

She huffed her disdain and glared in his direction. "No one who really knows me would ever, in the furthest stretch of their imagination, call me gooey."

Chapter Thirty-six

Once they returned to the house, Alia beetled into her room before temptation to pick up where they'd left off when Cassie called became too great. Anyway, she needed to have a Skype session with Ruby, one they'd planned before the woman left.

Alia had no doubts about Ruby's arrival at her home. Positive her family would welcome her back into their fold with grace and the forgiveness she craved, Alia's heart swelled for her best friend. Her biggest concern was that Ruby might not come back. Just thinking of that set all her nerves to clamoring.

How could she bring up Kean alone when she had so few qualifications for doing a good job? Hell, she even cringed when she knew a hug was needed. Overcoming her upbringing, her inability to be openly affectionate, would damage her and Kean's relationship. She knew it. But Jesus help her, most times it didn't feel natural, or easy... or possible.

With her laptop on her knee, propped against the wall and sitting on the bathroom floor so as not to disturb Kean, she made the connection.

Ruby glowed. And Alia had no choice but to celebrate with her friend. Ecstatic, her old nanny warbled on and on about her homecoming. Her father's tears of welcome had healed the breach and even her sisters had rallied around her with open arms and loving greetings. She talked non-stop for ten minutes about her happiness, her relief about her flight, which had proved to be arduous, before grilling Alia about Kean and her own situation. Once assured that both were fine, she'd passed on reminders, orders that Alia needed to follow, and then signed off.

Later, Alia lay in bed, trying to calm her mind, conscious that Sloan slept on the other side of her bedroom wall. If she listened closely enough, she could almost imagine hearing him breathe.

He disturbed her. Set all her pre-conceived notions of men, and especially male agents she'd known, upside down. Most of the guys where she'd previously worked wore suits, had slick hair and the personalities of sour green grapes.

Here was a man who was completely different.

His thick wavy hair constantly drew her attention to where her fingers itched to sift through and stroke. His everyday outfits, featuring khaki shorts, with either his Booker work tops or colorful Hawaiian shirts, caught her eye because any woman with good vision knew they covered a muscular frame most men would envy and females would lust over.

Then there were his slanted, chocolate-brown Hawaiian eyes, filled with gold and danger. This thought made her pull her legs together to stop the yearning hunger from drawing her fingers to help relieve sudden cravings.

She turned over on her back, bed creaking, wriggling uncomfortably and heard similar noises from behind the wall. Was that a moan? Yep. He'd moaned. *Good! I bloody hope you're having a hell of a time sleeping too, Mr. Sexy. Why should I be the only sufferer?*

Oh, cut it out! She needed to stop fantasising about screwing the man, for heaven's sake, and set her priorities straight. Right now her main goal was to do her job, while at the same time, keeping her ex-husband from getting close to Kean.

She'd die if Paul took her boy away from her. And the thought of giving in to his ludicrous demands to give him and his young bimbo a baby... well, she'd rather be dragged under the wheels of a bus.

If she thought for one tiny second that Paul had

any affection for his son, she might be willing to open a dialogue. One where he'd get to know Kean, even form a relationship that every boy needed with another male, especially a dad.

But she knew better. The jerk only wanted to please his rich, well-connected wife. With *her* eggs. No thank you very much! Her eggs were staying inside her body, and he could go to hell.

Libby's words intruded and their earlier conversation came back to haunt her. The PI had followed her to Sloan's house, but all the woman had to have seen was the taxi pulling away. Not their suitcases. Otherwise, she wouldn't still be stalking the old house.

So she didn't really know where Alia and Kean were living now. What Libby did know was her cell number. But that would be easy enough to get for anyone with Internet smarts.

Accepting the proficiency of the PI, Alia knew she'd soon figure out that they lived here now. When she passed that information on to Paul, Alia had no doubt that he would try something. The man didn't like being refused. And, according to his boasts, the law wouldn't stand in his way; he'd just use it to his benefit.

Friggin', shittin' hell!

Chapter Thirty-seven

"Mom, Roy's working in the yard, cutting the bushes. Can I go and help him? He wants me to. I promise not to get in his way." Kean stood in front of her, his blue eyes big as saucers and his soft bangs obscuring his vision. *He needs a haircut.* She remembered Ruby's instructions issued last night and winced because it should have happened days ago.

"Sure, kiddo. If you like."

"If he likes what?" Sloan appeared in the kitchen doorway, his body seeming overly large in the small space.

Kean stepped closer to her, his hand reaching for her bare leg where the white shorts didn't cover.

"He wants to help Roy in the yard." In a motherly fashion, she brushed his hair away from his eyes and noticed his surprise when she touched him.

Sloan stepped closer and crouched down so that Kean and he were eye to eye. "Hey, dude, wanna try cutting the grass with the riding lawn mower? It's a hoot. You'll love it."

"Can I?" Eyes glowing, Kean first checked with her. Only she had to confirm with Sloan because she honestly didn't know if it should be allowed or not. They'd always hired yard people to take care of their place.

"Sure. It's safe. Come on. I'll go and tell Roy we need to give the front yard a slight trim and he'll set you up." He reached for Kean's hand and smiled when the boy quickly grasped his, anxious to get started.

With a parting wink for Alia, he closed the door behind them, and she rushed to the window to see him piggyback Kean toward where Roy was setting up his gear in a wheel barrow.

Her boy's smile couldn't have been any bigger, stretching on his face from one ear to the other, his arms gripping Sloan's neck. And Alia felt the same smile light up her features. That man was getting to her.

She took a cup of coffee and made her way into the sunroom where they had the equipment set up. When they'd returned the night before, Don had reported that everything across the street had been normal. Lights had gone out early and there was no movement thereafter.

She examined the equipment closely, familiarizing herself with each piece and all three computers attached to the video feeds. They'd been set up on a table behind a decorative screen, so once turned on they couldn't be seen from outside. Making sure the recording device would work when she and Sloan each dictated their reports, she did a few tests.

Then she watched as Roy came from around the house, followed by Sloan and Kean riding on a lawn mower that wasn't too huge or too scary for a small boy. Face lit with excitement, Kean listened as Sloan gave directions and then slowly took over the controls, the machine lurching forward. They laughed and Sloan ruffled his hair, followed by a small hug that was given to show Kean he was doing just fine.

Alia's heart swelled and she couldn't take a deep breath because of the building emotion. *Oh, God!* This is what her boy needed. Not a mommy who babied him, but a dad who could teach him how to be a man. Sobs broke free before she even knew they were coming. Swiping at the rainfall on her checks, she bit her cheek to control the sudden onslaught and headed to the kitchen to clean up their breakfast dishes.

This job was going to break her. She knew it.

But how the hell could she build defenses when that handsome son of a bitch kept tearing them down?

***

Ten minutes later the call came. She answered the phone, recognizing the ringtone as Don checking in.

"Hi, Don. Did they arrive?"

"Yeah. I'm watching them here at the airport. Only Janna came to pick them up. There's a man and a woman. Both look to be in their mid-twenties, seem educated and have little baggage other than their carry-ons."

"You figure they're not staying?"

"Their return tickets indicate two weeks. They have their B-2s, all the documents they needed for their visas and their qualifications have been checked and okayed, including the papers on behalf of their relative, Janna Aman."

"So that's the connection."

"Yes. Looks like they're her brother's children."

"So we can't, in all good conscience, send them back to Pakistan?"

"Nope. They also have direct ties to an important Pakistani government official. Strangely, he employs them both. We certainly don't want to ruffle any feathers at that end when we have no evidence they're planning on waging Jihadi-type activities. Plus, having a relative here is part of their cover and it's perfectly legal for them to come and pay her a visit."

"But you're worried."

"Damn right. Homeland has flagged one of them as an activist in their own country. They have online connections to groups who're vocal but not operating in the sense that they've been physically involved in any fighting or subversive activities."

"So they're here to what...?"

"That's just it. We don't know. They could be holidaying or planning to attract other ideological fighters."

"It's important we don't take any chances. I get that."

"Yeah. Because of their interactions with some suspected terrorist sympathisers here in Oahu. DHS has kept their eye on these local groups with convincing online and social media campaigns that have grown. In fact, they've shut many down, only to have them immediately show up on new sites. Unfortunately, their rhetoric is dangerous and could be taken seriously by those crazy enough to carry out their own jihad, like the brothers in Boston."

"Cyberterrorism is hard to prove and equally hard to stop. I'm glad the various government agencies are on top of these kinds of situations."

"Me, too. Okay, they're heading out now and should be arriving there shortly. If you and Sloan have any trouble keeping up with the stakeout, I can always provide a break for you. What have you told Kean about that room?"

"Sloan made up a story about being a stargazer, and that he had exclusive equipment in there for that reason. Also told him he kept the room locked because the stuff was crazy expensive. Kean bought it."

"The French doors leading there from outside works perfectly, doesn't it? He won't even see anyone going in and out of the room from inside the house."

"True. Any time one of us is on duty, we can leave and then re-enter from outside so he doesn't know we're even in there. I'm glad, because I want to keep him completely unaware of the surveillance."

"Don't blame you. Not that it's a dangerous mission. These people don't pose any threat."

"None that you know of."

"Right. They're heading your way. Will trail them as far as the driveway and then they're all yours. Talk soon."

Alia stalked to the front window to see not only Kean on the mower working the controls, but Faisal, Janna's son, perched there with him, the two boys working the machine, laughing... bonding.

Roy and Sloan stood close by, watching their antics and laughing too.

Lonely confusion gripped her. She fingered the side of her eye, wiping away the moisture, knowing she'd have to fix her mascara yet again... twice in a matter of such a short time.

Chapter Thirty-eight

Sloan watched Alia at the window and saw her raise her hand and wipe at the corners of her eyes. *What... Why?*

He'd never met another woman who had so much emotion locked away behind such tough constraints. What the hell could have turned her like that? Appearing cold and standoffish and yet willing to put her life on the line for street kids in trouble, ones she'd never met before.

Or being afraid to reach out and touch her own son, and when she managed a caress, she acted like she'd taken liberties and was expecting a rejection.

He shook his head. The woman he'd held in his arms not that many hours ago had been coiled like a snake full of need and hunger. Her reaction to him had been passionate and giving, hot and ready. And... sweet.

So sweet.

He crouched over, pretending to check the grass. Roy had a keen eye and would wonder at the bulge in his pants if he didn't get rid of it soon. After the night before, he'd been walking around with his mascot ready and willing. All it took was one look at the woman and the nuisance swelled with interest.

Especially this morning.

She'd taken him at his word and had dressed appropriately for the island. White shorts, that made a man blink and then blink again, highlighted her heart-stopping tanned legs to perfection.

She'd cut down on the make-up, but now looked even more untouchable because what she'd revealed was the real person behind the mask. And that girl was stunningly beautiful and surprisingly shy.

Her look-but-no-touchie sign glowed bright as the red on her cheeks when she'd seen the appreciation he hadn't tried to hide. It was going to be hellish trying to keep his hands off her... at least until the kid hit the sack later and they were alone.

Suddenly, Faisal jumped off of the mower and headed across to where a car had pulled into the driveway.

"Bye, Kean. See you later." He turned to Sloan.

"If my mom says it's okay, can I come over later and watch TV with Kean?"

Sloan pretended he'd just noticed the visitors exiting Janna's car. "I'm not sure your mom will approve, Faisal. Looks like you have visitors."

Being a boy, Faisal hadn't cultivated the ability to hide his feelings well. His face dropped and confusion appeared. "They're not visitors. Well, not really. But they intrude and we must let them stay. My Dad has spoken."

Sloan took pity on the boy and gave his shoulders a squeeze. "If your mom says it's okay, you are welcome here anytime, brat. You know that, right?"

Cheerful again, Faisal grinned. "Thanks, Sloan. See you later, Kean."

Kean appeared a bit down and Roy picked up on it and stepped into the breach. "Hey, son, you wanna come to the garage with me? I have some work that needs doing and I'll be tidying up after Les, the old slob. You could be my handyman and earn a few bucks?"

Glowing, smiling again, Kean looked toward Sloan for permission. "Can I? Please."

"It's okay with me, bud. But only if you help Roy put away these tools first."

Already moving in the direction of Roy's truck, Kean skidded to a stop and reversed direction. He quickly picked up a rake and some clippers to put into the wheelbarrow, his young-boy's face grinning with enthusiasm.

"Then check with your mom."

That's when the grin faded and consternation appeared.

Sloan didn't know why Kean reacted this way, but he headed into the house too, wanting to be present when Kean asked for permission. He didn't quite understand the relationship between mother and son but he damn well intended to find out.

Alia came from her room, her light makeup restored, the upsweep of her hair pure perfection with every strand in place. Before he could warn her about Kean's request, the boy barrelled into the room and stopped dead, two feet away from her.

"Mom, Roy's asked me to go to the garage and help him with some chores. Can I go? Please, Mom. He wants me to. Please."

"No! Oh, no." Her reply followed his request without a second of hesitation. "I'm sure Roy doesn't want a boy around, getting in his way. You stay here with me. We'll do something together."

Alia, not too stupid, picked up on Kean's overwhelming disappointment immediately. Most likely the well of tears pouring from his eyes was an indication. So too could be the way he wailed the word *M-o-o-m-m* and then ran to his room.

Sloan never said a word, just watched to see what she would do. He wasn't disappointed either. This woman had no idea how to handle the boy's behavior or his angst.

None whatsoever.

She pressed her shaking hands to her mouth and blinked back her own tears before looking his way, a begging expression clear on her face. "I should have let him go. Now he hates me."

"No, he doesn't. The boy's disappointed, is all. You replied without asking him anything about the request. Just said no. He needs to know why you refused. And then he has to figure out if he should state his reasons for wanting to go or leave the matter alone. But you never gave him the chance to say anything."

"I made Roy's invitation sound insincere. I didn't mean to. I'm a terrible mother." She sniffed first and then let out a small sob. "I don't know what to do, how to talk to him, what to say. Ruby always did the mothering. I just loved him from behind the scene."

"Where it was safe. Where you couldn't get hurt."

She swung his way. "You don't know me." Her anger grew. "How dare you say that?"

He didn't retreat. Rather, he leaned into her space and watched her blue dazzlers grow huge "Because, it's true. Quit protecting yourself over the needs of your son. Take a few chances. If he hurts your feelings, pull up your big-girly thongs and get on with it. You're his mom, for Christ's sake. Act like it. Now go and talk to him and find out why this treat means so much to him, and make your decision based on that. And... just so you know, I spent my entire childhood in that garage and it's a fascinating way for a little guy to pass time. And... Roy and Les never let anything bad happen to me, so I'm sure they can be relied on to take care of Kean."

He stopped there. Ignored the pain on her face and left her to decide what she would do.

By the time he'd told Roy to give it a little while and had parked the mower in the garage, Kean came running out of the house. His small face was lit with excitement and his globby eyes had been wiped, leaving streaks on his smiles. "I can go. Mom said okay." He skidded to a stop in front of Roy and Sloan. Then he turned and waved.

Alia stopped at the door and waved back to him, her own track of tears blackened slightly with mascara... her smile enormous.

Chapter Thirty-nine

Alia made repairs to her face, though without putting on more mascara because it would take too long to do it properly. She needed to get to the sunroom now that Janna had arrived with her company.

Staring at her image, she hesitated. She had cut down on how much make-up she wore, but it felt weird to go out in public without her former mask, like she was naked, exposed—unprotected.

The scene earlier between her and Kean replayed over in her mind and she reached for another tissue. Her little boy had been on his bed crying when she'd knocked and opened their bedroom door. As soon as he'd seen who it was, he'd swiped at his tears and laid back down, facing the wall.

Not sure how to start, Alia had stood nearby, gathering her courage so she could come straight to the point. Finally, she cleared her throat and dove in. "You really wanted to go with Roy, didn't you?"

"Yes," Kean had sniffed and added, "He *likes* me."

His words had cut her in half, leaving the raw wounds bloody. She'd gone with being honest and hoped he'd hear her sincerity. "I do too, kiddo. You're pretty easy to like. When I said no to you, it was because I was trying to protect you. But in this case, I was wrong. Sloan says that he used to spend all his time at the garage when he was your age. So I guess it's safe."

Kean sat up and looked at her, his globby eyes earnest and full of hope. "Roy and Les wouldn't let anything bad happen to me, Mom."

"I know they wouldn't. But accidents can happen, so you must do exactly as they tell you and don't touch anything unless they give you permission."

"I'm not a baby, Mom. I know that."

"Sorry. You're right." Remembering Sloan's words, Alia had taken the discussion further. "Kean, when you really want something, I mean something that well... that means a lot to you, you gotta tell me. Explain it to me so I understand. I'm not too good at picking up signals sometimes so it would really help me if you like, told me."

"Ruby says I mustn't argue when I don't get my way."

"She's right… to a point. But you're growing up and you need to be able to, ahh… discuss things with me. For instance, when I know something means a lot to you, I promise I'll give it more consideration and we can… ahh, hash it over, like adults. Okay?"

"Sure. That's good, Mom. We can hash a lot if you like. So can I go with Roy?"

Well, that wasn't so hard. "Uh, huh. He's waiting for you."

Kean had dashed over to where she'd stood, arms crossed over her middle to keep the rioting emotions inside her stomach from making her hurl. *God this parenting was hard shit!*

When he'd come at her, his arms had been stretched wide. She'd opened hers and he'd moved right in, wrapped his arms around her waist, brushed his face against her stomach and hugged her hard. She'd kinda thought he might have left his tears on the front of her top—hopefully no other bodily fluids—but that didn't matter. The desperate hug he'd given her would keep her going for days.

She'd followed him to the patio to wave as he'd flown at the two men who were waiting. *God, I love that boy. He's so damn precious, how did I ever get so lucky?*

Sloan stepped up behind her as she entered the kitchen for a coffee to take with her to the front. "Do you want me to watch the Amans' place so that you can have dinner ready for when the kid gets back?"

Dinner?

Friggin', shittin' hell!

"You want me to prepare the meal?"

Having picked up on her terror, he chuckled. "You can't cook either, can you?"

"I can make hot dogs. Or French toast. Once I made an omelette and after we scooped it from the stovetop, it actually tasted pretty good."

"Let me guess. Ruby cooked. And you let her."

On the defensive now, she admitted, "There's no *letting* that girl do anything. The kitchen became her domain and I respected her rules."

"And...?"

"And it was easier to stand back and let her take over. Okay, I'm a failure as a mom and a housekeeper. But that's my personal life. Please don't imagine I'm a pushover when it comes to my career. I'm a good agent."

"So I've heard. Tough as nails." The man's voice turned husky, and she had to grip the handle of her mug tighter.

He grinned, and she wasn't too sure if he was teasing her or making fun. Not willing to push buttons, she said, "I'll order pizzas later and take this shift so when Kean returns, I can spend time with him until he goes to bed. And, so you don't think me totally incapable, I made my own coffee." She headed toward the far doorway. Fully aware of his heated stare, her skin pebbled with delightful tingles. Preventing the swaying of her hips from becoming provocative was difficult but she managed.

His words followed her into the hallway. "Glad you conquered the coffee machine. Those little pods can be really difficult, fitting them into their slot." This time, his laugh echoed until she closed the door. Her answering grin, she kept to herself.

It was only minutes later that she spied him sauntering across the street, an empty measuring cup in his hand.

That sneaky bastard!

Why hadn't she thought of that? She quickly headed out to catch up with him.

"Why didn't you tell me you had intentions of going over there?"

"I knew you'd see me and follow."

"I'm that predictable?"

"I wish." He nudged her with his shoulder in a friendly way so she couldn't take offense. "I really didn't have any sugar left and my first instinct was to go there and get some. Why change habits, right? Plus, it makes sense for us to go and make the visitors' acquaintance as soon as possible and see just what we're up against."

"If anything?"

"Exactly. They could be here for a Hawaiian vacation, like the thousands of other tourists who come to the islands."

"Or not."

"Well, at least, this way, we can do a bit of analysis on a personal level. I'm a pretty good judge of character most times."

"Me, too."

He stopped on the sidewalk and stared at her cheeky smile; his questioning look drilled her confidence to bits.

"Are you playing with me?" His hand snaked out to pull her close. Their mouths were angling to feel the taste of the other, their need a vibrant emotion sizzling between them.

"Quit bullying your sister, Sloan. Be nice."

Sister?

Well, hell!

"Yeah, bro. Be nice." Alia couldn't stop the comment even if she'd wanted to.

Janna had seen them coming and had stepped out onto her porch in welcome, though she was too far away to feel the spiralling tension. "Please come in and meet my visitors from home: my brother's children."

Sloan backed away and waved Alia forward. "You first, *sis*."

Chapter
Forty

Kean had never felt this way before. Being the center of attention from two old guys, who... made
him laugh, made him feel safe, and best of all, made
him feel worthy, boggled his mind. He didn't know
how to behave. And was scared he'd step out of
line.

He circled a car that stood off to the side; the
paintwork was eye-catching due to its bright colors
and Polynesian scenes. Waves of frothy turquoise
water flowed up to a shoreline where palm trees
and sand dunes waited. Whales and other sea life
frolicked in the water. The bright sky dazzled from
sunshine and multi-colored clouds invested with
pinks, mauves and yellow. And every so often, one
saw the brown and black Maori symbols like tat-

toos painted against this soft background.

"Did you paint this, Les?" Awe filled him and sounded in his voice.

"Yep. Still working on it." Les stood close by, hands on hips, waiting.

Kean liked the attention and felt comfortable to ask more questions. He stepped over to a strange-looking machine that was connected to one of the scattered tools on the counter. "What's this?"

"It's the compressor for my airbrush." Les picked up one of the instruments. "I have a few different kits but this here is my favorite." He held up a chrome airbrush that intrigued Kean. It looked like a weird pen, but with a cup on the top beside a lever and with a cord attached. "With this sucker, I can create the smallest details and it keeps a steady spray."

Before he could stop himself, Kean asked, "How does it work?" Les gave him a very brief lesson while actually using the instrument. The words became jumbled together, but when Les actually let him try, he understood that one had to press down on the top lever to make it spray and pull back on the same lever to bring the paint out thicker.

"He's a natural." Roy joined them and sat next to Kean. "You like painting at school?"

"Nah! This is way more fun." Kean noticed the two men grin at each other and his pride swelled. They liked him.

"Where do you work, Roy?" For some reason, Kean felt connected to Roy the most. The older man looked like Santa Claus, had blue eyes like his and his mom's and a smile that soaked right inside a person.

Somehow, he just knew that Roy liked him too. No, it was better than like. Whenever he was in Roy's presence, he knew *he* mattered. Not Kean the son, or Ruby's Kean. But the person *he* was, his ideas... shoot. He didn't know the words.

Les gestured for him to get up off the high bench and settle himself down next to Roy. "See, now you've gone and done it, kid. He's gonna yak your ear off, and all the time he's bragging, he'll get you to clean up the place."

Roy stiffened and came back at Les as usual. "Only because you leave a gawd-awful mess everywhere, so someone's gotta pick it up. If we left it up to you, we'd be tripping over your crap and... Hey, Kean, it's no biggie. We talk like this all the time. Old Les would live in a pigpen if we let him." Roy grinned and pointed at himself. "Me, I like order."

"You should get a Ruby. She looks after all of that for me and my mom."

Les began laughing. "We do have a Ruby. Only we call him Roy."

"Is this a private joke or can anyone join in?" A woman had come into the shop and now stood facing them. Kean recognized her as the lady who sometimes parked on his street. Only this time, her blonde hair wasn't quite so poofy.

"Sorry, we're actually closed on Sundays." Roy stepped forward.

"Darn. I wanted to talk to the man who repairs fenders. Last night, I cut off some jerks and they smashed into my front end. It's not a biggie but it kinda looks bad."

Les had stood back, his arm around Kean's shoulders. But now he stepped forward. "It's okay, Roy. I'll take her to the office and fill out some forms so she can bring the car in tomorrow."

Kean thought that Roy looked stunned. He even mumbled, "You will?" But he moved aside and let Les take over.

Once they were out of hearing, he shook his head at Kean. "Some days that Les blows my mind. I would have bet a million bucks that he'd have brushed her off. He does that, you know, doesn't care who people are. But this time, he put on the charm. It's strange."

"Maybe he likes her."

"Or maybe he's learning some manners in his old age." He winked at Kean. "*Pffft!* Just kidding." Grinning, he waved his arm. "What do you say we leave this mess for now and get us some ice cream? I just bought a big tub of Rocky Road."

Kean loved Rocky Road and headed in the direction Roy had pointed out. They went through a back door that led into an apartment. There was a kitchen that opened into the sitting room full of old-man chairs, coffee tables and a huge TV. "Is this where you live?"

"Uh, huh. Used to be where everyone lived at one time. Sloan and his Dad shared that area and Les and I had those two bedrooms. We were a bit crowded but they were the good old days. Until Sloan bought his own house and moved. Then his dad was killed in a car accident, and now it's just me and ole pain-in-the butt Les."

A kitten's meow cut off their conversation and Kean swiveled in time to see the fluffy tabby jump to the windowsill near the kitchen door. It sat, peering inside, yowling for attention.

"Awww. It's a baby cat. It's so pretty." Kean's heart swelled and his excitement grew until he noticed that Roy was watching him. He cooled it, not wanting to seem like a little kid. But cats were special animals. His classmate had brought his to school the other day for Show and Tell, and the cat had been really smart, even came when it was called.

Roy opened the door and lifted the kitten off its perch. "She's homeless, the poor little thing, keeps coming around to get fed." He passed her into Kean's waiting arms. "She needs a good owner who can look after her."

"You can take care of her, can't you?"

"Well, you see there's a slight problem with allergies. Nothing that can't be handled with some shots, but when you're dealing with a stubborn jackass, one who's scared of needles, well... let's just say, this little girl and I have been keeping our relationship on the sly."

Chapter
Forty-one

Sloan walked into the Amans' summer kitchen behind Alia, his embarrassing discomfort likely noticeable after their interaction on the street. *Shit, man, you need to get control of this predicament. Tonight... For sure. Jesus!*

He quickly leaned against the side of the couch and crossed one leg over the other, trying to appear nonchalant.

Janna, unaware of his suffering, called to her husband. "Sam, we have company." Anya, who had been playing with her toys, spotted Sloan and her tiny face lit up with a huge grin. She scrambled to her feet, fell once and then crawled to him instead. Moving like a speeding train, babbling with joy, she reached up, her intentions clear, and they were instantly obeyed.

Sloan passed the empty measuring cup over to Alia and gladly picked up the beaming infant, nuzzling her tummy the way she loved and chuckling at her screams of delight.

Janna spotted the cup in Alia's hand and reached for it. "I know what you have come to borrow. Your sugar was empty yesterday. You're very welcome to some of mine." She hustled to the counter and filled the container and put it on the small table by the doorway." Then she scurried around, loading the table with mugs and plates. Doilies decorated the table center and there she placed platters of cookies and cakes.

Sam entered the room and rushed to Sloan, his hand outstretched to shake and welcome his neighbor. "Please come in. Faisal, take your sister for her nap." The boy collected the little girl from Sloan's arms and ignored her wails of dismay. Once Anya saw the bottle her mom held out, she reached for it and settled right down while her brother took her from the room.

To Sloan, Janna appeared anxious, even nervous, as did Sam. Wanting to reassure, he admitted. "Yes. We're out of sugar and I've come begging. But please don't fuss." He pointed to the small suitcases by the entrance. "You have company. We'll leave you to your guests."

"Nonsense. You must meet my niece and nephew, right, Sam?"

"Of course. Dina, go and ask your cousins to come and join us." Sam touched his five-year-old on her shoulder and she rushed from the room.

A few seconds later, a twenty-something man entered, walking in front of a young woman. His skin was dark, hair black and his mahogany eyes appeared furtive, almost shifty.

Sam made the introductions, and Sloan reacted as he would with any stranger he'd just met. But Yasir hesitated before shaking hands. He wouldn't look at Sloan. The floor held more interest.

When Alia stepped forward, Yasir nodded, and then brushed rudely past her and took a seat at the table.

Leah, the young woman who'd followed held more interest for Sloan. She looked like her brother but with one difference: her eyes held hatred, cold and simple. She didn't like him, and he instinctively returned the sentiment. *What a disagreeable witch!* She was nothing like her aunt, who was showing her discomfort by talking much louder than normal.

"Please, everyone sit." Janna gently led Alia to the chair next to her and graciously pulled it out for her guest.

Sam, anger covering his face at the disrespect shown to his neighbors, followed and sat next to Sloan. The other two guests slumped into their seats next to Alia and began conversing in their own language.

Janna fussed, making sure that everyone had a chance to select some baked goodies. She blushed at the obvious disrespect of her family, and Sloan applauded Alia's attempts to open a conversation with Yasir and Leah.

"Are you here for a long visit, Yasir?"

"Two weeks. We have time off from our jobs."

Alia continued, still trying hard to make a connection. "I hope you get to see as much of Hawaii as you can during your stay. The island is beautiful."

"Yes."

The following silence was wrought with discomfort. Leah began talking with Yasir in their own language, their voices low, leaving the others out of the conversation.

Suddenly Sam banged his fist down hard. The contents on the table rattled and Janna's expressed dismay rang in the silence. "We will speak in English. That is the language of this country, and we will respect it. Understood?"

"Yes, Uncle." Both his relatives spoke together, their disrespect appearing on their faces rather than in the tones of their voices.

"Now, pass the plates and let us eat."

Sloan let Sam lead him into conversation, but all the while he watched the others. Yasir and Leah ignored attempts from their aunt to draw them out by answering in terse, short sentences. Within a short time, they thanked their aunt for the food, excused themselves and left the room.

Janna had the last word on the subject. "I'm very sorry for my niece and nephew's bad manners. Truly, they are like strangers to me. Once we married, my brother and I didn't live close and we seldom saw each other. I'm sure after they have a sleep and recuperate from the long flight, they will behave better."

Sloan knew that Sam had felt offended by their behavior and disgraced by the pair, and he wished to smooth things over. But he wasn't sure how to go about doing so without appearing rude.

Thankfully, Alia knew exactly what to say.

"Please. You mustn't be annoyed with them. They're new to the U.S. and maybe they've heard misleading information about how we live. Let them experience for themselves that most people here on the Islands are kind and friendly. No doubt, they will go home with a completely different attitude."

Breathing a huge sigh of relief, Janna's eyes gleamed with unshed tears and she reached across for her husband's hand. "You see, Sam. It will all work out fine. We must have patience."

Chapter
Forty-two

Alia stepped out of the house first, waved one last time and turned to Sloan. As they made their way across the street, she whispered. "We'll need the car tonight."

"Seriously, what did they say?"

"Those two rascals are up to no good. They're being picked up and going to a meeting, where they'll be assigned some sort of equipment. I couldn't hear everything they said, but it's true that they have connections in Honolulu, and there's mischief brewing."

"Okay. I'll get the car and park it around the corner so when they leave, they won't pick up on our tail."

"I'm going with you."

"Guess we'll be needing Roy to babysit then."

"Guess so." She grinned up at him, interest glowing in her teasing look.

Accepting her invitation, he rushed her into the house, or at least it seemed that way. Once the door closed, he had her in his arms and his lips were taking full advantage of her surprise, her open mouth and her willingness to play.

"I can't get enough of this, of you, your taste..."

"You like me."

"Now you sound like your son."

She laughed, her lips moving against his. And she felt his grin form too. They stood there, lips glued together, smiling and it was a sweet moment. "Sugar."

"Yes?"

"Not you. The sugar. You're spilling it."

She jumped away and righted the mug, her expression of dismay comical once she spied the white granules spread over the tiles. "Oh, no. What a mess? I'm sorry. Where's your broom? I'll clean it up."

"Leave it, who cares about a bit of mess? Come here." He yanked her back into his arms. He was gentle, yet forceful.

"You do."

"Says who?"

"Says Don, Roy, Les —"

"Big-mouthed bastards. I'm not that bad."

"OCD was the term they warned me with."

"Okay, I'm a little fussy, sometimes. But at this exact moment, I seem to have overcome my psychosis." He nuzzled her neck and worked at her ear, kissing and sucking the lobe into his hot mouth. Then he whispered, "The only sugar I want to pick up is you—and put you in my bed, naked and willing."

She couldn't have stopped her moan of agreement even if she'd tried. "We can't."

"Yes we can." His hands travelled to her bare legs and then cradled her ass. Seconds later, he lifted her close to him as he rubbed against her body.

"No."

As if she'd spilled ice water over his head, he wrenched back and glared. "No? Are you kidding me?"

"No. You don't understand. Yasir and Leah are being picked up in a few minutes."

"Aw, fuck." He actually whined.

She laughed. Her lover sounded exactly the way she felt. "Sorry, bro. We've got to get out of here now and set up around the corner if we're going to tail them."

He kissed her hard once more and, as if he couldn't help himself, he did it yet again. Then turned her toward the garage door and slapped her gently on the ass. "Let's go. And enough with the 'bro.' Instead, start figuring out how you're going to explain our close relationship to your son."

***

Alia went to follow Sloan to where he stored the car, but hesitated at the door.

"What's up?" He saw her stop.

"Wait here for a second. I'm going to get my firearm. You never know what we might be heading into. I've learned over time not to go unprepared."

"Right. I keep a spare in the glove box."

She joined him a few minutes later in the vehicle, this time wearing her uniform yoga pants and a black island T-shirt, her hair swept back in a ponytail.

"Whoa. You look different; all businesslike now."

"Yeah. Well, it's best not to stand out too much from the crowd. Don't know where we'll end up, so just taking precautions."

He looked down at himself. His shorts were navy but the golf shirt was white. He reached into the seat behind and whipped out an article of clothing. She couldn't make out what it was until he shrugged out of his shirt.

His muscles gleamed in the light of the garage and his tanned skin had her fingers itching to touch. Good Lord, the man was well built. Saliva pooled in her mouth and she swallowed rapidly. Then gripped her fingers to stop from following her instincts to touch and caress.

"Quit looking at me like that." He quickly donned the black golf-shirt with the word *Booker's* embroidered discreetly in white on the pocket.

"Like what?" Dazed, she'd heard the words but hadn't taken in the meaning.

"Like you want to eat me." Voice husky, he pushed the lever that opened the garage door and started the car, winking at her before putting it in reverse.

"I do." *Too much! Back off, or he'll get the wrong impression and think you're needy.* "I mean, I am?" This time she formed a question, and made it sound like it was an outrageous thing for him to say. "Looking at you like that? You exaggerate. How can you think I'd want to eat you?"

Sloan chuckled. "Methinks the chick doth protest a whole lot more than she really needs to."

"That's just silly." Did her voice sound as squeaky to him as it did to her?

"Not to me. I'm planning to do the same to you just as soon as we can get some privacy."

A gush of moisture pooled low down, and she squirmed from the image she'd visualized. "Stop talking like that. It – it's annoying."

Sloan chuckled and headed around the corner to park under a palm tree. Once stopped, he reached for her hand and twined his fingers around it, swallowing hers in his large palm.

Both stared at their joined hands. He swiveled his palm so he could rub the skin gently, stroking it in such a tender way as to wrench her heart right out of its normal place and rev it up to where she couldn't breathe.

She knew it was foolish but she imagined swirls of energy around their connection and wondered if he felt the same.

"You don't wear any rings."

"Not since my divorce six years ago."

"Was it an amicable separation?"

"Yes... No. I don't know. I guess it was." She pulled back but he held on. "Paul, my husband, Kean's father, couldn't have cared less about me leaving him. He was so wrapped up in his job, we didn't matter. At all. In fact, I have no doubt he was glad to see us go, even signed over full custody of Kean without making any demands."

"Were you still in love with him?" Sloan switched his gaze from checking the street to looking at her, measuring her reaction to his question.

"Good God, no. He wasn't easy to love. A narcissist like him takes care of that all on his own. He'd become closely associated with the type of people I wasn't comfortable with. Unless I was arresting them, that is."

"He's broken the law?"

"Let's just say he skims very close to the edge. He's a contractor and pays off a lot of scumbags to keep the filth from rubbing off on his thousand-dollar, silk suits."

"Sounds pretty much the opposite of my kind of dude."

Considering that Alia had only seen Sloan in

a suit once, the shoulders ill-fitting and the jacket creased, no tie and his shirt open-collared, she could truthfully agree. "No. He's not up to your standard whatsoever."

His eyes narrowed as he read her expression. She hoped he'd recognize her sincerity because she wasn't too good at giving compliments. But this was the pure, unaltered truth. There wasn't a hope in hell for Paul to ever be half the man that Sloan Booker was. Not now, not ever.

"I hope you mean that in a good way."

"Are you soliciting compliments?"

"Yeah. I need to know the lady's feeling some of this crazy-assed shit that's been blowing my mind ever since I met her."

"Crazy-assed shit" Alia laughed. His voice had expressed a whole different feeling than his words had spoken. "Is that supposed to be good or... not-so good?"

"Baby, it's beautiful and we both know it." Just then a car drove by and stopped across the street from his house. He squeezed her hand hard before letting it go. "Remember where we left off." He put the car in gear, and they both watched as the two young Pakistanis walked away from their distraught aunt who had followed them to the curb.

Alia edged forward in her seat. "Friggin', shittin' hell. We can't follow them until Janna goes back into the house, or she'll recognize the car."

"I know." He sat ready. "What was that you just

said? It's an expression you use frequently." The laughter in his voice made her grin.

"I don't know. It's just an expression I say whenever shit happens."

"And it just did. Can you read their license plates?"

"Not from this far away."

"Okay, I'm going to circle over to the next block and try and pick up the trail from there. Hold on."

Sloan pulled a wheelie, actually riding over the curb, and headed to the intersection just ahead. Then he took a right and flew up that street, only to be forced to stop when a car pulled out of their driveway and cut him off. The white-haired oldie took so long angling the car around to head in the right direction that Alia found herself grinding her teeth with vexation.

Finally, the old guy straightened the car enough so Sloan could pass him. As they flew by, she ignored the open mouth and waving fist, though she had no doubt the poor senior had gotten a fright.

Sloan sped around the stop sign, took another right and headed to that corner, only to see the empty street and Janna entering her house. He quickly headed in the direction Yasir and Leah's friends had most likely taken, but there were no vehicles anywhere in sight. By the time he'd reversed, that road too was empty.

"We lost them."

"I know." She groaned with frustration.

"Blasted old fart just had to leave at that exact time."

"Go figure. But there was nothing you could do."

He hit the steering wheel. "That's what makes it so damn frustrating."

Chapter Forty-three

"Where are we going?" Alia knew Sloan was upset. Hell, she felt the same. They had screwed up on their first task and it didn't sit well with her at all.

Sloan turned her way and answered. "First I'm going to the office and get a couple of microphones that we can plant in the room where those two are staying. Sam said they opted to take the guest suite off the summer kitchen and wanted to sleep in the bunk beds there."

"I remember they both came out of the same room when Dina called them earlier."

"I figure if one of us can get in there and plant the tap, you can listen to their conversations and we can get a better idea of what we're up against. I know that Homeland can't step on toes when trying to get intel about possible suspects, but it's hard to fathom that those two mixed-up young people are involved in espionage or terrorism."

"That's true. But then again, they weren't being open about their activities. I'm not sure if you heard – you were talking with Sam – but when Janna tried to explain about the arrangements she'd made for them to go sight-seeing, they told her to cancel them. They had friends who would be taking them around. When she'd asked who they were, they made up a story about people they'd met back home."

"And that's a lie because...?"

"Because when I overheard them talking in their own language, Leah asked how they'd know the people who were picking them up were the ones from Facebook. And Yasir had answered, 'Who else would know the address?'"

"Okay, that puts a different spin on things. We'll go and get that equipment."

"Agreed. Just have one other question."

"Shoot."

"You're going in the wrong direction, why?"

"That's because I'm heading for the garage where you keep your extra wheels hidden. I think it's time we did another switch."

Alia began to laugh. "You're full of good ideas tonight." She gazed at him and saw his hair blowing every which way before he gathered it to tuck it behind his ear. His muscular frame at ease behind the wheel, his arm now riding the open window sill, fingers tapping against the leather, he looked relaxed and in charge.

He grinned at her. "Are you talking about my earlier brainwave?"

"Oh, you mean where I'm naked and willing in your bed." Alia had no idea what possessed her to say the words but she loved his reaction. Like he'd been shot. Watching him squirm satisfied the devil in her as she waited for his reply.

"You're a wicked, wicked woman, you know that?"

Giggling softly, she kinda liked that impression. She put her arm on her windowsill also and let the balmy ocean breeze cool her hot skin. Watching the tourists wandering along the pavement, catching the distinct odor of meat barbecuing from a beachside luau nearby, all intermixing with the sea-smell that she'd begun to love, her heart lifted and for the first time in many long years, she felt young and happy... and thrillingly alive.

Chapter
Forty-four

Alia pulled her SUV over on the street corner where they'd parked earlier and watched as Sloan headed his GTO into his garage. They'd decided they needed both vehicles if they were to avoid any curiosity. Plus, it would be good to have two sets of wheels and she wouldn't need to rent a car now.

A niggling thought hit her. What if she had to use the switch car?

Right! Priority. Next day she would rent a car exactly the same as hers and park it in the lot. Better to be safe than sorry.

Decision made, she met up with Sloan, who was heading through the French doors of the sunroom. He went straight to the video feed on the screen to see if, by any chance, the license number of the car that had picked up Leah and Yasir had been captured.

His sound of disgust was an indication that it hadn't.

Alia moved close to him and caught a whiff of his personal scent: coconut mixed with oils or soap. Whatever he used, it was fresh and smelled like Hawaii, and for her it was an aphrodisiac.

She leaned in to see the computer screen for herself just as he moved, and they brushed up against each other. Combustion sparked. He stood looking down into her upturned face. She wondered if her eyes broadcast her hunger to be back in his arms where she'd felt like a princess for such a short time. The large, gentle man had a way of making her feel protected and adored.

Maybe that's the way he acts with every woman... She started to back away.

He reached for her. His hands tender as they pulled her into his arms. "I like it when you're close to me. You smell good." He smiled down into her eyes, his soft with promises.

She chuckled because he'd been thinking exactly what had been in her mind. "It's my perfume." *Hey Einstein, no kidding.* She swallowed, wanting to take back her dumb reply.

"It's not *Pure Poison*."

"Pure... Oh right, the other perfume I wear. No. It's new.

"It suits you."

"It's called *Wicked Wahine*."

He chuckled. "Do you know what that means?"

"No."

"It means wicked woman."

"Oh. Does it still suit me?" She had to know.

"Depends on whether you can live up to the name." He winked at her and she caught her breath. The man oozed charm and his attraction was making her knees weak.

He lowered his head, slowly, as if waiting to see if he had her permission. She kinda liked his politeness. But on the other hand, she decided if he didn't make his move soon, she'd have to shoot the bastard.

She whimpered.

His smile disappeared. And his lips swooped in and devastated her completely. His hunger was huge, overwhelming...wonderful. It left her in no doubt that he wanted her as much as she desired him.

She couldn't catch her breath. He was consuming her with his lips and tongue, and she loved every second of feeding his needs.

"Oh, baby, I want you so much, I won't be able to stop."

"Stop!? No, don't do that. Please."

"I won't, not now. You're in my blood, Alia. It's unbelievable how much you've come to mean to me."

"That's a good thing, right?"

"Damn right."

They sunk to the carpet at the same time, both pulling at each other's clothes, both breathing hard.

She was trembling with her needs, and she loved that he wasn't so cool either. Her yoga pants fit tightly and he was having a hell of a time divesting her of them. She brushed his hands away so she could help. He couldn't seem to stop stroking her legs and that made the endeavor much more difficult.

Finally, she grabbed his hands and switched them to her now naked chest so she could remove her pants, and he willingly followed her initiative. His mouth soon got involved in the process and she forgot what she'd been doing. She arched her back wanting him to have total access and he bathed her skin, sucked her nipples, and his big warm hands caressed every inch of her front and back.

Soon, he was again tugging at her pants. His groans of frustration made her grin with delight. This man wanted her badly if his moans were anything to go by.

"Let me. You take off your own jeans."

"I hate your pants even if they make your body mouth-watering. Burn every fucking pair."

"Right. Burn them with my dress. I will. Okay, they're gone."

Her words lingered. He was naked now also

and he looked his fill before he scooped her under him so his hot body could cover hers.

She had seen his naked chest before but she hadn't seen the rest of the man. From the moonlight streaming in through the French doors, he was magnificent. Broad in the shoulders, his stomach was firm and strong hips cradled his penis. Fully engorged, it was impressive. *Friggin', shittin', I'm-in- heaven impressive.*

She reached for him, guiding him home and he came gladly. Perfectly matched, they fitted together as if they'd been made for each other. With sighs and gasps, they fulfilled each other's wants, some spoken out loud and others hinted at with gestures or groans of approval.

By the time they'd satisfied each other, both lay sweat-covered and limp. Suddenly a noise was heard coming from the other part of the house, a warning that their time together was at an end. A quick last kiss of thanks turned into a hot and heavy embrace.

She pushed at his chest. "Sloan." She turned her head so his lips landed on her neck. "Slo-an, there's someone here. Ahh... God, I love it when you do that." She let him lick the pebbled skin under her ear as his breath tickled.

"Your skin is so soft, you wicked woman of mine."

"I'm yours?"

"Yep. I'm keeping you forever 'cause I... like

you." His chuckle twined with hers.

She knew he was referring to Kean's way of talking and she loved him for it. She loved him.... Oh, God! *She loved him.* Not like *he's okay for a lover.* She adored him. This time she seriously pushed at him so they could break apart.

"What? What did I say?"

"Nothing. It's time we saw who's home."

"Baby, come here. No way we're going to end these beautiful moments this way. Now tell me, what put your tail in a trap?"

How could she admit that she'd fallen big time for the idiot when the word he'd used was 'like' not love.

She stopped fussing with her clothes and looked into his worried eyes, soft with a glint of emotion that she'd swear was adoration. She took his cheeks in both hands and kissed his lips, and then his nose and forehead. "I like you too."

Satisfied, he grinned, then dove in for another kiss, which she stopped by the simple means of putting her hand in between their lips. "Get dressed you rascal. Now! We need to see if they put Kean to bed, and whether he drove Roy crazy with all his questions."

They left the room and went to the front door to enter the house. Lights were blazing in the kitchen, living room and in her and Kean's room. *Goodness! He should go to bed now.* Roy was being lenient with him and that was fine, but not on a school night.

Once the door closed behind them, Les appeared and held up his hand. "Nothing to be worried about. He's fine. And so is Kean."

Sloan stiffened. Alia felt his concern even before he spoke. "Who's fine? What the hell are you talking about?"

Chapter
Forty-five

"Roy had a bit of a scare. The old fool fell outta the big tree behind the garage. We got him to Emerg and they took care of it. But, he's staying overnight so they can monitor him."

"What? Why the hell did he fall out of a tree?"

"Seems a bulldog chased some kitten up the tree and he went after it. According to what Kean said, Roy hit his head on the way down, silly bastard. The kid came running for me, and thank goodness, by the time I got to him, Roy'd gained consciousness. Had a big gash and lost some blood. As you know, he has a weird blood type, AB, and the hospital was short because of that bus accident recently, and also a multiple car crash that happened last night."

"Jesus."

"Yeah. Not to worry, they're having more blood flown in from one of the other islands, but until he gets a transfusion, they won't release him. In the meantime, I figured the kid should hit the sack for school tomorrow but he's unsettled. Something's up? He's being kinda cagey but he won't spill."

Alia interrupted, her voice wobbling with concern. "Strangely enough, I'm AB too. I can donate some blood for Roy. Sloan, I'll just check on Kean, and then will you take me to the hospital?"

"Sure." Suddenly Sloan sneezed. "Les will stay with him." Another sneeze. "And let him skip school for one day. If he's fussing, Les, let him hang out with you. It'll keep his mind off what he saw."

"Bless you." She looked at Sloan, who sneezed again. "I'll be right back." Alia went to her and Kean's room, listening to yet another series of sneezes from Sloan, who cussed after each one. She opened the door to find Kean on his hands and knees, looking under the bed. He jumped up quickly. "Mom, Roy fell outta the tree. There was blood everywhere. Lots of blood."

She rushed to him. "Oh, baby. I'm so sorry about Roy. I know you're worried but I have the same blood type as he does." She put her arm around him and he hid his face in her stomach. "Sloan is going to take me to the hospital so I can donate some blood for him. It'll make him feel a lot stronger."

He leaned back, but his frantic look hadn't faded. His blue eyes were huge and not far from tears. "I have to tell you something, Mom. You have to help me find her."

Not understanding his words but picking up on his misery, she smoothed the shaggy hair back from his face and cupped his pale cheeks in her hands. "Of course I'll help you. Explain what you're talking about."

Sloan stood in the open doorway and interrupted. "He's talking about this." A bedraggled, very unhappy kitten hung limply from his hands. The minute she spied Kean, she began thrashing and meowing piteously.

Kean ran to Sloan, his hands reaching. "You found her! Thanks, Sloan. I thought she'd run away and gotten lost." Kean lifted the kitten to his chest and ever so gently gathered her to him. The tears in his eyes turned them to blue-glowing saucers of adoration as he shone them at his hero.

Sloan turned away and sneezed.

Alia caught on immediately. "You're allergic to cats."

Sloan went to speak but the next sneeze cut him off. So he nodded instead. Les had followed him and his grin didn't make the matter any better. Sloan glared at him before he sneezed again.

"The pussy won't go and get a shot. He's scared of needles. Roy kept the blasted animal hidden."

Kean piped up. "The pussy's not scared. She'll

get a needle so Sloan won't sneeze. She wouldn't mind. She has no home, Mom, no one to love her. And she–she likes me."

Everyone in the room stopped and stared at the kid embracing the kitten, who lay happily in his arms with her paws wrapped around each side of his neck as if she were giving him a human hug. Alia thought it one of the most beautiful sights she'd ever seen and her heart melted.

But she also knew the unfairness to Sloan, who'd grabbed his nose to stop the next sneeze but to no avail. It bust out so loud that everyone jumped.

"Kean, you can't keep the cat. It's Sloan who would have to get the needle because he's allergic, and besides, the kitten belongs to Roy. Give her to Les and he'll take her back to the garage."

"But, Mom, Roy said she's a stray. That he fed her because he felt sorry for her. She has no home, no one to care for her, and its dark outside and lonely and she likes—"

Sloan interrupted, the words forced. "And she likes you. We get it, kid." He pushed his hand through his long hair and glared at Les, and then turned to Alia, softening his expression before stepping closer to Kean. "You can look after her until Roy is better, if you promise to keep her in this room or in the garden. I'll take care of my problem. Deal?"

Flinging himself and the cat toward Sloan

before anyone could stop him, Kean clung to the man's neck and only pulled away when Sloan gave the biggest sneeze of the night.

Alia rushed forward to get the kitten off of Sloan's chest where it had transferred and now clung. "Bless you."

He glared at her and she repeated her words, only this time with a hand to his cheek so he'd know how sincere she was. "I really mean it. Bless you."

Sloan sneezed again, and Les snickered and left the room. His words drifted back to them. "Gazoontite ... and comes out loose."

***

Smiling at Les's silliness, Alia opened Kean's bedcovers. "Sloan said you can skip school tomorrow so you can take care of the kitten. But you need to get to sleep now. I have to close your bedroom door so she won't wander into the other part of the house, but I'll leave the bathroom door open a smidge and the light on in there. You get it that Sloan is allergic, right?"

"It means he sneezes when he's near her. And his eyes get swollen."

Alia had noticed but wasn't sure if Kean had. His observational skills pleased her and she patted his shoulder lovingly. "Good boy. You can understand how hard it was for Sloan to agree for you to keep the cat here, then. It makes things very uncomfortable for him."

"He's getting a needle he said. Will he be better then?"

"I don't really know, honey. But I think he's being very generous, so we can't take his kindness for granted. You do as he says and keep the kitten here or in the garden for now. Once Roy is better, he can take her home."

Kean's face fell but he nodded. "Maybe when we move back to our house, we can adopt her. Can we, Mom?"

Not wanting to disappoint her son, she used the same answer that all mothers fell back on. "Let's wait and see, okay?"

He looked at her closely, so she made her expression firm. "We're going to the hospital now. You behave for Les and go straight to sleep. Promise?"

"I promise. Me and Kitty are kinda tired." He got into bed, and before he lay down fully, he lifted his head for her kiss and she gladly co-operated, and then tucked him and the tired little animal into the covers.

Once she stepped out of the room, she followed the sneezes to the kitchen. "I'm ready. And we should get you away from this house."

"I took an allergy pill. It'll kick in soon. Les has a visitor. You went to Kean before you saw her. Come meet her before we go." He motioned toward the sitting room where she heard a woman's voice and Les laughing.

Libby?

The blonde turned from where she sat on the couch next to Les and stood when Alia dashed into the room.

"What the fuck? How did you get in here?"

Chapter
Forty-six

Libby held out her hand toward Alia, palm up. "Don't get your undies in a twist. My car was in the driveway of the garage when Roy fell. It was the obvious vehicle for us to use to take him to the hospital. Then I dropped Les and Kean here and was just leaving." She reached for her purse and stepped past Les, who backed up to let her by.

"If anything happens to my son because of you, I'll—"

"Hey, doll," Libby moved closer to Alia. "Your slime-ball hubby fired me. I'm off the case. Last information I passed on was that you'd left with the boy. No forwarding address."

"He fired you?"

"Yep. Said I wasn't worth the money he was

paying me. So screw him. When I went to the nearest garage to get my car fixed, imagine my shock when I saw the kid there."

Alia pierced the woman with the look others cringed from. She stared her down and could see no lies until at the last moment when Libby broke their connection and turned to Les. "Gotta go, sugar. I'll call you about bringing the car in for those repairs."

She made her way to the front door and stepped out without a backward glance. Her high heels clicked on the floors and her jasmine perfume hung in the air.

Les targeted Sloan with the open-handed gesture that meant, *What the fuck?* And when Sloan shrugged, he turned to Alia. "What's going on?"

"Libby's working for my ex."

"Was working you mean. She said he fired her."

"I don't believe that. She's still working for him. And now that Paul knows where Kean is, he's in danger."

Sloan and Les both stiffened, but it was Sloan who asked the obvious question. "Why?"

"Because he's threatened me. Either I give him a baby, or he'll take my son."

Chapter
Forty-seven

On the way to the hospital, Alia told Sloan about Paul, and what a prick her ex-husband was. About him wanting to give his rich, infertile wife a baby, but being picky about whose baby he'd be willing to raise.

She also explained that she'd done a lot of digging into his affairs and he was so close to being arrested for fraud and dirty business practices that she didn't know what had kept him out of jail, other than bribery and payoffs.

"Why don't you press charges?"

"Because I have no proof. It's there and the authorities know it but we'd have to prove it in a court of law."

"And when a person is as rich as sin, not only

does he have those in power by the short hairs but he can afford the best scum-lawyers."

"Exactly."

"Why did he all of a sudden want to be a father again?"

"His pretty, well-connected wife, who's young and very rich, wants a baby. Desperately, if he's telling the truth. Somewhere in his twisted mind, Paul decided that Kean was a smart kid, good-looking, worthy of being his son and so, rather than using donor eggs, he's willing to bring up another kid with the same genetic background."

Alia had to stop talking or choke. She had no intentions of letting Paul anywhere near her or her eggs, the sick bastard.

Sloan's medication had finally kicked in and he'd stopped sneezing. Now he only had to deal with the occasional annoying sniffle. But his eyes were still affected. In the lights of the oncoming cars, his expression appeared full of anger; his eyes were red and weepy.

Watching him wipe away the gathering moisture did something to her visceral reactions. Her heart ached from seeing this strong man's human weakness, his vulnerability. His next sentence brought her mind back to the subject.

"So you told him to piss off, that you weren't interested, and then what?"

"He didn't like it, threatened to go to the courts for shared custody of Kean. Warned me that if he wanted to, he could even take him away from me for good."

"The bastard."

"I got nervous. He's a big shot in Chicago. Has a lot of murky friends who owe him and I couldn't ignore their power. If he says he can get the courts on his side to gain custody of Kean, I have no doubt that it's true. Or that he'd do just as he says. There's a streak of narcissistic insanity in him that he uses to justify his wants. He gave me a son. Now he wants me to give him another one. Plain and simple."

"And screwy."

Alia nodded. "I get that. And thank the good Lord, you do too. But he doesn't. He truly believes it's no big deal. I should just hand over my eggs so he can fertilize them and get his wife pregnant. Then they'll raise the baby, and we'll all live happily ever after."

Sloan drove the car into the hospital parking lot, pulled the key from the ignition and turned to her. "He's certifiable."

"Yes."

"Plus, he has no legal right to force you to do anything you don't want to do."

"I know. And your point is...?"

Sloan's eyes widened. "It won't stop him. He'll take Kean and blackmail you."

"Oh, yes, he will." She swallowed the sob itching to get out and hardened her voice. "But he'll have to kill me first. I wouldn't let that degenerate bastard anywhere near my son or my eggs. I'll see him dead first."

Sloan got out of the car and came around to her side to open the door. With his hand extended, he waited for her to take hold and then he helped her out.

Once she stood in front of him, he gathered her close and wrapped his large arms around her shivering body, his warmth penetrating her iciness, her fear. She let go of her anger and nestled as close as she could, soaking up his strength and his gentleness, enjoying the slight coconut smell from his shaving lotion.

She whispered her fears. "I'm strong when it comes to anyone else's kid. I can fight off the bad guys without a second thought. But when it comes to my own, I'm a mess. I can't even think straight."

"Don't worry. I'm thinking straight and this is what I know. Not only will the son of a bitch have to get past you, but there'll be a lineup. He'll have to come through me first."

Chapter
Forty-eight

Once inside, a male nurse recognized Sloan and reached to shake hands and do a man-hug. "Hey, Booker. Figured you'd be here soon. Nice to see you again."

"You too, man." Sloan recognized Ryan from high school. They'd hung out but hadn't caught up with each other for a few years. "Hey, bro, how're things with you?"

"All good on my side, married now and got a kid on the way. How about you?"

"Not so lucky." He glanced at Alia and then back to Ryan. "But I'm working on it. Meet Alia Hawkins, a friend from the Bureau. How's the ole man?"

"Hi, Alia." Ryan shook hands with her. "Roy's

in 404 and he's making a fuss. Says he needs to get home; something about a kid he's taking care of."

"Okay, thanks." Sloan stopped Ryan from hurrying away. "Hey, man, two questions. One – where can I get an allergy shot for felines? I have a blasted cat in the house and it's almost killing me."

"Where? How about in the ass." Ryan laughed at Sloan's darkening expression and thumped him on the arm. "Just kidding, dude. Lighten up. They're working on a new product named Cat-SPIRE. It's promising to stop the symptoms after only four shots but the producers are still doing case studies now. Other than that, there're needles, but it isn't only one shot. It can take many." Watching Sloan's face drop, he added. "You're probably better off just using the over-the-counter medication for now and getting rid of the cat."

"Shit."

Alia stepped closer. "We'll take her back to the garage, Sloan. Kean will understand."

"Yeah. Well, we'll talk about it. In the meantime, can you tell us how Miss Hawkins can donate some blood for Roy? Les said he needs a transfusion and she's his blood type, AB."

Ryan perked up, looking interested. "Come with me, Alia, and I'll take you to the lab. It'll be good for the old guy to get some of the fresh red stuff. He's pretty lethargic as well as argumentative."

Sloan let go of her hand and watched Alia follow the blue-garbed nurse before he headed to room 404.

Roy was lying back on the white pillow, his hair a billowing cloud of silver framing his tanned face. The vivid blue of his eyes had paled slightly and his usual happy glow seemed less happy.

Chapter
Forty-nine

"Blasted arthritis!" Roy spoke before Sloan could say a word and watched warily as the younger man moved to sit on the nearby chair. "I used to be able to climb any tree. Why in my youth, I was—"

"Don't even start, Roy. Climbing trees like a young kid, at your age. Are you senile or just crazy?"

"Hey! You don't get to talk to me like that. Show some respect."

Sloan had played this game before, but this time he wasn't going along. "No, Roy. You need to show some respect. To your body, and to me and Les. If you don't take care of yourself, how can we trust you?"

Roy's sheepishness appeared and he looked

over Sloan's head at the far wall. He waited. Usually when he did this, Sloan would give in and break the silence first because he hated being on the outs with either of his old dads.

But this time, Sloan didn't play. He also waited.

Finally, Roy huffed and reached for Sloan's hand. "I'm a dumb old fool. Sorry, son. It's just that Kean had been holding the kitten. And when that blasted old bulldog from across the way headed over, she started flailing around in a panic and he let her go. She headed right for the tree. Shot up into the top branches like she had a firecracker up her... ahh, back end."

"Surely you knew she'd come down eventually. I've seen her up on those branches myself a few times."

"I know. But when the kid started crying, I couldn't stand it. He gets to me. Like you used to. I just wanted to make him happy again. I'd coaxed the kitten down, but when she ran past me I lost my footing and hit the ground."

Sloan listened and then he added. "Do you remember when I fell out of that same tree? I was ten."

Roy's expression showed his distress, his bandaged head came off the pillow and his voice rose. "Don't remind me. You broke your arm. It was a terrible time. I couldn't sleep for days thinking how close you came to getting killed."

Sloan just kept staring. Then he pointed at

himself. "That's where I am right now, Dad. Feeling what you did then."

Roy paled, his hand shook as he held Sloan's. "God, I'm sorry, son."

The nurse and Alia entered just then, and Sloan had time to blink the moisture away before he caught Alia's eye.

She nodded toward the back of the room and he joined her there while Ryan set up some equipment next to Roy. "They've taken and tested my blood and they'll give him the transfusion. He's pretty weak. They were happy to see me come in. The flight from Maui was still an hour out and according to the chart I caught a glimpse of, his blood pressure has dropped. It's best if they don't have to wait."

"I'm so glad you were here. And could help him."

"I know. In San Diego, I was a blood donor and they called me in a few times during dire situations. I've been meaning to sign up here in Honolulu. Now I will for sure."

Sloan watched the nurse setting up the transfusion paraphernalia and hesitated to go back to Roy. A thought came to him out of the blue and he voiced the question. "I guess parents have the same blood type as their kids."

"I think that's how it works, but I really have no idea. I was adopted. Never did find out about my genetic pool, so to speak. I only know that I was born in San Francisco and my parents had to fly there from Chicago to pick me up. They always told me that my mother had been a young girl who'd decided she'd rather follow an acting career than be a mom. Her name was Scarlet Honor. She gave me up for a private adoption."

"And you didn't go after more information once you had the opportunities with the bureau?"

She bit her lip and searched his gaze that only showed interest. "Okay, I did. Found out that the adoption agency had shut down and the records had been passed on to the government agency that looked after Child Services. When I accessed those records, it seems Scarlet had died by the time I was two; she'd caught pneumonia and had serious complications. Poor girl never stood a chance."

"And your adoptive parents?"

"What about them?"

"Are they in San Diego?"

"Nope. They've both passed. They were quite a bit older when they adopted me and cancer took both of them years ago."

Sloan reached for her, his arms cuddling. "I'm so sorry."

"Me too. They were nice people, Brits. Quiet and scholarly, both teachers. Sadly, I have no idea what made them decide they needed a baby. By the time I joined their little circle, they had various babysitters look after me most of the time and the rest, well... they just made sure I behaved."

"And you did."

"I had no choice."

"How sad."

"I was well fed, had nice clothes. Lots of kids had it far worse than me."

"I never heard you add that you were loved."

"Oh, I'm sure I was. It's just that they couldn't seem to show their affection. Not even with each other."

"Like I said, how sad."

Ryan called out to them and interrupted their conversation. "Sloan, Alia. We're finished the transfusion."

Roy piped up. "I feel surprisingly stronger. So, I'm thinking I want to go home."

They both moved over to stand by the bed and Sloan glanced at the nurse who shook his head very slightly. "Not a good idea, Roy. We'll take you back tomorrow. Tonight you rest up here and let them watch over you."

Ryan added. "Yeah, man. There's a little matter of a concussion. The doc has ordered us to monitor that for the night."

Roy reached for Alia's hand and squeezed her fingers as soon as they joined. "Thank you for giving an old man your blood. I feel like a new person already."

She laughed and squeezed him back. "You're so very welcome, Roy. I can see your coloring is better. You sleep well, and I'll be around tomorrow with

Kean who begged to come tonight. If the doc says we can take you home, we'll break you outta here then."

He laughed at her teasing, his blue eyes shining again. "You got it. I'll be waiting. Now take this bully with you, or he'll sit here all night, watching to be sure I don't mess up again."

"Oh, you're not getting away with that nonsense, old man. I'm not going anywhere. Now shut up and go to sleep or I'll cut off your Netflix."

Alia looked amused and Roy added, "He's always bugging me about how many movies I watch."

She leaned in closer. "Far as I'm concerned, that's pretty damn low. If the scoundrel messes with your viewing, you call me and I'll fix it for you."

"You're my kind of girl." Roy laughed and patted her cheek.

Sloan led Alia to the door and grudgingly passed over the car keys. "I'll be staying here tonight, but you'll need to get home for Kean. I can't believe I'm letting you drive my baby again."

As she took the keys from him, Alia patted his hand. "I'll guard her with my life, I promise."

He sighed, pretending to be hugely distressed. Meanwhile, he covered the very real dismay he was experiencing with witticism. "Just so you know; Don's at the house doing the stakeout. I called him before we came to the hospital. He promised to sneak in and take over tonight's vigil."

"Oh, God, I forgot all about the case." Alia's shock wasn't feigned. She had forgotten.

"I know. Not to worry. I told him to try and get the license number when the relatives are dropped off back at the Amans'. You grab some sleep now, then take over from him early and he'll pick us up in the morning."

He went to hug her but suddenly, he felt her shy away. Roy was there and so was Ryan, who still hovered around, tidying the room. Alia stepped out of the zone and shot him a sad smile before she blew Roy a kiss and left. The woman's barriers drove him crazy. When they were alone, she was like another person, warm and open and willing.

But that wasn't her nature, and he knew she had a long way to go to be as affectionate as he expected.

Chapter Fifty

Once he was sure that Roy had settled down comfortably, Sloan made his way to the hospital cafeteria. His allergy medication sometimes made him drowsy so he needed some caffeine to keep from dropping off.

At this time of the night, the restaurant was only open for pre-packaged sandwiches, hot drinks, sodas and some wrapped desserts, but there was enough choice for him to grab a little something.

A man came up behind him at the coffee machine and started up a conversation. "You have someone here in hospital?"

"My dad. He fell out of a tree trying to save a cat. How about you?" Sloan noticed the other man's eyes narrow as soon as he turned his way. Recognition filled his expression which made Sloan look twice himself. "Do I know you?"

The Hawaiian fellow stepped back and shook his head. "Nah, man. I don't think so."

Sloan couldn't stop. He felt drawn to find out more about the guy. "You have someone in here?"

"My boss. He got sh- hurt earlier. But I think he's gonna recover. Gotta go." The man stopped in the hallway and turned. "Your dad?"

"Pardon me?"

"You said your dad fell out of a tree."

"Yeah. He's not my real dad, but he brought me up and so I think of him that way. Why?"

"No reason. Hope he gets better." The words followed the man as he rushed to the elevator, two coffees in his hand.

Sloan knew that whole exchange had been weird but he wasn't sure why. As far as he knew the guy was a stranger. And yet he'd gotten the bizarre feeling that the other man knew him. In fact, knew him enough to question him about Roy being his father.

Accepting that people were odd at the best of times, he headed to the lounge close to Roy's room and sat down with his food and drink. The TV was playing low and the breaking news caught his notice.

"Earlier tonight, Nick Kroller was shot in a gang war. The leader of the Kroller gang was attacked in

*front of his restaurant by unknown gunmen. He was
rushed to hospital where he's currently on life support.
Sadly, an innocent bystander wasn't as fortunate and
was killed, as was one of Kroller's bodyguards. No
names will be released at this time until police have
informed the families of the deceased. Witnesses say they
saw a red Camaro leaving the scene. Police are investi-
gating the crime and would like anyone who might have
further information to come forward."*

Sloan's shock slammed him so hard he dropped
his sandwich and barely saved the coffee from end-
ing on his lap too. A jolt of understanding pene-
trated and he started to rise, only to sink back into
the orange leather chair.

Fuck me. He'd been talking to Tadeo Kealoha,
his mother's brother. His friggin' uncle. Of that
he had no doubt. The man had recognized him.
According to Les, the shmuck worked for Kroller
and had been his right-hand man for years.

He had to contact his superior, Jack Harrison.
Tell him that the guy they'd been after for so long
was not only in the hospital but that he was pretty
sure he knew who'd shot Kroller.

First, he needed to confront his uncle.

Chapter
Fifty-one

He waited for Ryan to come back to the work station and then started in on him. "You have a patient, name of Kroller, who was admitted earlier tonight."

"Okay."

"He was shot. I need his room number."

"Are you asking in your official capacity?"

Sloan realized that Ryan hadn't heard about him stepping down to take over the garage and so he nodded. "Of course. I just ran into one of his sidekicks in the restaurant and then I saw the news. He's here. I need to check on him."

"I'll tell you the same thing I told the city cops. He's not able to answer any questions, bro. The guy's mortally wounded. We're not sure he'll last the night."

"Who brought him in?"

"An ambulance was called to the scene right after the incident. Kroller'd just stepped out of the restaurant, him and his bodyguards. One is dead, another wounded and the other was waiting in the car. He's fine. There was a man walking his dog. Dog's fine. The dog-walker's deceased. Crazy-assed shit, man. Here in Honolulu? Are you kidding me? It's supposed to be the safest playground in the world. We can't be having these kinds of incidents before people decide it's not so great after all. Then where will we be with no tourism?"

"Calm down, bro. As long as we have the ocean, warm weather and friendly service, people will always come. Look, have the police set up a guard by his room?"

"Shit, man, yeah he's got police protection, plus his own guy's there too. I'd say he's been looked after better than he deserves if the rumors he's a trafficker is true."

"Judge not, my friend." Sloan patted Ryan's arm.

"Fuck that, bro. I just hope they keep their gang wars outta this hospital." A bell buzzed on the desk computer and Ryan rushed off.

While he was gone, Sloan bent over the screen and found the information he'd requested. Kroller was on this floor. He headed in the same direction that Ryan had disappeared to moments earlier.

Very few staff were visible in the equipment-filled corridor, nor were visitors. The quiet was eerie.

When Sloan approached the room, an officer was slouched in a chair outside in the hall. He was half asleep.

"Hey, Pat. How're you?" Sloan was glad he recognized the younger cop as someone he'd worked with before.

Pat stretched his lean form, sat further up in the chair and grinned his welcome. "Hey, Agent Sloan. What's up?"

"Just found out about Kroller. It's all over the news. Were you there at the scene?"

"My partner and I were the first responders. It was a bloodbath, man. Two people killed. One an innocent bystander. And Kroller's barely holding on from what I overheard the doc tell the nurse just now when he gave him instructions. This guy's been on our radar for a long time."

"I know. He's a bad one."

"We've attributed more drugs brought to the island by him than the rest of the sources put together." The cop leaned forward to clasp his hands between his knees and he glanced up. "Mind you, there's another prick who's making moves to take over, and I wouldn't be at all surprised if this wasn't a bid to do so. Kill the gang boss and move in on the territory."

"No doubt. Have you heard the names Joey or Roger – no last names – being connected to the red

Camaro that CNN reported was seen at the shooting?"

"No, sir."

Suddenly, the door burst open and Tadeo rushed out, his face contorted with grief. He didn't even see Sloan. Or the cop. He was in too big of a hurry.

Ryan followed behind him into the corridor, his hand raised as if to protest but he dropped it as soon as Tadeo turned the corner.

Sloan knew something was up, and he was right when Ryan signalled that Kroller had died by shaking his head.

"Dan, do you have a squad car here?"

"Yeah, sure. Why?"

"No time for questions. Either give me your keys, or let's go. We have to follow Tadeo. He's second-in-command to Kroller, and his boss's just died. I believe he's after retaliation for the assassination."

Not too stupid, Pat kept up with Sloan as they rushed the elevators, pounding the lit button frustratingly. Sloan had his cell phone in his hand and was passing on his information to the FBI's SWAT team's leader on shift at the bureau. "There's going to be trouble, Henry. I'm at the hospital and John Kroller just died. His long-time body guard, Tadeo Kealoha, just shot outta here with a look of revenge plastered over his ugly face."

"Shit. Kroller's one of the worst degenerates

out there, but at least he's old-fashioned, a known entity, unlike this newer gang who's trying to take over. They're total dirt-bags, as rotten as they come."

"I'm on Kealoha's tail right now but not sure if we'll catch up with him. We're just leaving the hospital. Can you get some squad cars to intercept? If he gets to where he's headed, there could be a whole lot more people getting killed."

"I'll contact dispatch and have them put out an APB for him. Do you know what he's driving?"

"Not yet. I'll get back to you but get those squad cars closest to the hospital to respond. Stop him for whatever reason they can, speeding, suspected bank robbery, who cares as long as he isn't free to organize revenge for his boss's death."

"On it. We'll hold him as long as we can."

"Thanks, man. I'll keep you posted." Sloan and Pat rushed the door. He saw Pat's squad car at once and blessed the fact that the cops had special parking privileges at the hospital. They both bounded into the vehicle and Pat started up and headed to the exit, where they arrived in time to see a black SUV speeding toward the gate. Sloan called it in, the make and model of the vehicle before buckling in.

"That must be him. Follow and don't let him make us. We'll just keep him in sight until the officers can make an arrest."

No sooner were the words out of his mouth,

than a HPD Ford Fusion pulled out from a side road and took up the chase, sirens blaring.

Rather than Tadeo pulling over, he sped up and took the next right at a dangerous angle.

And the chase was on.

Chapter
Fifty-two

Pat turned up a horizontal street, expecting to cut off the SUV at the next intersection, and he would have too, if it hadn't been for an asshole on his bike. Slowed down by the seconds needed to blockade the SUV, they had to pull in behind the HPD Fusion and soon realized that the cop in the car ahead wasn't an experienced driver. He was erratic, foolishly taking chances. Sloan grabbed the latch-handle over the passenger seat as a precaution.

Thankfully, Pat's driving skills were good and he hit the brakes at each stupid maneuver taken by the car in front to stop from slamming into it. "He's getting away. Those idiots can't keep up."

"I'm not surprised. Tadeo's been Kroller's dri-

ver for years. I'm sure it's not the first car chase he's
been involved in. Look, there's a side street in the
next block. See if you can cut off there and pick
him up on the other side." Sloan had his cell in his
hand, waiting on his boss, AD Jack Harrison, to
answer.

"Okay. But I think I know where he's going.
We got a call to a warehouse on the east side a
while back, saying that they were storing guns and
drugs there. We were too late. The place had been
cleaned out, but they could have returned after the
heat was off. Looks to me like he's headed in that
direction."

"What's the name of the street? I'll call it in
and have them send the SWAT guys there." Once
Sloan had his boss on the line, he briefed him
about what was going down and where they were
headed, told him he'd called out Henry and his
team and gave him the news of Kroller's death.

"Sloan, I can't say I'm sorry about that bastard
being killed, figured he'd get his dues in exactly
that way. But we can't afford a bloodbath, so we
need to stop this now."

"Yes, sir. We'll do our best."

"Keep me posted. And keep your head down."

"Right. Head down. Talk soon."

By the time they pulled over behind another
building, Sloan saw Tadeo's SUV drive through a
garage-like door that automatically opened for his
car.

"This isn't the same place I remember. It was two doors over. I guess they decided to move here after the dust settled from the raid."

"Kroller owns a few of these buildings. Agent Howard and I have a file thick as your arm on this gang. On the books it looks like it's being rented to a perfectly legit organization, but in fact, Kroller was renting to himself. It's complicated."

"No kidding. These assholes hire high-priced accountants and legal scum who know every law inside and out, so they can get away with breaking them without being charged."

"You got that right."

"Hold it. Here they come." All of the various warehouse doors were sliding up revealing a line-up of cars, waiting to pull out. "Tadeo must have rounded up their men just in case."

"Jesus. We can't stop them on our own. Where's the calvary?"

No sooner had the words left his mouth than the compound was inundated with SWAT vehicles, blocking the gang trying to exit the huge warehouse and the loading area.

Both of them exited the car, taking cover behind the safer SWAT vehicles.

Thinking the game was up, Sloan never figured on the gunshots, or that the lawbreakers would take a stance. They were opening fire on federal agents, for crissakes. And they were outnumbered. "Who in their right mind would have given the order to shoot?"

Then he heard his uncle's voice. "Take 'em down, boys."

Sloan crouched and ran from where he'd been protected to behind one of the team's SUV's. He called out before approaching. "Hey, man. It's me, Booker. I need a firearm."

The agent who knew him well reached to his ankle and handed over the smaller weapon and a fresh reload. "Here. Stay low. We figure there's at least a dozen armed with rifles and they don't seem to care if they shoot a cop."

"Their old boss died. You know that, right?"

"And I'm supposed be sorry? Not me, man. The guy deserved everything he got and more."

The fresh spurt of bullets stopped their conversation and Sloan took off, heading in the direction where he'd heard his uncle call out. He bypassed one of the police vehicles and ran around to the next, staying low and cussing every time another spurt of rifle fire pelted the area. Fucking modern automatic weapons were a menace.

He waited until the agents returned fire and then ran for the building, hiding along the side. A movement drew his attention and he ducked just in time to avoid the bullet that would have taken off the top of his head. He fired back in that direction, and heard a man scream first and then thrash around as if he'd hit the ground.

He peeked into the side window of the building

and saw Tadeo. He'd gone back inside and was rushing to another door that headed out of the back.

Sloan quickly followed him, running hard, his breath coming in gasps.

Just as he rounded the far side of the place, he spied the dark shadow and called out. "FBI. Stop where you are and put your hands up."

Tadeo turned. He saw Sloan and the gun in his hand wavered for a few seconds. "You don't know who I am."

"I don't give a fuck who you are, either. You're under arrest. Drop your weapon."

"I'm Tadeo Kealoha, your uncle. I used to play with you when you were a baby. Your mama brought you to visit me before she left."

Sloan held his gun steady in both hands, stepping closer, ready to shoot. He didn't trust Tadeo one little bit. "Yeah. She left. And you killed my dad. So there's nothing stopping me from shooting you, is there? In fact, I'm itching to pull the trigger, so maybe you should just do as I say and drop the gu—"

When Tadeo pulled the trigger, Sloan returned fire instinctively. He saw his uncle go down, and the flash of pain he'd expected never came. Quickly, he turned and saw the man sprawled to his left, one of Kroller's men. The one his uncle had just shot to protect him.

Rushing forward, he skidded to the ground

beside Tadeo and lifted him into his arms. "I'm sorry, Uncle. I thought you'd opened fire on me."

His uncle was bleeding slightly from the mouth, but mostly from the gunshot wound in his chest. "We didn't ki-kill Tommy. His car crashed. We just wanted him to pu-pull over, kid. He was so stub..."

Tadeo's head lolled over, and a wash of pain slammed into Sloan. Not understanding if it was truly grief he experienced, he decided rather that it was regret. He should have known this man.

The gunfire had stopped and the night's silence was welcoming. He could hear the voices of the FBI giving orders to the survivors. Seems like tonight, they'd stopped a gang war. A thump sounded and Sloan instinctively turned to fire, only to realize a coconut had hit the ground from an old tree close by.

Sloan continued to rock the man who'd saved his life. Ignoring the carnage nearby, men calling back and forth, a siren blaring in the distance and screams of the wounded, he paid no attention.

Finally, he looked at the face of the man in his arms. He couldn't put him down. Instead he studied him and saw the family resemblance. Tears gathered while he fought with the knowledge that he'd done what he had to do.

His phone rang, breaking into the silence. It took him a few moments to retrieve it and take the call. "Yeah?"

Alia screamed. "Sloan. My God. Kean's gone."

"*Friggin', shittin'... friggin'...*"

Chapter
Fifty-three

Alia arrived back at the house and sat in her car for a short while, reliving those earlier precious moments with Sloan. He'd been everything a woman could wish for in a lover, thoughtful of her comfort and caring about her being satisfied before reaching his own climax.

She had no idea how she was going to explain their new relationship to Kean, who was probably more observant than most boys his age. She'd lied and told him Sloan was her brother. Actually, she'd said stepbrother but even still, that left a sour taste in her mouth when it came to explaining things to an eight-year-old.

Maybe she'd leave it up to Sloan. He had a way of getting through to her son that she'd never had.

The enormous love she had for the boy didn't change the difficulties she experienced every time she had to show her emotions. For her, talking to him was excruciating because she kept thinking she'd screw up. And he'd push her away. God! What a baby she was.

Suddenly, she had the overwhelming urge to go see him and tuck him under the covers he'd often kick off during sleep.

She went into the house, directly to his room and couldn't believe her eyes when she found it empty. Heart pounding, she looked everywhere, under the bed, in all the other rooms. Screams rang inside her head, wanting to burst out but she maintained the control that she'd been trained for. Sobbing under her breath, she finally pulled Don into the search.

"He's gone? What the fuck? I had the door open to the house so I could hear him call if he woke up. He knew I was in here. I went and told him so he wouldn't be scared after you guys and Les left. Maybe the cat wandered off and he's chasing her. I'll go outside and look."

While he checked the yards nearby, she combed the house again, calling Kean's name, this time going through closets and every nook and cranny she'd missed earlier.

There was no sign of the boy.

The kitten.

She searched again for the tiny animal, calling,

"Kitty, Kitty, here Kitty," all to no avail. The cat was missing too. Collapsing into a kitchen chair, she pushed her hands through her messy hair.

How the hell could anyone have come into the house and taken Kean without Don hearing them? When they'd first moved here, she'd wondered at Sloan's lack of security but hadn't worried overly because she'd argued with herself that there would normally be two agents in the house, both with firearms if necessary. And yet, Kean was gone.

Paul! The bastard had threatened, said he'd take Kean away from her, and she hadn't fully believed he'd be able to pull it off.

Libby's image popped into her mind. She fitted into the slot as the perfect suspect. The woman had been here earlier. She knew the layout of the house. All she'd had to do was wait until Sloan and Alia had gone to the hospital. In her mind, that would have left Les to get past. But she could bide her time waiting for him to doze off and if she came in through the back door, she'd be home free.

And to make things even easier, Sloan had told Don to relieve Les, so Les would have left after Don had arrived. Not having to deal with Les would have made taking Kean even easier. No doubt Don was concentrating on his surveillance in the sunroom, or snoozing, and the PI would have had an easy time breaking in.

Hell, with her boy being small for his age, and Libby being so strong, she could have simply carried him if he was asleep. Since Kean knew her voice, he probably wouldn't make any fuss.

Deciding she had it all worked out, there was only one other person Alia needed to contact.

Sloan.

Chapter
Fifty-four

Her cell phone rang again just a few moments after she'd called Sloan the first time. "Honey," his calm voice eased her apprehension. "I'm with a SWAT team now. It's a long story; I won't get into it. We can be at the airport in the same time as it takes you to get there from the house."

"But, Sloan, would he head for the airport? That would be the first place we'd be looking for him."

"Not if he flew in a private jet. My take is he'd have to get Kean off the island right away because he'd know we could shut down all exits in a very short time. In fact, I've already issued the Amber Alert and it's being put in place as we speak."

"Thank God."

"I took those pictures of Kean at the barbecue on Sunday and I've given his likeness to the team, and they're being sent to every known exit point from the island, including marinas and helicopter companies. There's a cruise ship that docked earlier at the Honolulu pier located in the harbor. We've sent agents there too."

"Thank God! I'm a mess, I can't think straight. Sloan, I think that Libby came back and took him. She's working for Paul and, after being at the house earlier, she'd know her way in and out."

The silence from Sloan was nerve-wracking. "You think so? How about checking the video feed from after we left the house and see if you can make out the person. Unfortunately, I have the cameras pointing at the Amans' place, but on the center cam you might just be able to pick up anyone sneaking around in the yard."

"Good idea! I'll do that and get back to you."

"I'll go with the team to the airport and let you know what we find as soon as we arrive. And, baby. Don't be scared. Paul only wants him to force you to do his bidding. He won't hurt him."

"I know. It's the only thing keeping me breathing." She hung up the phone and ran to the front room, meeting Don as he returned after his search.

"Did you see the kitten?" She asked him just in case his theory about Kean searching for a runaway cat could be true.

"No. I called for both Kean and the cat. Woke

up Sam and Janna and they're out there searching too. Did you get in touch with Sloan?"

"Just hung up. He's headed for the airport, and he's initiated an Amber Alert so everyone is on the lookout for Kean."

"Why in the world would he do that? The kid's obviously taken off on his own, no doubt chasing his cat."

"You don't understand, Don. His father threatened to take him away from me and I'm sure he's kidnapped Kean."

"His father? Shit, why didn't you say something earlier? I'd have gotten the agency involved right from the get-go."

"Sloan's taken care of that now. I think a woman called Libby is in on the abduction. She works for my husband." Alia held out her phone to Don, showing the PI's website.

"How could she have been here earlier? This says she works out of Chicago."

"Les brought her over."

Don looked completely dumbfounded. "What? How does she know Les?" Confusion lit up his face and he shook his head as if to clear the cobwebs.

"Right. You don't know this part. It seems that she's been in Honolulu tailing me and got into a little fender-bender. So she took her car into Sloan's garage for repairs and when Roy fell, they used it to take him to the hospital. Then Les and Libby brought Kean back here."

"So you figure she's taken Kean." He scratched his head. "I'm thinking you might want to call Les. He has a way with women, and if I know him, he'll have gotten her phone number. In the meantime, I'll play back the video feed and see if we picked up anyone near the premises earlier."

"Thanks, Don. Sloan suggested checking that too." Alia swallowed hard, controlling the hysteria hovering on the edge of sanity and whipped her phone from his hand. "I'll call Les now. I'm so rattled, I never thought of it. Do you have his number?"

She frantically began hitting the numbers on the screen until she'd screwed up the second time, and he took the phone from her and hit the right ones himself. Then he pushed speaker phone and held it up.

Les answered on the second ring, his voice raspy from just being woken. "Yeah?"

"Les, do you happen to have Libby's phone number?"

"Hold on, I'll ask her."

Chapter
Fifty-five

"What was that all about?" Libby seemed shaken. Les figured she'd heard his end of the conversation.

He slid out of the bed they'd just shared and started pulling on his jeans. "Shit's happening. Kean's gone missing, and Alia's losing her cool. When I told her you were here, she started bawling and Don took the phone. Don, not Sloan. I don't know what the fuck is going on, but I'm heading over there right now to find out."

Libby rolled out from under the covers, her naked skin glowing in the light from the candles he'd lit to romance her. He stopped for a second and felt his body reengage. He couldn't get over how perfect she was. The old doll had kept her figure and she looked good for her fifty-something years.

Breaking out from her spell, he began hauling on his Booker's shirt and grabbed the brush to get his hair tied back. By the time he'd finished, she'd gotten into her clothes and was looking for her cell phone. "I think I know where he might be."

"Who?"

"Kean. The kid."

"How in hell would you know?"

"I used to work for his dad, the asshole."

Still not getting the connection, Les stopped and grabbed her arms. "Tell me."

Libby fiddled with her phone and it took a few seconds before she met his gaze. Her eyes were full of regret, and from the amount of tears that had gathered he knew it wouldn't be long before they spilled over onto her cheeks.

"He's a real number, that one. I'm talking about Paul Landon, Alia's husband. He hired me to find his son, told me this long bullshit story about how Kean's mother was a workaholic, a drug addict, and that he needed to save the kid from her, bring him back to Chicago where he had a judge willing to grant him full custody."

"Alia? Seriously? One look at the broad and anyone with a brain could see she loves her kid."

"I know that now, but I didn't when I took the job. I'd been overworking. Looking for runaway kids, finding evidence on cheating wives, mostly bitches who didn't deserve the lives their hardworking men were providing. When Landon came along, I'd just finished with a horrible case where a mother had been abusing her kid, locking him in the basement for punishment. I needed a break from all the sadness. So when Landon called, I jumped at the chance to come to Hawaii and keep tabs on his Kean."

Les had started to pull away. "*You* gave him Sloan's address."

"Yeah, after I tailed the taxi to the house, I gave him that address. It was listed in the details from the investigation but I hadn't known they'd moved in. You saw me then, didn't you?"

"Uh, huh."

"You knew who I was when I came into the garage earlier. I thought you recognized me."

"Yep."

"Les you've got to know this. I also reported that Kean was happy. That Alia was a great mom and to leave them the hell alone. He got so mad, the prick fired me. The bastard didn't deserve a kid like Kean."

"Okay. I believe you. But that still doesn't get the kid back. I've gotta go."

"Wait. I think I might know where he might be. If Paul actually took him that is. When he first hired me, we were shooting the shit and he said once I had located the boy, he would come and pick him up himself because the kid knew him and would listen to what he said. Then he mentioned a boat he often rented for deep-sea fishing when he was here on the island. He could have rented the boat today and taken Kean to one of the other islands where he could get the kid away without anyone knowing."

"Shit, woman, with his money, he could do anything. Do you know the name of the boat?" Les held his breath. *Could they be this lucky?*

Libby swiped at her eyes, sniffed and grinned. "Actually, I don't. But I know where the marina's located." She passed on the information.

"I know the place, been there myself with Roy and Sloan."

"Paul had bragged about a restaurant that served fresh fish close by, and I went there to try it. I'm thinking if we checked the place out, we could find if my hunch is right. If I remember correctly, when I strolled by, there was a guard at the gate. He might have seen something."

Les hugged her and then swung away to grab for his phone. "I'm calling Sloan. Either back your car out of the drive so I can get mine out, or we'll take my bike. Your choice."

Within minutes, Les could tell Libby loved riding passenger on his Harley. It made his heart kinda sing. Most women her age wouldn't have anything to do with motorcycles or the men who rode them. Her arms encircling his chest made his heart swell. And her laughter ringing in his ears had him grinning like a youngster on his first ride.

Pre-dawn in the city was normally gray and bleak, even on the magical island of Oahu, but this early in the new day they were fortunate with a full moon guiding them.

A Banyan tree – majestic with its foliage spreading wide, its aerial roots drooping to the ground like clusters of pale legs holding the weight – never failed to catch his attention when he traveled this street. Today, it seemed extra magnificent having the sky's golden sphere as a backdrop.

Streetlights began dimming as the sun broke the horizon and traffic appeared to double with each minute. The drivers at this hour weren't in a rush and consideration for the next guy was still in evidence.

They made it to the marina in time to see the last of the lights fade and the place looked deserted. No one policed the guard's small hut at this early morning hour.

"What should we do?" Libby's question caught him off guard.

"We'll wait until Sloan arrives. He has the authority to throw his weight around and make things happen."

"Look, I know a way we can sneak in and check things out in the meantime."

He couldn't stop the chuckle that broke free. This woman amazed him. "Okay, I'm game. What do you have in mind?"

"When I was here yesterday, I sat at the café,

outside, and watched some of the kids crawl in through that chain link fence back there. It's broken away from the post. If we sneak in now and find anyone around at this hour, maybe someone has seen something that might help us find Kean."

"Okay. Lead the way." Les sent a text to let Sloan know they were going into the marina, in case they weren't back in time to meet up with him out front.

Chapter Fifty-six

"You're going where?" Sloan couldn't believe that Les was involved in Kean's disappearance until he explained about Libby and him getting together. Once he'd told Sloan everything, Sloan jumped into action. "Thanks, Les. I'm on my way." He ended the call.

"Pat, can you head back to the city?" He'd commandeered Pat to be his driver when they'd planned to search the airport. After passing on his change of plans to the SWAT team leader, Henry, who already had uniforms searching the departure lounges at the airport and the airline manifests, he explained his new information.

"Good luck, Booker. I'll send back-up. Keep me informed."

Sloan took a minute to call Alia and let her know his change of plans. "There're men at the airport right now, baby. They have Kean's photo and will stop him being taken off the island. In the meantime, I have a new lead that he might be at the marina. Turns out, Paul bragged to Libby that he likes to go deep-sea fishing whenever he's here in Hawaii."

"It's true, Sloan. He had a picture of the boat in his office. Mind you that's a lot of years ago. It was called *Lia Mine*. I'll never forget it because Paul made a joke about the name when we met. I'm coming right now. I'll meet you there."

"Good. We'll probably arrive at the same time. I'll watch for you. And Alia? I... ahhh, you know I'll do whatever it takes to get Kean back. Trust me."

"I do. That's why I... I like you so damn much."

"I *like* you too, baby. See you soon."

Sloan sat on tenterhooks all the way to the marina, and by the time Pat peeled into the lot, he'd lost his cool multiple times and had to swallow back the acid gathering in his throat. Who knew fear had a taste? Guess he'd never been on a job before that mattered so fucking much.

Sensing his issues, Pat hadn't said a word but now he spoke. "What's the plan?"

"Alia will be arriving soon. But I'm not waiting. The guard's just starting his shift so I'm going to ask him about a boat called *Lia Mine*. It's the one that Alia remembers Paul used to hire."

"What do you want me to do?"

Sloan searched his phone's photo gallery for Kean's picture, got Pat's number and sent it to him. "Can you stay here and wait for backup. And, if anyone tries to leave with this kid, stop them."

"You got it."

Sloan ran over to speak to the arriving guard who was unlocking the gate. "I'm Agent Sloan Booker with the FBI. He flashed his badge. Did anyone come in the late hours of the night with a boy who looks like this?"

The guard, a Hawaiian that Sloan had seen around occasionally, shook his head. "We close the gates at midnight. After that, anyone who comes and goes has a key. Besides, I wasn't on duty last night. I work dayshift."

"Do you have a boat moored here called *Lia Mine*?"

"Used to. She's gone now."

"What do you mean gone?"

"That old girl hit the rocks a few years back. Sunk off the reefs near Maui."

Shit! "Did the owners replace her?"

"Oh sure. They called her replacement *My Lia II*."

"Can you tell me which slip she docks from?"

"Yep. But you won't find her there. She left on a trip about a week ago. Haven't seen her return."

Suddenly a text message dinged and Sloan

checked to see it was from Les.

Bingo!

Chapter Fifty-seven

Before Sloan could text back, Alia rushed up to where he was, her face full of the same fear that had ridden him since he'd heard that Kean was missing.

"Did you find the boat?"

"According to the guard, *Lia Mine* sunk a while back, and *My Lia II* replaced her but it left the marina a week ago."

"Oh no." Her eyes filled.

Swollen and blotchy from previous tears, they broke his heart. This woman had suffered enough because of her bastard ex-husband. He needed to get back her son, needed to do it badly.

His priorities had shifted since they'd met. He'd fallen for her, no two ways about it. Now she was his everything—her and the boy.

He wrapped one arm around her to pull her close and give her comfort. She stiffened, as if by habit, but he didn't let go and then she sagged gratefully, seeking his warmth. He held his phone in the other hand.

"Honey, Libby and Les are here looking for him, and I just got a text from Les that they found something." While he talked his thumb flew over the screen and he hit send.

They waited, hardly breathing. The ding let them know that Les had answered.

Sloan read aloud the message. "Slip #4, Boat #6."

He quickly asked the guard where that location would be and they followed his directions, arriving in time to see Libby and Les crouched behind another boat berthed around the corner.

Sloan squatted next to Les, with Alia bringing up the rear. He pointed to the craft they were watching. "What makes you think he's there? How did you find the boat?"

Libby answered. "Pure bloody luck. The kid's giving his dad a hell of a time. He was yelling his head off. We just happened past and heard the ruckus."

Alia started forward. "Is Paul hurting him?"

Les held her back and spoke quickly. "No. Nothing like that. The kid's madder'n a hornet for being taken away from you."

Sloan and Alia stood up and headed for the

boat that Les and Libby had indicated. No sooner were they in front, the engine started up and a man appeared to untie the lines.

Sloan pulled out his badge. "FBI. Just stop what you're doing. We need to talk."

Looking relieved, the fellow threw down the ropes and walked over to the controls on the deck. He turned off the motor. "What can I do for you, officer?"

"Agent Sloan Booker and this is my partner, Agent Hawkins. We'd like to come aboard and talk with you, sir."

"As you can see, I'm headed out on a day trip. Have a customer who's paying the shot and time's a-wastin'."

"It's that customer I'm interested in. Can I come aboard?"

"Sure. I haven't done anything wrong that I'm aware of."

Sloan climbed the ladder onto the boat and helped Alia aboard also. Les and Libby brought up the rear. "Have you seen this boy?"

The captain seemed uncomfortable as he studied the photo. Before he could answer, Kean yelled, "Sloan, I'm in here. Ow! Let me go, you creep."

Kean appeared on the stairs leading down into a cabin. He held the tabby kitten protectively. Close behind came Paul, his face full of fury, he cheek bearing scratches and his whole manner that of a man close to losing it completely.

Kean ran to his mother, to her open arms, and his telltale sob awakened every protective cell in Sloan's body. Before he could step forward, Paul had moved into Alia's space. "You. What kind of mother are you? The kid's a freaking brat." Paul pointed his finger and continued his rant. "He kicked me, bit me, wouldn't take orders and go to sleep. He's a—"

Suddenly, before anyone could stop her, the kitten flew out of Kean's arms and tore a strip of skin off Paul's face.

"Goddamnit!" Paul screamed and flung the cat away from him. It landed on its feet, back arched, its fangs still showing. Paul's finger again poked in front of Alia's face. "That blasted cat's as big a menace as the kid."

Sloan reached for the stupid prick, but Alia beat him to it. He'd never seen anyone get flipped over so fast and all because his finger had been where it didn't belong.

The shmuck ended up face down on the deck, her knee in his back, his cheek being ground into the netting where he'd landed. Alia, her beautiful face full of determination, her blue eyes spitting revenge, leaned over him and her words made him proud.

"You ever come near my son again, you prick, and I'll see you in hell. He's mine. And, once and for all, my eggs are mine."

The idiot sputtered, frothed, and his howl of

indignation broke loose. "If you think I want another brat like him, you can think again. Let me go and get out. I never want to see either one of you again."

Alia flung Paul's arm down and stepped purposely on his back as she walked over him. That made him yell yet again.

It made Libby laugh.

Les added, "You go, girl."

Kean cheered. "Yeah... Mo-om."

The commotion got worse when two more agents suddenly jumped onto the boat, one being Nigel Dullen. "FBI. Everyone stop what you're doing, drop your weapons and put your hands up." The idiot had his gun pulled, held out front in both hands, while the agent behind him shook his head disgustedly.

"Nigel, I think Al has the perp under control. Maybe we don't need to use force in this situation."

Nigel, seeing that everyone was staring at him with shock, disgust or amusement, lowered his weapon. "What the hell is going on here? We had a report that there was a kidnapping in progress."

Alia spoke calmly to her co-workers and within a few minutes had control back in her capable hands. They were pulling out handcuffs to make the arrest, take Paul into custody, but after seeing the horror on Kean's face, Alia waved them down.

"It's been a big misunderstanding, Nigel. No harm done. Kean's fine and we're just going to go home and take care of the other little bit of business we're working on."

When Nigel went to argue, she stepped close and whispered something that had him backing off and nodding.

Sloan, who'd pulled Kean protectively close, his arms shielding the boy during the scuffle, sneezed.

Chapter
Fifty-eight

Alia couldn't stop hugging Kean. She was so proud of him. Once they'd left the marina, Kean had gone over to speak to Libby and Les, who'd stood by waiting.

She'd watched him pass over the kitten, and saw Les grin and nod. Libby had crouched down and given Kean a hug that he'd returned. Then they'd waved their goodbyes and mounted a motorcycle, taking Kean's pet with them.

By the time Sloan had thanked the officer who'd been waiting in the background and they'd gotten in her car, she'd gladly handed over the keys for Sloan to drive. With Kean on her knee held close, the seatbelt wrapped around them both, the three of them made their way through the traffic.

Sloan looked over to them. "Thanks, son. You didn't have to hand over the kitten. I understand that she meant a lot to you."

Kean's head rested against his mother's chest, his eyes droopy. "Not as much as you mean, Sloan. Kitty can't help making you sneeze. I asked Les to look after her for Roy... for when he gets out of the hospital." He looked up at Alia. "Can we go and see Roy now?"

Alia glanced over to Sloan and saw him shake his head ever so slightly. "Not now, babe. We'll go later when Roy's awake. It's still really very early and I think we all need to go home and try and catch a few hours' sleep."

Kean snuggled closer to her, his little-boy's voice full of the compliance and trust that she knew best. "Okay."

Her curiosity lit up and she wanted to settle the issue now so they'd never have to refer to this night again. "I need to ask you one thing, Kean? How come you went with Paul last night?"

"He's my dad."

She couldn't hide her shock. "Yes. But you didn't know him. You were a little baby last time he was with us."

"No. He came to my school sometimes and we talked. He showed me a family picture. I was small, and he had his arms around you, and you were holding me. I thought he liked us."

"But when he took you last night, weren't you

kind of shocked?"

"I was sleepy, and he said you wanted me to go with him and he was bringing me to where you were. So I didn't stop him. He even let me bring Kitty."

Sloan hadn't said anything, but now he broke in. "What happened? When we got there, you were fighting with him."

"He slapped Kitty and yelled at me when I told him I wasn't going anywhere with him until Mom got there. He got so mad at me that I kicked him, and when he stuck his finger in my face I bit it."

Sloan grinned at Alia. "He's definitely your son."

At this point, Kean looked up into her face. "Am I in trouble for biting, Mom? I know it's bad, but he scared me."

Alia hugged him, raining kisses on his hair and cheeks, her usual reserve totally forgotten. "You have my permission to bite any bas... anyone who tries to take you away from me. And kick him too."

Kean giggled and nestled closer. His long eyelids drifted to his cheeks and his breathing evened out.

Sloan's hand reached out to smooth Kean's overly long hair away from his eyes. "I need to take him to my barber as soon as I find the time to go myself."

Alia smiled at him, a sob very close. His gentleness made the inevitable tears that still lingered return.

Sloan took her hand, his thumb smoothing her skin gently. "Right now, all I want to do is take you home, put you both in my bed and have all three of us get some much needed sleep. Then we'll take Kean for breakfast and go pick up Roy. Are you game?"

She squeezed his hand. "That sounds like heaven."

"Unfortunately I need to ask you a question first, and I know you won't like it."

She stiffened at his serious tone. "Try me."

"I need you to tell me your Cassie's address."

"You're kidding me. Right?"

"Not even a little." The look in his eyes said it all. He was as serious as a bullet in the chest.

"You know I can't tell you that information. I've explained that we keep the police away from the kids for a reason. If we didn't, the word would get out and no one would trust us again. We'd lose our creds, and all the work the women have put into helping those street kids will be for nothing."

"You also said, unless it was a dire situation. And at this point, I figure it's a matter of life or death."

Alia heard the seriousness in his tone. "Whose life?"

"Sara's. She can identify Roger and Joey. And they're suspects in a gang war shooting that took place earlier tonight where two people died. The witnesses said that the shooters fled the crime scene in a red Camaro. Remind you of anyone?"

"Friggin', shi...." She glanced down at the sleeping boy in her arms. "Well, hell!"

"You got that right. We need to get her into custody. And then we need to question her. See if she knows where we can find those two murdering perverts."

"Tell me." She knew he understood what she was asking and he gave her a watered down version of what he'd been through earlier. "I'll tell you more details later, but for now, you need to know how important it is that we get those two behind bars. After tonight, there's a huge gap on the streets where the Kroller gang had power. No way do we want those slimy badasses to take their place."

Alia pulled out her phone and dialed a number. "Cassie? Sorry to wake you up. It's Alia. Is Sara there with you?"

"Sure, kid. She was pretty shaken over what went down. I figured it was best to keep her close by."

"Can you do me a favor?"

"You got it."

"If I arrange to have a service car sent to your address, will you go with her to the FBI office and ask for Assistant Director Jack Harrison? He'll be waiting for you. He needs to speak with her."

"She in any trouble I need to know about?"

"Not her. It could be for her protection. She has some information that they need. There's a couple of murderers out there who'd love to get their dirty hands on her. We need to get her protection. Can you take care of it?"

"You bet, kiddo. I'll get her up now and we'll be ready."

Alia put her cell away and looked toward Sloan. "You want to call Jack, or do you want me to?"

His expression was so full of approval that a warm tenderness overwhelmed her. He pulled out his phone and with a few sentences, he gave the address to his boss that Alia supplied, brought him up to date on his suspicions regarding the red Camaro and breathed a sigh of relief that she found herself seconding.

By this time, they'd arrived at his driveway. The house looked welcoming in the early dawn. The rising sun brightened the red tiles on the roof and made the opening blossoms on the bushes appear as if they searched for warmth.

Don stepped out and came to Sloan's side of the car. He opened the door. "Thank God you found the boy. I appreciate you asking Nigel to let me know. The guy's a bit of an idiot but he means well."

Sloan looked at Alia. "Is that what you said to him?"

She nodded.

Sloan was slow getting out of the SUV. "No problem. I'm glad you were here to take over the stakeout."

"Yeah, well, about that. Sam wants to see you."

Chapter Fifty-nine

Sloan held up his hand to Don. "Can it wait? We're bushed." He opened the door on Alia's side and gently scooped Kean into his arms, the boy's head lolling onto his chest. When Kean looked up for a split second and saw who held him, he wrapped his arms around Sloan's neck, a sigh of contentment following as he drifted off once again.

Once in Sloan's bedroom, Alia turned down the covers on his king-sized bed and Sloan slid the boy under them, only removing his flip-flops. He turned to her. "Leave this to me. You need to be with Kean right now in case he wakes up."

She nodded, stepped in for a hug that he was more than happy to bestow, and kicking off her own sandals, she crawled in next to her boy. She gathered him into her arms and, with a happy sigh, her eyes closed.

Sloan stood, looking down at the two asleep in his bed. A mass of emotions churned in his body that could bring him to his knees. *Alia and Kean.*

How had he ever lived without them? Without the mess the boy left in his wake. Without the perfume she wore to sweeten his world. Without these two, he'd still be the empty shell of a man he used to be.

He swallowed the lump that had formed, blinked a few times and unclenched his hands. No one would ever take them from him again. A grin lit his face as he scrubbed at the beard forming. *Face it, Booker. You like them way too much, both of them.* Fighting off the powerful craving to slide in with them, he turned.

Stepping from the room, closing the door quietly, he went to the kitchen where Don had brewed the morning coffee. Grabbing a mug, he sat at the counter and saw the kitchen clock had struck seven.

Again, he scrubbed at the tiredness that hovered, waiting to descend, and wished with all his might that he could say good-bye to his old partner and head back into his bedroom to join his family. Instead he started the ball rolling.

"What's up?"

The beginnings of a beard colored Don's face darker than usual and his forehead wrinkled with worry lines.

"After Janna and Sam searched for the kitten, they stopped by to see if we'd found Kean, and if the animal had come back. It was once they got home that they realized that their relatives still hadn't returned. So they waited for them."

Sloan added, "It was pretty late by then, almost midnight."

"I know."

"Did the two return?"

"Yeah. A little while after that they showed up."

"Did you get anything from the cameras? Any pictures of the passengers in the car or the plates?"

"Only Leah and Yasir got out of the car, no one else. I managed to focus on the license plate, but when I zoomed in, they'd covered it with mud or something. It was completely blurry so I couldn't make out the numbers."

"Man, we just can't cut a break with this investigation, can we?"

"I'm thinking we might have one now. Sam was pretty disgusted when he came looking for you ten minutes ago."

"Was he surprised to see you were still here?"

"I bullshitted that you didn't know how long you'd be at the hospital with Roy, and in case you wanted me to babysit, I'd slept over."

"Good. That's good. Did he buy it?"

"Sure. Why wouldn't he? It's not the first time

I've bunked here."

"Right, when you were too drunk to walk home." Sloan teased. "How come he wanted to talk with me?"

"He wouldn't go into any details other than he's angry about his visitors. I'm thinking he remembers that you worked for the agency and he trusts you."

"Hell. He knows you're an agent too. Why didn't he share with you?"

"I figure it's because I still work for them, and he's trying to protect Janna. Whereas, he knows you're a private citizen now, one who understands the system. That's my take, anyway."

"Okay. Can you stay for the rest of the morning? I'll call him over, but then I need to get a couple of hours sleep and go pick up Roy. He'll be wondering why I wasn't there all night. I'd planned on it and he knew that."

"Sure. No problem. I'll just borrow some cereal and get out of your way."

"Borrow some? Don't you intend to eat it?"

Don looked at Sloan and grinned. "You're an ass, you know that?"

He went to the cupboard, grabbed a bowl, hauled down the box of Cheerios he knew from previous visits that Sloan always kept and made himself breakfast. He motioned to Sloan if he wanted some also.

Shaking his head, Sloan pulled out his cell

phone and scrolled for Sam's number, knowing his buddy was an early riser who'd already paid a visit.

"Hi, Sam. Don said you wanted to talk to me. Sure, come over now. The coffee's on."

***

"They're not Janna's relatives, Sloan. Those two are strangers. And they're dangerous. I want them out of my house." Sam had arrived full to bursting with frustrated anger, needing an outlet.

Sloan couldn't blame him. "Calm down, Sam. Tell me how you know this."

"Last night, after we went to search for Kean, and Don said you had a lead on his whereabouts, we came back into the house and fixed coffee. It was then we realized the light was on in the guest room. Janna worried we'd made noise and so she knocked on the door to invite Leah and Yasir for a snack. Both looked upset, as if they'd been fighting. They came and joined us, but weren't very communicative when we tried to ask them about their evening."

"I remember. They'd been going out with friends."

"Yes. Janna tried to ask about her brother and his wife but they became rather unfriendly and soon excused themselves."

"And this was a problem?"

"Even though we haven't spent a lot of time with her family, Janna recalls that her brother always referred to his wife by a special endearment,

Baalam, which means beloved in our language. When she asked Leah what Baalam did to keep herself busy, Leah appeared mystified. And so did Yasir. Neither of them were aware that it was the nickname their father used for their mother."

"So you don't believe they are who they say."

"Exactly. This morning, we tried to contact my brother-in-law but his phone seems to be disconnected. After Janna's e-mail bounced back, she asked Faisal to send one of those Facebook messages, but their page has been discontinued too."

"Okay. I see why you're worried now. But truthfully, Sam, I noticed your lack of welcome and Janna's dismay way back when you first mentioned they were coming to see you."

Sam looked uncomfortable. He clasped his hands together between his knees and thought deeply for some time before he looked up. His deep brown eyes were clear with conviction and truth. "I want to explain. Life at home was very frightening for us before we were able to escape. Any reminders of those days make us nervous. If Janna's brother and his wife had been coming with their children, we would have been overjoyed and welcoming."

"I don't understand."

"For them to come alone seemed wrong, especially when it wasn't their parents who reached out to us, as is our custom. We are worried that something has happened to them and to their real children."

"Is there no one you can ask who knew both your families?"

"Not anyone we trust."

"I'm sorry about all this, Sam. I understand your fears. What can I do to help?"

"I do not want to bring in the FBI, not yet. But neither do I want to sit by and see anything happen because I wore blinders. Those two need to be watched. You used to be an agent. Can you help us?"

"Yes. But you need to know the truth. I'm still an agent."

"Of course, my friend, I understand. A man can never stop being what he was trained to be."

Not sure how to continue, Sloan decided to leave it alone. He'd told the truth, and even if Sam didn't want to listen, he felt somewhat vindicated. "I'm thinking we can put a tap in their room. Tape their conversations. Find out what they're up to once and for all. If they're planning anything harmful to the city or its citizens, we'll have evidence and can move in to prevent it from happening. Are you willing to plant this equipment where they won't see it?"

"Absolutely. With the bombings going on lately by crazy Jihadists, I'm more than prepared to set them up. We can't take any chances. All I ask is that if we find there's anything dangerous, I can remove my family to where they'll be safe."

"Alia has had a terrible scare just recently with Kean's disappearance. His father kidnapped him and, no doubt by the grace of an *Aumakua*, a Hawaiian family god, we were able to stop him in time from taking the boy off the island. So I'm sure she could use some company later today if Janna feels up to visiting and bringing the children."

Sam's face cleared. A smile began in earnest. "Then she will be happy to do so. Give me these gadgets and show me what I must do."

Sloan went and fetched both of the small devices he'd had Don bring to the house and passed them over to Sam. Within a few seconds, he'd explained how to set them up and where they should be placed.

"This is good. I will put one in the bathroom and the other in the bedroom. And I will send you a text when it is done." Sam stood to leave.

Sloan shook the hand that Sam held out. "Wait until it's clear. Don't take any chances. Those two might be young but we don't know if they're dangerous."

"I'll be careful. Thank you, my friend. I feel a huge weight has been shared."

Chapter Sixty

Sloan's eyes felt like two balls of burning mush in their sockets. All he wanted to do was lie down and close out the world. But first he placed a call to the hospital. "Hey, Ryan. Thank goodness you're still on duty. I need a favor."

"Whatever you want, dude, unless it's against the law like the last time you asked."

"You found out I'm not with the FBI any longer."

"Roy mentioned something." The peevishness in Ryan's voice said it all.

"He forgot to mention I'm on special assignment. Look, he expected me to be there all night. As you know, I had to leave."

"Yeah. He asked where you were."

Worry slammed into Sloan and made the muscles in his stomach grip tight to fight off the rising bile. "What did you tell him?"

"Are you kidding me? I'm not completely stupid, man. The dude's already unsteady, so you figure I'm gonna add to his problems by telling him you went after a bunch of murdering scum? I told him that Kean wouldn't settle unless you were there and so you had to go home."

"Good. Great. He believed you?"

"Not one lyin' word."

"Dammit. I knew he'd be a handful."

"Not really. Once we knew for sure his concussion hadn't done any lasting damage, I gave him a sleeping pill. Man's in lullaby-land and will probably stay that way for a couple hours. By the way, Les and his lady just got here and they're hanging out."

"Tell them we'll be there soon. I owe you. Big time."

"Right. In case you weren't aware, my family and I really enjoy barbecues like the one Roy was talking about earlier."

"Consider yourself invited. See you later."

***

When they arrived at the hospital a few hours later, Sloan watched Kean rush past everyone to hug Roy, his face lit with the excitement of seeing his old friend looking a heck of a lot better than he'd seemed the day before.

"Les took the kitty back to the garage, Roy. She has to stay there with you 'cause Sloan sneezes when she comes near him."

Les joined them and pretended to whisper. "He's a real wienie about getting the needles to stop the allergies."

Sloan turned his head and glared but saw three pretend angels grinning back at him. How could a man hold a grudge when all three pairs of eyes were filled with glee mixed with affection?

"You guys messing with me over there? I can tell by your expressions you're up to something."

"Nah! Just having a guy's conversation. Nuthin' ya need to worry your little head about." Les at his best was a pain in the ass but when he was in a playful mood, like this morning, he ragged on a person something terrible.

Roy's grin was worth being the butt of jokes. He looked positively radiant, if a grizzled-looking old Santa Claus could appear so glowing.

Sloan shot them his best pretend glare. Then he offered to go for coffees. "Ryan said that they're waiting for the last x-rays to be delivered and if everything looked okay, you'd be free to go Roy. In the meantime, anyone want a treat from the cafeteria?"

Plus, he needed to check in with Don and see if they had picked up anything yet on the audio listening devices Sam was going to hide in the guest room.

"I'll come with you." Alia had appeared shy this morning, back to her reticent self, but he wasn't letting her get away with it. He reached for her hand and hesitantly, she gave in.

"Good." They gathered everyone's orders; Kean's plea for a milkshake got an eyebrow lift from his mom and a wink from himself, and they headed down the hallway.

"I couldn't tell you earlier with the boy there, but Sam came to see me this morning." He filled her in on their discussion and ended with his suggestion about Janna and the children coming to stay with her at the house. "That's a good idea. Of course I kept Kean home from school again, so he'll be glad to have the kids around later. He'll be bored by then. I was hoping we could have Roy come home with us for at least a day or two, if you don't mind. He can sleep in one of the twin beds in Kean's room and I'll sleep on the couch."

"Good idea about Roy but there's a much more comfortable bed for you to sleep in, sweetheart. It's king-sized and the mattress is firm."

She pushed against his shoulder with her own. Her sassy grin warned him she'd have a comeback. "Then where will you sleep? Don't forget, Kean thinks you're his uncle and so does everyone else. Didn't you notice the looks we got when you held out your hand to me in the room earlier?"

"Shit! You're right." He came to a sudden stop and she stood next to him. "I forgot all about the undercover roles we were playing. So much has happened." He tucked his long hair behind his ears and continued to run his fingers through to link at the back of his neck. Then he looked down at her teasing playfulness. "So what are you going to tell them?"

"Not me, my friend. They're your family. Until we get this case solved though, we'll have to keep up the pretense. So no more of this affectionate stuff."

A little hurt at her words, he couldn't help his comeback. "You don't like it?"

She pushed him again, a little harder this time. "I love it, you big baby. Now call Sam and let's see if they've collected any data yet. I suppose the idea was for Sam to come over and listen to the tapes and translate?"

Sloan nodded, happy again after her teasing comeback. "What he doesn't know is that you'll be translating them also. We'll see for once and for all if he is to be trusted." Just thinking that his friend could be a liar, Sloan felt his stomach react and a headache form.

"Don't worry, Sloan. He's a good man. I'd bet money on it."

"But would you bet the safety of your family? Because that's what I've done and I'm beginning to wonder if it was the right thing to do."

She stared at him and he saw the reaction his words had evoked.

By the time they returned to the room with everyone's orders, root beer replacing the actual request Les had given, Ryan came to inform them that Roy was good to go. He transferred Roy's clothes to the bathroom so the old man could get dressed in private, and then left them with a last reminder about his love of hamburgers cooked on the grill.

Sloan went over to where Les and Kean still hovered around Roy's bed, and noticed that Libby took the moment to sidle over to Alia.

***

"I want to tell you how sorry I am about Paul taking Kean last night. He's an asshole. I'm sorry I ever took his money or that my firm did any work for the prick."

Alia read the truth in Libby's expression, her gray eyes wide and this time hiding nothing. She spoke low, so only they could hear. "You helped us find Kean. Without your information, he'd most likely be in Chicago with Paul by now and I'd be the one up against the courts trying to win him back. I'll never be able to thank you enough for your help."

Libby looked uncomfortable but earnest. "Just so we're straight. I would have taken him away from you myself at the beginning. Paul had described you in a very unflattering light and I have a soft spot for kids in trouble. If I hadn't done my homework and seen what you did for that street kid, things could have turned out a lot different."

Alia stiffened, thought over Libby's words and made a decision. "Those street kids need us. I only do what I know best. Protect them. But there's a hell of a lot more that's needed after I get them to safety. And they're looking for people willing to help."

"What are you saying? That I could pitch in. Honey-girl, I'd love to but I have a business to run back home, a life, even if it's a shitty one."

"You can bring the business here, to Hawaii. There's always room for a good PI firm. And... truthfully, I doubt if Les is going to let you go. He seems to me like a man who keeps what belongs to him."

Libby reacted. She stiffened. "I don't belong to anyone. I'm my own girl, always have been and always will be." Her voice had roughened but there was a false bravado as well.

"And how's that worked for you so far?" Alia couldn't help her response. It seemed appropriate and she knew the truth when Libby deflated and shrugged.

"Okay. You might have something. I'll see what the big guy thinks. If he wants me to stick around, I could do it for a while I guess, see how the wind blows."

"As a good friend said to me while I was still making up my mind whether to take the job or not – *Aloha!* Welcome to Hawaii."

Chapter
Sixty-one

All the way back to their house, in the rear seat, Roy and Kean talked in low voices, youthful giggles and lower tone chuckles emanating, while Alia thought over the conversation she'd had with Libby. There was something about the woman that intrigued her. No doubt, she'd had a checkered past, but Alia felt deeply that she was also suffering.

In today's harsh world, most everyone had something they regretted or wanted to forget, and Libby appeared to be a woman who fit into that mold. She only hoped when the time came, she'd make the right decision and give Les a chance.

From the way her face had lit up when he'd come to suggest they take a ride to a beach he knew and maybe hit the waves before he had to open the garage, Alia had decided that whether Libby was aware of his power over her or not, she had no doubts. Les would be a very strong motivation for the woman when making future choices.

Good. Once I go back to my real life, I'll need a lot of friends to help me get over Sloan.

Thinking of the devil, he turned to break the silence. Ever since she'd warned him about their behavior, he'd been standoffish, almost comical in trying to behave. Except it wasn't funny to her. She missed his special smiles and easy hugs.

"I'll set up the barbecue out back and settle Roy and Kean in the yard. We can take turns in the sunroom watching the house. Don needs to be relieved."

Guilt flooded and she quickly agreed. "I forgot about Don. He's covered for us a long time. He must be exhausted."

"Actually, don't feel sorry for him. I'm sure he got more sleep than either of us did. But it's time we let him have a break. I'll make some lunch and you can watch Sam's house. Then I'll relieve you."

She couldn't argue with him, it made total sense. "I guess that's how it's got to be for the next while. Each of us taking turns and sleeping when we can. But you need to take the first break, not me. I actually got a few hours last night. You only had a short nap."

"We'll see. Thank goodness Don will be here

tomorrow. I have to get back to the garage."

"How's the fellow working out that Jack found for you?"

"Truthfully, he's a genius and being young he's full of energy. And... he gets along with both the old brats, keeps them from killing each other when I'm not there. I don't know how he's managed, but the records are all up to date and the paperwork is correct from what I can see. He's good with the customers and he's a great mechanic. I've decided to keep him on after I return."

"I'm so glad. You work too many hours, Sloan. You need to slow down."

"I know. I've just felt so damn guilty after my dad died because I wasn't here. I knew he'd kept the place running, and without him things wouldn't go smooth. Roy and Les need to work; neither of them is ready for retirement yet. So there didn't seem to be a choice. Either I pitched in, or *Booker's* would close."

"But that's not your nirvana. You miss working for the agency."

"Yeah, well, shit happens to everyone."

***

Alia left Kean with Roy and Sloan, and made her way to the sunroom to deliver Don a hamburger before he left. "Sloan says you like it with just mustard and onions." She passed the aromatic plate over and watched his eyes widen before he took his first bite.

"I don't know what's better – the smell or the taste." She forgave him for talking with his mouth full and went to study the screens they had erected behind the room divider.

"It's been quiet since they came home last night. Have you heard any discussion yet?"

"Not a lot. Here's one conversation." Alia listened with earphones and shook her head. "It's nothing, just talk about whose turn it was to be nice to Janna and Sam. Neither wants to go and visit with their hosts but they're arguing that it needs to be done."

"Pathetic."

"No kidding. They're referring to Sam and Janna as Auntie and Uncle, as they should. Yasir wants to read something they got from their meeting last night. Leah agrees to go out into the kitchen, but says she needs to read the information also."

Alia removed the apparatus from her head. "There's nothing here."

"I'd like to get a hold of whatever he's reading that's so important."

"Me too. Maybe Sam can be convinced to check it once they leave again."

"They're going out?"

"Yes. Tonight. Same time. He's told her to be ready; they're to be picked up."

"Good. I think I'll borrow the neighbor's Doberman, do a little dog-walking and show up about that time."

She grinned. "Get closer to the vehicle so you can make out the numbers, you mean."

"That too." He brushed the crumbs from his hands, winked at her and walked to the outside door. "See you later."

"Maybe not. I might be in my own car, waiting to tail them."

"Good. You can pick me up."

"Or you can stay here while Sloan and I do our jobs."

"Or that." He waved and left.

***

Alia had a hard time keeping her eyes open. Watching a house where nothing was happening called for a person who was wide awake and not one ready to pass out. Her head kept nodding and she lifted her millionth cup of coffee to her lips only to find it had turned cold.

Her stomach churned, making her nauseous. Not partial to the constant stress over the last few days, it had decided to repay her now with intermittent cramps. She stood and did another set of bends and stretches, hoping against hope that the exercise would keep her from falling asleep.

The door opened and she turned to give Sloan a piece of her mind. She'd fought with him over whose watch it had been and he'd given in, but not gracefully. The man wanted to protect her; she got it, but she was an FBI agent who had a job to do, and by golly, she'd be doing it.

She'd gotten twice as much sleep as he had. Fair's fair. He'd finally agreed to go into his room and she'd wake him in a few hours. In the meantime, he'd left Kean with Roy, fed and happy to be together.

"Sloan, give it up. I'm good here."

"It's not Sloan. Can I come in?" Roy stood waiting for permission. Alia glanced around the room and gave the sliding screen a yank, hoping it covered the equipment behind sufficiently. She pushed the binoculars under her chair and slid the camera behind it.

"Sure, Roy. Of course. I was just dozing anyway."

"Kean decided to have a nap. I coaxed him after he'd fallen asleep for the tenth time during our chess game."

Alia pointed to the wicker chair across from hers. "I'm so glad you like chess. Kean picked up the game at his last school and when we moved here, he had no one to play with. He loves it."

"He's almost as good as I was at his age. Maybe better. I have to go to the senior's home around the corner to be able to play anymore. Les never did enjoy games, he's an outdoor freak, loves the water and his Harley. And Sloan, he never wanted to learn, too busy with his drawings and sports."

"Roy, where does your family originate from?"

"I was born in San Francisco, and came to

Hawaii as a young man with Lester and Tommy Booker. I'd left a girl back home, one I wanted to make my wife, but when she chose to have an acting career rather than marry an old farm boy like me, I took my broken heart to the docks, signed up to crew on a ship and met up with those other two." He pulled his wallet from his pocket and showed her a black and white photo of a pretty girl, dressed in a costume and her signature scrawled illegibly across the bottom.

Suddenly, Alia's interest heightened. Before she could ask Roy if the girl's name was the one she suspected it was, she saw the door across the street open and Yasir and Leah appear.

Reaching across to touch him, she stopped halfway and let her hand drop. "I *really* want to talk to you more about your travels, Roy, but something has come up. I just need to go out for a short time. Can you tell Sloan, I'm leaving for a while when he wakes up?"

Not totally understanding her, but being a gentleman who didn't argue with women, Roy quickly stood as she rushed out. "Sure, Alia. I'll tell him."

She only had time to grab her sandals and her cellphone and rush through the French doors. Making sure they wouldn't see her, she stayed on her side of the street and held her phone in her hand in case they turned around. She planned to pretend she was taking pictures, hoping her phone would hide her face.

The pair walked slowly, meandering as if they had all the time in the world. Until suddenly, a car pulled up next to them.

Friggin', shittin' hell! If they got in, she'd be screwed. By the time she could run to get her vehicle, they'd be gone.

Wait. They weren't getting in. Something strange was going on. She ducked behind the nearby bushes and started taking a video. Two younger men got out of the car and met up with the couple on the sidewalk.

They carried on a conversation, one she wished she could hear. Quickly, she skimmed though the gardens in front of her and drew closer. She couldn't chance going any further without drawing their attention and so she stopped.

Aiming her phone, she took shot after shot of all four gathered together.

Leah appeared upset, while the three men overrode her protests. Then she nodded and they retrieved a small package from the back seat of the car and handed it to Yasir. One last hand clasp and they withdrew into their vehicle and drove off. Alia took a picture of the license plate, and this time the numbers showed up clearly.

Leah still appeared upset, and Alia waited while Yasir listened to his sister's tirade. The other girl was speaking in Urdu, their official language, her hands gesturing her obvious disagreement. Alia recognized the sounds but she wasn't close enough to hear the words.

Finally finished arguing, Leah whirled toward their aunt's house and Alia only had a few seconds to duck and hide. Waiting for them to pass by her, she made up her mind.

"Leah! Yasir... hello!" She ran toward them, waving wildly. "Are you taking in the sights of the neighborhood too? It's nice around here in this residential area, isn't it?"

Yasir appeared happier to see her than Leah. He answered cordially, "Yes. We're very lucky to come to Hawaii. It's a beautiful place."

"Have you been to Waikiki and seen the beaches there? I'd be happy to take you."

"We will be going with friends tonight."

Leah hissed a warning only Yasir was supposed to hear, but Alia was trained to pick up on such things. "Your friends, they live on the island?"

Looking slightly subdued, Yasir nodded. "Yes. They live here."

"I'm glad you have people you know in Hawaii. It makes a vacation more fun when you can spend time with those you care about. Were they originally from Pakistan?"

Uncomfortable now, Yasir looked to Leah as if he wasn't sure of the meaning of Alia's words, which was crazy since he spoke perfect English. Leah chimed in. "They're acquaintances who I met online. Yasir was only introduced to them last night. We must return to my aunt's house now.

They're expecting us for tea."

Walking along with them, Alia wished she could see what was inside the parcel that Yasir had shoved into the waistline of his shorts and then covered up with his new Hawaiian shirt.

Purposely, she tripped on the jutting sidewalk and flung her hands toward him to break her fall. In doing so, she managed to pull at the brown envelope from where he'd tucked it and it fell to the ground. Righting herself, she scooped it up as soon as it landed.

"Oh, I'm sorry, Yasir. Thank you for saving me from a nasty fall."

He stuck out his hand, knowing she held his parcel. Quickly, she passed it from one hand to the other and handed it over. "I think I made you drop this. I'm just glad you were there to break my fall. Thank you again."

She turned to go towards Sloan's, and saw him at the open door, watching her make her way over. His expression was welcoming. Smiles lit up his face and he waved to the pair, who glanced over and then returned the gesture before disappearing.

Alia stepped through the French doors and was instantly devoured by arms that wrapped around her and lifted her off her feet.

"Roy came and told me you went out. I was worried. I knew you wouldn't leave unless something had happened."

She returned his hugs and kisses, happy to be

where she never wanted to leave. When she could finally speak, she gently stepped back, and her outstretched hands stopped him from following. "I'm sorry. I didn't mean for him to tell you right then. I just wanted him to let you know where I was *after* you woke up."

The passion in her voice was noticeable. The man could turn her on in seconds. Her lips wanted more of his special brand of kisses and her swollen breasts ached. Budding desire buckled her knees and a throbbing sensation clawed low down, engaging her body, releasing fluids, preparing her for the inevitable. She cleared her throat and gathered her wits so she could stop daydreaming and pay attention to his words.

"He didn't wake me. Jack did. He wanted to report that they caught Joey and Roger, thanks to Sara's information. It led them directly to the apartment where the two were holed up. They came out without a fight."

Alia felt some of her stress ease. "I'm so glad. She needs to understand that cops aren't all bad. Will she be a witness?"

"She told them she'll take the stand if you're with her. And, she'll only talk to the District Attorney if you're there too."

"I guess that can be arranged. They'll need to take my statement also, as well as yours. When did they set up the appointment?"

"Jack says he'll give us some time to get this

mess here organized and he'll send in backup if we need it."

"As long as we can have Don covering for us, we should be able to work it out between us. Right?"

"Exactly what I told him. By the way, Roy had his say after the end of the call. I suspect he overheard some of our conversation about the garage in the car while we drove here earlier. The man has ears like a rabbit when he wants to listen in."

Alia grinned. "I gotta tell you, I love that old man."

"Me too." Sloan's smile, full of tenderness, ignited her desire again. "Roy said seeing as how the doctor had told him he was getting on and he needed to cut back on working so many hours, perhaps he should retire. But Roy said he wasn't quite ready for that. However, he did admit to thinking a shorter day would suit his lifestyle as a nanny."

"As a what?"

"Seems he's taken a strong attachment to my nephew and intends to apply for a position as your babysitter, since Ruby's not here anymore. He believes you'll be staying with me for the foreseeable future, no reason why not – his words – and he figures he'll hang out with Kean while we're at work.

"Did you tell him I'm an agent?"

"Nope. But I think Kean's been sharing some of your secrets."

"Ahhh. That makes sense. Truthfully, I can't think of anyone I'd rather have look after Kean, especially after my last Skype with Ruby. Her father is left with a long-term disability and she says there's no possibility of her being able to leave him. She's also started working in her community, setting up help for the street kids there. I think she's home now."

He searched her eyes and she opened to him. "It's okay. I told her she must stay where she's happy. But that does leave me without someone to be with Kean after school hours."

"Guess you can stop worrying." He brushed the tendrils of hair away from her cheeks. "Did I just see you fall? It looked like you did."

"Right! I almost forgot. I need to talk." She led him to the chairs where they could watch out the window and she took the seat across from him, not trusting herself to be any closer.

She explained the conversation she'd over-heard, and about Yasir and Leah's plans for this evening. Then she showed him the footage she'd taken with her phone. Together they downloaded the video and then sent it to the office so it could be passed through the computers there for facial recognition. They needed to know if any of the people in the pictures were known to the FBI.

Once they'd decided to take her vehicle to fol-low the others later, he led her to the door. "I got a couple of hours, now it's your turn. Go lie down, baby. You must be tired if a sidewalk can trip you."

She laughed. "I didn't trip. Well, not by accident. I wanted to get hold of the parcel I told you
about, that those two people earlier gave to Yasir."

"You devious little devil!" He laughed loudly,
his eyes sparkling with humor. "What did you find
out?"

She kissed his cheek and opened the door, then
stopped before leaving the room. "As far as I could
make out, it felt like a couple of passports. I find
that rather interesting, don't you? Wake me when
Janna comes to call."

Chapter
Sixty-two

Sloan had to stop himself from following the sexy diva, scooping her into his arms and locking them in his bedroom away from the world. But it wasn't possible. In the future, the way he envisioned it, he had plans where Kean would have a lot of overnighters with his faux grandpas, while he and his little missus could have the house to themselves. And do whatever they pleased, whenever they wanted to.

His body reacted to his imagination and he had to drag his mind away from the wonderful notions. He called the bureau and got the lowdown on the images they'd recently fired over, only to be disappointed that nothing had come up.

Neither did Homeland Security have anything

in their data bases.

Shit! It looked like they'd be playing the game without having any real knowledge about wrong-doing by the people who were involved.

One thing the agent he'd contacted was able to tell him: they'd tracked Janna's brother's family from Pakistan, and it seems that they were settled safely in California under new names.

Her brother had asked for asylum with the US Government in exchange for some badly-needed information about ISIS informants, and now that the dust had settled on the issue, he and his wife were safe and well. And so were his two children. Until it was deemed otherwise, they would be staying in seclusion.

So now they had tangible proof that Yasir and Leah were not who they pretended to be. That alone was a crime: entering the country illegally under an alias.

But the bosses wanted more than just these two. They wanted to know what plans were in place, and who else was involved.

Just then Sam knocked at the French doors and, taking a chance that any damning equipment was out of sight, he let him into the room.

"Hi, Sam. Come in. Has anything happened?"

"No. It's quiet. Leah and Yasir went for a walk and so I was able to install the listening device in the bedroom also. The earlier one, I could just put in the bathroom because it also has a door leading into the hall and we all use it."

"Good. We did hear a bit of their conversation. Do you want to listen and tell me what they're saying?"

"Yes. That's why I came over. And to let you know that they have made plans to go out again tonight with the same people they were with yesterday. When Janna tried to make them explain to us where they were going, they made excuses to leave the room. I think they're starting to feel uncomfortable in our home. I wish they'd just leave."

Sam listened to the brief tape and confirmed what Alia had already translated.

Sloan hesitated to say anything and then took a leap of faith. "I have some information on Janna's family: her brother, his wife and the real Yasir and Leah. They're well, and they've sought asylum in the United States. Until their special circumstances are changed and the restrictions lifted I can't tell you anything more, but I thought you should know. It's probably best not to mention this to Janna until your two intruders have left."

"You are right. I'm very, very relieved, and I will keep this to myself until you tell me it's safe to share. Thank you, Sloan. You've been a good friend. I will never forget."

"Alia and Kean have just settled, trying to catch up on the sleep they missed last night. Can Janna's visit happen a little later in the afternoon?"

"Of course. She is looking forward to it."

Sloan let the man out and caught up on the video surveillance from the night before. There was a very short scene, where the camera had picked up a male intruder coming through the gardens, most likely Paul. The rest was empty except for the birds, the wind blowing the palm fronds and the moon's shadows playing over the scene of tranquility.

He set up the binoculars, checked to make sure all was quiet across the street and went to find another cup of coffee. It was going to be one hell of a long shift.

Chapter
Sixty-three

Alia sat next to Sloan in her vehicle at the appointed hour that evening, waiting for Yasir and Leah to be picked up. They'd both spent a restful afternoon for a change. She with Janna and the children, while Roy and Sloan had checked out things at *Booker's*.

The more time she spent with the Muslim woman, the more Alia liked and trusted her. Janna's soft brown eyes held only respect and caring. She had a lovely spirit, and like most other mothers throughout the wold, all she wanted was the best for her family.

Don had taken up residence in the front room again, and all was quiet.

Alia knew Sloan had a lot on his mind. She

decided to ask rather than sit and stew. "Was everything running smoothly at the shop?"

He reached for her hand and squeezed gently. "Surprisingly, yes. I had a talk with our new guy and he's really keen. Loves working there, even has a few friends he went to school with who're interested in helping out on the more detailed, pricey contracts. I've refused a lot of those intricate renos because we were already pushed to the limits. Maybe now we can think about taking on those fun jobs."

"Would it be possible for you to quit working there and go back to doing what you love?"

"Truthfully, I kinda wondered about that. If Roy seriously cuts his hours, it would mean that Les and Roy wouldn't be running the place alone. I'm thinking I could cut back, do a bit of the detailing work I really enjoy as a hobby rather than a full-time job. Les seems happy with his life. He's talked Libby into sticking around for some time. Roy can hang out at the house with us to look after the kid and—"

Alia stiffened. "You're forgetting something, Booker. When this job is over, Kean and I'll be going home."

He swung her way, his voice hardening. "Over my dead body, *Hawkins*... Shit! They're on the move." He pointed at her and she noticed that his hand wasn't steady. "Lady, we'll talk about this later."

Grinning happily, Alia chirped. "Okay. Later." Relief flooded and she couldn't stop smiling. He was making all kinds of plans and she was a part of them. She loved it.

The car in front took a corner to the left and sped toward the on ramp to the Kamehameha highway. This road travelled for miles around the island and Sloan settled in behind a gray Corolla, one car removed from the vehicle they were following. Suddenly, the perp's car passed two more and the double yellow line in the center stopped Sloan from keeping up.

Alia sat forward. "They're driving erratically. Do you figure they made us?"

"How could they? Just keep your eye on them in case they decide to turn off." He finally got the opportunity to cut ahead of the van in front but had to pull in before they were in the place where he would have liked to be.

"Sloan, there, he's turning off – by that roadside restaurant. They're stopping. Can you pull over by those bushes ahead? I'll go and see if they're actually getting out of the car and going inside."

Sloan drove off the road and stopped. Alia slid out, darted to the edge and crouched down behind the covering leaves. She watched as all four exited the car and entered the ramshackle building.

There were a number of vehicles gathered in the parking area and that surprised her. At one time, it might have been a good place to eat, but now, it looked run down and uncared for, a place where either those less fortunate, or less caring, might hang out.

Running closer, peering through a dirty window, she watched them weave their way toward the back of the restaurant and walk past a lopsided curtain at the back.

Something pressing into her side warned her she wasn't alone. "Well, miss. You are being a nosey-rosy, and for this, I think we must have a little talk. This way, if you please." The Muslim sounded polite but the gun he held belied his tone.

"I *don't* please."

"For that I am sorry. But you must do as I say."

Alia tried out her best don't-be-mean-to-me smile on the guy. "I was just looking for a menu."

"I doubt that very much. People who want a menu step into the restaurant. They don't sneak from behind bushes and peer into windows. I believe you must come with me." He pointed toward the back of the place and she knew the minute Leah and Yasir saw her, they'd know the gig was up.

She worked to create tears, gulping and blinking as hard as she could until rivulets gushed from her eyes to flow down her cheeks. "No, please don't hurt me. I'm sorry for being nosey. It's a problem I have. I promise not to come back here if you let me go." Her hands taking a prayer-like position helped with her act. And when she pushed forward for the final scene, she caught him completely off-guard.

Before the man knew it, she'd grabbed his gun and her uppercut left him writhing on the ground. A quick blow to the side of his head with the gun barrel cleared away the problem. Now to just hide him before anyone came. She heard a soft chuckle.

"Do you need any help, ma'am?" Sloan stood a few feet away, a smart-ass grin lighting up his face.

She swiped at her wet cheeks and sniffed. "You could have shown up a bit earlier before I had to pull out act two."

"And miss the best performance I've ever seen? No way. Here, let me pull him to the ravine there. We'll hide him behind the rocks and he'll be out of sight. So what happened?"

"They met up with another man and went through into the back of the café. This one caught me watching through the window and took offense. Some people are so picky about their privacy."

"Go figure." He chuckled and, crouching low, he led the way around to the back of the yard. Watching carefully for any other guards, they breathed easily when no one came forward. A window was open, the curtains only pulled halfway and Alia could hear every word spoken.

It sounded as if there was a meeting of many more than the four she knew about. There were a lot of voices all spouting Jihadi crap and plans to teach the infidels not to mess with Allah's chosen.

Suddenly an argument sprung up as to the best place to set their bombs. *Shit!* These wackos were serious... if they had fire power. Then she heard Yasir speak. "What bombs? You have nothing but dreams and talk. I don't want anything to do with a group of complainers who speak of war and do nothing."

Her anxiety lessened tenfold and she continued to pay attention. Sloan had his phone out and was recording everything, but only after he'd sent a text with the address and a request for backup.

When they heard the sirens approaching, so did the people inside and many would have run if not for the fact that Sloan called out. "FBI. Stay where you are. We have you surrounded. If you have any weapons, throw them into the restaurant area and then lie down with your hands over your heads. Do it, *now!*"

Alia circled back out front and added her orders to his. "Weapons forward. Come on folks. We'll be searching you and the premises so just save yourself from being charged with possession of a firearm." A small handgun appeared from behind the curtain and then another.

Screams turned to arguments as everyone started to blame each other. It was a shit-show, a bunch of untrained, unknowledgeable complainers who'd decided to form a group and rant their hate.

Sloan waited by the window to make sure no one tried getting out that way and soon passed over his spot to an officer Alia had sent to cover for him.

She watched him walk up to Nigel and pass on his phone so they could upload his files into the computers, making sure not to delete anything that would be proof against these numbskulls.

Then he walked up to Alia. She had taken a moment to talk with Leah who had begged for her attention. "Alia, please help us. We just want to go home."

"I'm sorry, whoever you are. I do know your name isn't Leah. Look, people can't come into this country and behave in a subversive manner. It's considered treason and it's against our laws. There'll be a trial and you will be charged. What they'll do to you, I don't know. But if I were you, I'd start praying to Allah because you're going to need all the help you can get."

Disgusted with the whole sick situation, Alia walked away and stifled the pity the other girl's anguished cry generated. In her head, she knew her sympathy was misplaced. But her heart did clench for the future of the young woman who'd probably been brainwashed all her life by zealots who'd lied and bent the truth for their own advantage, and to support their own beliefs.

As if he knew about the fight raging inside her, Sloan approached, slipped his arm around her waist and led her to the SUV. "We'll go and tell Sam the good news, shall we?"

Chapter
Sixty-four

Alia could see that Sam was ecstatic when he learned his visitors would not be returning. He quickly fetched their belongings and passed both bags to Sloan. "How can I thank you for the peace you have given this family, Sloan?"

"No thanks needed, Samir, just doing my job."

When Janna opened her mouth to argue, Alia held up her hand. "It's a long story. And we'll share it with you one day soon. For now, we need to get back to Kean and make sure he's not too worried about me leaving him again tonight. The last time I did, he was kidnapped. I'm still a little nervous."

They said their goodbyes and left. Sloan's free arm rounded her waist but she knocked it away. "Stop it. They might be watching."

"Dammit, woman. I'm telling everyone the truth tonight. I can't keep my hands off you."

"Sounds good to me." She giggled and then ran in front of him as soon as he tried again to encircle her around the neck.

When they entered the house, they saw Kean engrossed in a Transformers movie, surrounded by a bunch of adults all with bowls of popcorn.

Seeing this and knowing that no one had paid any attention to their arrival, Sloan put his hand over her mouth gently and dragged her back into the kitchen where he kissed her so deeply, her legs lifted around his hips so her lower body could grind against his. Completely absorbed by the wonders of his mischievous tongue, she didn't hear a thing until her son yelled, "Mo-om!"

Sloan's arm stiffened and he let her down slowly. They stared for a second into each other's eyes and then both turned to see five faces filled with various expressions.

Kean was horrified.

Don was laughing.

Libby, Roy and Les were all grinning like baboons.

Alia pushed Sloan in front of her and waited.

His hands came up as if to ward off enemies and he spoke calmly. "I can explain."

Les's smart-alecky "Uh, huh?" seemed to be the only response.

"First, I'm really not Alia's stepbrother, we're

not actually related. Just pretending. It was the job."

Kean appeared worried. "You're not my uncle?"

"Nope. The FBI wanted us to act as if we were, so you and your mom could move in here with me. We were working undercover but that assignment is over as of tonight."

Kean's sudden sob and face full of tears shocked them all.

Roy, whose hand had shot out to cover Kean's eyes, now shook his finger at Sloan, the anger in his tone most unusual. "Well, son, you've gone and done it now."

***

Alia rushed to gather Kean close. "Why are you crying, honey?"

"Because we won't be staying here with Sloan anymore, and I like living here. A lot."

Sloan stepped into their space and crouched down next to them. "Hey kid, if I have my way and your mama agrees, you'll never have to leave."

Roy's mood reversed and his happy chuckle caught her attention. She couldn't help but notice the twinkle in those blue eyes that were so similar to hers and Kean's.

A wave of fear suddenly swept over her. *Son?* Why did Roy refer to Sloan as his son? And then she remembered. Sloan had called Roy 'Dad' in the hospital. In fact, Sloan said that he had three dads and didn't know for sure which one was his paternal father. Didn't care. But if her suspicions were correct, that small detail could be a deal breaker to them ever being able to be together. She needed to find out the truth – right now – before they went any further with his plans.

Her heartbeats sped up. Taking a deep breath became impossible. Pain slammed into her almost doubling her over and a sick foreboding thrummed throughout her body.

She caressed Sloan's cheek for a second and then shocked the hell out of everyone, including the man who had started to reach for her.

"Roy, can I see you alone for a minute?"

The room went silent. Sloan's arm dropped and his questioning stare unnerved her but it didn't stop her. Everyone else shuffled uncomfortably and Sloan picked up Kean who kept aiming his stare between his mom and the man who now held him. Then his small arms wrapped around Sloan's neck and he hid his face.

Chapter
Sixty-five

Roy, confused but willing, followed her to the bedroom she shared with Kean and she pulled out her
laptop. In a few seconds, she found the files for her
mother and held out the screen so he could read
the information.

A cry broke from him, one that tore at her
heartstrings. He dropped to the bed as if all the
strength in his legs had vanished. She sat next to
him.

His voice came out raspy, hoarse with emotion.
"Who is this woman to you?" His blue lasers, the
ones that reminded her of what she saw in the mirror every day, searched her expression.

"She's my real mother, Roy. Her name is Scarlet
Honor and she lived in San Francisco. According

to the file I was able to obtain, she gave me up for adoption because her dream was to be an actress. Regrettably, she passed away two years later and was never able to achieve her goal."

"Lordy, lordy." He shook his head sadly. "How terrible. Scarlet was the reason I left San Francisco. She wouldn't marry me, said she never wanted kids. All she wanted was to be an actress."

"How long did you and Scarlet know each other?"

"We were together for six months, night and day. I thought we were in love. But when I wanted to get married, she refused. Said she had just been notified that her audition to act in a play on Broadway had been successful and it was the answer to all her dreams. I was stunned and heartbroken. I offered to wait but she would have none of it. Left me. Just walked out. I never saw her again."

"So you came to Honolulu."

"I had to. Everywhere I went in 'Frisco, I saw her. The memories were killing me."

"When did you leave San Francisco?"

"It was two weeks after Christmas; January 1986."

"I was born in August 1986."

Roy's stunned cry broke through within a few seconds, and his sob of joy left her in no doubt as to his delight. "You're my *daughter*?"

"I believe so. We can always get a test—"

Stiffening, he gently took her face into his

shaking hands and they stared into each other's tear-filled eyes. His tender smile twisted her heart into a big, happy, glowing knot of love. "Do you truly feel that's necessary?"

She whispered the words. "Not for one second." They hugged. He rocked her and she patted his back. The feeling of sweet acknowledgement would never occur again and they both wanted to savor the moment.

Releasing each other, they again stared, grinned and he kissed her forehead so lovingly that the sniffles returned.

"How can a man be so blessed with an instant family? All in a few magical moments, I'm a father and a grandfather." His unsteady hands cupped her face and his thumbs wiped away the tears on her cheeks. He gazed into her eyes. "How long have you suspected?"

"From when you told me about your earlier life in the sunroom. About the actress you wanted to marry in San Francisco but that she wanted a career."

"This is the most wonderful thing that could have ever happened to me. I'm not even going to dwell on the years we've missed, the years I could have watched my child growing up."

"You've never been a father before?" She held her breath, the sudden increase in her heart's thudding came close to choking her.

His startled questioning look passed the conversation back to her.

"Sloan. He calls you 'Dad'. He has three fathers—"

"Oh, sweetheart. Now I know why you were so pale earlier, and it also accounts for your fearful expression when I called Sloan 'son'." He again wiped at the new deluge of tears. "Alia, I'm not his father."

"But how do you know for sure? He said all three of you were with Wai." Hope filled her and began to replace the ugly fear from moments earlier.

"Because, though I loved Wai, I was never *in love* with her and we never slept together. I was and always will be in love with your mother. So there is absolutely no chance that the boy is mine."

"Why haven't you ever told him? He believes that any one of you could be his dad."

Roy's cheeks filled with color and he lowered his head so he could break away from her searching gaze. "I never admitted to the others that we hadn't been intimate. That way I had as much right to be Sloan's father as Tommy and Les." He held her shoulders firmly. "When he was first born and Wai needed a babysitter, she turned to me for help. And after she left, Tommy and Les did the same. As a farm boy with lots of siblings, I had the most experience and they were terrified they'd do something wrong. So, in those days, I ended up spending more time with him than either of the others.

As the months went by, he became my boy as if he were of my blood. Never doubt it. I do consider him my son, but he is not your half-brother."

"I can't tell you how relieved I am, Roy. I mean Dad." She grinned at his look of delight.

"Me too, sweetheart. Me too."

Chapter Sixty-six

When Alia and Roy returned to the living room, the silence deepened as the others looked up expectantly. She felt their eyes trying to gauge her and Roy's expressions.

The fact that Roy's arm was wrapped around her waist and she leaned in close to her Santa-like father allowed them all to sigh with relief.

Kean was on Sloan's lap snuggled in his arms, his expression revealing the fear all kids have of thinking maybe he'd done something wrong.

Les and Libby were sitting very close together on the couch, Les's arm around her shoulder. Both looked quizzical and yet strained.

Don looked around the room, picking up the tension. "I'm outta here." He waved and headed for the front door. It closed softly behind him.

Sloan's face was pale, his eyes hard, but his hands were gentle as he rubbed Kean's arm. "Wanna share your secret with the rest of us?"

Roy had Alia's paper file that she'd given him to read in private. He held it up, waved it once, saying, "Of course we'll tell you our news. You're all family."

Libby started to rise. "I'll leave you to it, then."

Les hauled her back into his hug. "Not so fast, woman. If I have my way and I usually do, soon you'll belong in the circle as much as the rest of us. Let the old man ramble."

Roy grinned at Les. "Tonight you can't mess with me, you jackass. I've just learned that I'm a father and a grandfather, and nothing can blunt my happiness."

"Say what?" Les came back at him, his body jackknifing forward.

"Alia is my daughter. Her mother was Scarlet Honor, the girl I left behind in San Francisco all those years ago. She was pregnant and never said a word. Broke off with me and gave our baby up for adoption."

Kean sat up suddenly. "Does that mean you're my real grandpa?"

"Yep. It sure does, boy. I'm your grandpa alright and I couldn't be happier." He went over to take Kean from Sloan and hugged the boy tight.

"Christ, we'll never hear the end of this now."

Les's unexpected comment made everyone laugh. Then he added another sentence and Alia saw Sloan's reaction. "It's a bloody good thing, I'll be a grandpa too as soon as Sloan marries Alia. Or I'd have to shoot you to stop the crowing."

Chapter Sixty-seven

Sloan couldn't believe the words Les said. Was he admitting something, or just using his surrogate status to give him rights as Kean's grandpa too?

"Les, do we need to talk?" He pinned Les with a hard stare and watched Les wither and then straighten his shoulders.

"You want we should go in there?" Les nodded his head at the room that Roy and Alia had just returned from.

"You got something to say to me?"

"Yeah. I guess I do."

Sloan stood and waited for Les to pass in front of him and then he gestured to the others to give them a minute. As he passed Alia, he kissed her and whispered three words that lit up her face.

Les waited for him to close the door, his hands in his front jeans' pocket, his stance solid, in the same way that Sloan often stood when he knew something was coming that he needed to be strong for.

For the first time in Sloan's life, he saw fear lurking in Les's straight-forward gaze. "So... I'm your real dad. Are you okay with that?"

Sloan felt a tremendous burst of happiness flood his body. "Why didn't you ever tell me?"

"How could I? After Tommy died, Roy needed you in his life as much as I did, maybe more. As long as he never knew for sure which one of us was your father, he could keep up the pretense."

Sloan reached out to grip Les's shoulder. "I knew you loved that old guy, I just never realized how much."

"Look, kid. We were all there for you. Tommy – he needed you to cling to after Wai left. Without the belief that you were his son, he'd have drunk himself to death. And Roy... well, the sorry son of a bitch was so in love with Scarlet, he never even touched your mom. She told me so, and I believed her."

"Why say anything now?" Sloan thought he knew but he just had to ask.

"Enough with the fucking secrets in this family. Besides, I couldn't stand the thought of Roy's bragging, ragging on me about his new status. Hell, if he's gonna be a grandpa, then you'd better get that girl to the altar and make me one too as soon as it can be arranged."

"Okay, Okay. Come here, you old bastard." Sloan grabbed Les in the hug they'd often shared before but never with as much emotion.

"Go on, now. Go get your girl and tell her you love her." Les gave Sloan a push toward the doorway.

"Hey, give me credit for being *your* son, Dad. I already did."

***

Sloan entered the room first and headed straight to where Kean was comfy on his grandpa's lap.

As soon as he saw Sloan, he reached for him, and once safely held in Sloan's strong arms, he searched his face. "Are you going to be my dad?"

Sloan looked over at Alia and her happy nod lit up his insides. "Looks like it's a yes, kid."

Kean hugged him, then pulled away so he could look him in the eye. "I'm glad. I really lo-like you Sloan."

"I lo-like you too, kid. A lot! But there's one thing we need to get straight. Roy gets to keep the kitten, and you get to play with it when you're at his house."

Kean's face fell but he nodded in agreement. "Okay."

Sloan added, his tone serious, "The thing is – I'm allergic to cats but... I've got no problem with other animals."

"You don't?" Kean's smile lit up his face, his blue eyes blazing with excitement.

"Nope. No problem at all. In fact, I'm kind of partial to puppies. And I know a great place where they always have a litter ready to sell. Deal?"

"Deal! I really, *really* like puppies."

Afterword

Thank you so much for reading *Special Agent Booker.*

I loved writing this story and I hope you enjoyed reading it. If so, I would ask you for a favor. Wherever you purchased this book, please take a few minutes and leave an honest review. Authors enjoy hearing that readers like their stories, and hopefully, others will read your words and choose to buy the because of your sentiments.

My website at http://mimibarbour.com now has all my books listed with links to the various publishers to make it easy for you to return to where you bought the book and to find my other work.

While you're there, I'd really appreciate it if you would sign up for my newsletter so I can keep in touch.

http://mimibarbour.com/con-tact.html#newsletter

I only send out newsletters approximately once a month and you have my word that your address will never be shared.

Hugs, Mimi

Special
Agent
Kandice

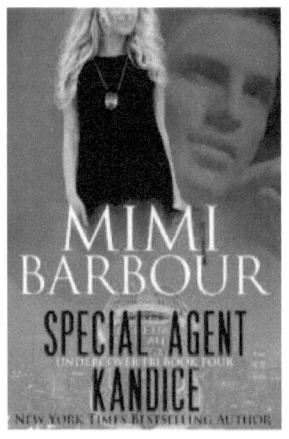

Undercover FBI Series Book #4
by New York Times Best-selling author, Mimi Bar-
bour

~*~*~

Powerful, thrilling and character-driven, this roman-
tic suspense is a real page-turner.

Special Agent indeed, Kandice Warner is everyone's best friend. Talk about a Barbie doll! This female might have the same pretty-girl looks but even though she has a tender heart, she also has the resilience needed for a very successful FBI Hostage Negotiator. Feelings of inadequacy constantly force her to prove that she's tough, and she demonstrates her courage when dealing with a murderous bank robber, a desperate jumper, being stalked, kidnapped and beaten. But her tender heart can get her in trouble and she needs to grow a thicker skin. Almost impossible when her obstinate new boss, for reasons of his own, interferes in everything she does.

Assistant Director of the Criminal Investigative Division in Washington, Dan Black is as hard as they come. With the grit of a street youth stiffening his resolve, he's worked his way up through the ranks, his personal space shields as strong as ever. Until he sees the sweetest things on two legs! A girl from his past. The one he's never been able to forget. Working undercover in the Seattle bureau, he tries to protect his childhood fantasy but she refuses to stay put or take orders. Faced with a woman like that, what's a mere man to do?

Special
Agent
Maximilian

Undercover FBI Series Book #3
by New York Times Best-selling author, Mimi Bar-
bour

~*~*~

Intrigue, complex characters and more fun than
you'll expect from a romantic suspense barn-burner!

In this electrifying romantic suspense set in the steamy streets of New Orleans, Lieutenant Commander Nik Baudin, accidently meets up with an identical twin he never knew existed. When his brother Max goes missing, Nik assumes his identity as Special Agent Maximilian. This gives him access to FBI files making it easier to arrest the gangsters who attacked his brother and to stop their trafficking of underage girls. Being that Nik has specialized commando training, he's the perfect man for the job – that's if his PTSD doesn't kick in and leave him cowering in a corner.

Special Agent Maya Barnes can't believe it when she spots her partner, Max Foster, wandering along the French market without a care in the world. Since he'd been beaten and had gone missing weeks earlier, they all believed him dead. There's only one problem… though this man might look exactly like the missing agent, she knows differently. In all the years they've worked together, she's never wanted to have mind-blowing sex with her partner before.

The Vegas Series

Romantic Suspense at its best
by New York Times Best-selling author, Mimi Bar-
bour

This sizzling box set for the Vegas Series starts off where we meet up with hardworking, hard-assed Detective Aurora Morelli. Attempting to arrest a rapist who attacks her colleague then continually thwarts her attempts to bring him to justice—to a horrific nightmare where her new baby is kidnapped—this scrappy detective does everything in her power to control these events. Kai Lawson, a partner she doesn't want, fights against and in the end accepts (in her job and in her bed) is the hero in these first few stories. The bald-headed, purse-carrying hotshot knows just how to pull her crank and the outcome is entertaining. Their blockbuster story will get you totally invested in this series.

In the last three books, along comes Lisa Jordan, a kick-ass kinda gal who loves wearing the shield as a Vegas detective and enjoys the more strenuous aspects of her job. She steps in for a while as Aurora's partner while Kai is MIA. Her story begins here and ends the series as she fights her attraction for wealthy casino owner, Jeff Waters. After one wild night, the charismatic charmer digs his way into her heart and that of the three-year-old nephew in her care. The fact that he leaves her speechless, literally, detracts from his appeal for Lisa since as a self-professed chatterbox, it's the first time ever. On the other hand, everything else about the man is fascinating. She can no more fight her memories than stop herself from rescuing him from two killers holding him hostage in revenge for the mistakes of his father.

Praise for the Vegas series:

"Cops & drama, absolutely loved this series!" ~ reviewed by luvbooks

"Good action and great stories. What a bargain!" ~ reviewed by Johnny Rotten Apples

"Great story lines, wonderful characters!" ~ reviewed by Rachel Larson

"Bloody fantastic!" ~ reviewed by Bernadette Boyce

A word about the author:

Mimi is an incredibly busy New York Times, USA Today and award-winning, best-selling author who has five series to her credit. The Vicarage Bench Series – Spirit/Time -Travel tales that have a surprising twist / The Angels with Attitude Series – Angels Love Romance / The Elvis Series – Make an Elvis song a book / Vegas Series – 6 books full of romantic suspense, humor and gritty conflicts / and... the fast-paced, edgy yet humorous romantic suspense, Undercover FBI Series. She also has numerous box collections and single titles to add to her credits. Mob Tracker is a new series she's working on now and the first book in that series called *"Sweet Retaliation"* will be published in January 2017.

Mimi lives on the East coast of Vancouver Island with her loving husband and a son who makes her glad she was born a woman. Also in a niece whose family adds greatly to her enjoyment of life, and she's a happy soul. Gardening lights her inner fires, but alas, there's just not enough time to be outside when fictional characters vie to be heard.

Contact me:

My website: http://www.mimibarbour.com/

Or my blogspot: http://mimibarbour.blogspot.com

Or follow me on twitter: https://twitter.com/Mimi-iBarbour

Or on Facebook: Mimi Barbour Fan page

Please sign up for my fun Newsletter: http://mimibarbour.com/contact.html#newsletter